IF YOU CAN'T
TAKE THE
HEAT

IF YOU CAN'T TAKE THE HEAT

MICHAEL RUHLMAN

Penguin Workshop

PENGUIN WORKSHOP
An imprint of Penguin Random House LLC, New York

First published in the United States of America by Penguin Workshop, an imprint of Penguin Random House LLC, New York, 2024

Visit us online at penguinrandomhouse.com.

Library of Congress Cataloging-in-Publication Data is available.

Printed in the United States of America

ISBN 9780593523445

1st Printing

LSCH

Design by Mary Claire Cruz

FOR LES JACOBS

PROLOGUE

New Year's Eve. Time to end this horrible, miraculous year and start a new one.

Chef didn't do a special menu for the last service of the year. But despite the fact that this was *the* French restaurant in town, he did send to every table a bowl of Hoppin' John and collard greens with hog jowl in their pot liquor, which he said was for good luck. Chef had asked me to make enough for staff meal, which was my main job at Restaurant Margaux.

"Ordering, two steaks mid-rare, one salmon, one lamb, two lardons!" Chef called to the line, and the three cooks shouted back the order they were responsible for.

"Order fire two pâtés!" he called. "Picking up two halibuts, salmon, steak rare!"

New Year's Eve was not like any other night. It was busier, for one, and guests had higher expectations than usual, which made things tense in the kitchen. This was a money-maker night. Paul, Reggie, and Amanda were turning and burning on the line; a lot of hot pans all under control. The festive mood of the dining room flowed into the kitchen whenever a server pushed through the swinging door, calling out "Order in!" handing the ticket to Chef. Most important, the silent partner, Jimmy Holliday, with his pinky ring and jewelry and slicked back hair, was laughing it up at table four with his wife, oblivious of the theft and what it had cost me.

I plated the Hoppin' John and collards in small dishes for deuces and small soup tureens for larger tables, which went out with chunks of corn bread and soft, salted butter as soon as the table was seated.

And there were only two desserts: a chocolate tart with a raspberry coulis and the usual crème brûlée. Both got a stenciled "1981!" in decorative sugar. A new year. When the last dessert went out, about fifteen minutes before midnight, I found sous chef Paul and told him, "I'm going out for a smoke." He gave me a thumbs-up.

"But, hey," he called before I reached the door. "Come midnight, cooks do a champagne toast with Chef. They're humping in the dining room and refilling glasses for the countdown, but our work is done. So back in fifteen, okay?"

I didn't even take off my apron, which was smeared with blood from breaking down Amanda's strip steaks. I was allowed to practice on them as those were left over and would go to the cooks to take home, since this was the last service before the restaurant shut down for two weeks.

I sat on the back steps of the house below the shingled awning, which kept me from getting wet from snow. Starting Christmas Eve, we'd gotten a ton of snow, and tonight would add a couple more inches. It was cold but not frigid and the air felt good. You build up a reserve of heat in the kitchen, so I didn't need a coat. I shook out a cigarette and lit it.

Dad told me shortly after my leg shattered that some ancient cultures believed the gods had to take something away from you in order to give you more of something else. For a while, I thought he might be right. Now that Julia's gone, I don't know anymore.

I blew a plume of smoke into the snowy air, lit up by the back-door light, and thought how crazy it was—just six months since it happened. Felt like a lifetime. In a way it was. Another life.

I was a jock. I'd been given a body that was perfect for sports, especially football. Coach said I had a "gift," and that's how I'd come to think of it—and a lucky thing, too, because I wasn't exactly a gifted student. I was a three-sport athlete, including basketball and baseball, but I endured winter, spring, and summer waiting for football. I hung out with the other jocks at school. I still had my best pals from elementary school, Johnny Williams and Roger Schmitt, who were cool in their own, unjocklike way, but I spent so much time on the fields, the court, and in the weight room that I hardly saw them during the school year. That changed, too.

Sous chef Paul stuck his head out the back door. The apron over his shoulder meant he was done for the night. He said, "Dude, it's champagne time."

"Be right in," I said.

Julia. I loved her. I hated her. I was furious. Crushed. Most of all, I *missed* her. She was still everywhere in this restaurant. She would haunt it, and me, forever.

This left me with the only thing I knew for certain: Sometimes you jump up, and when you land, your world has changed.

I took a last drag on my cigarette and flicked it as far as I could, watching the ember arc into fresh snow.

Cleveland, 1980

Roger and Johnny kidnapped me on the last Saturday of June.

Roger's car idled innocently in my driveway at 5:20, just as I arrived home from my job at Heinen's, where I bagged groceries and loaded them into cars—my first genuine job. I was still the only one without a driver's license. But that would change in two days, when I turned sixteen.

"Theo! Mickey D's!" Roger shouted like a ringside announcer, extending the *Deeeeee's* in a false baritone. They loved McDonald's. I did not, but Roger and Johnny would keep my mind off Heather for a while. I could join them, not eat, and be back in time for the dinner I was looking forward to making: a rib steak on the grill and a baked potato, heaped with butter, along with *The Love Boat* and *Fantasy Island* on television. If I were going to be miserable and alone, I would at least eat well.

"I need to be back by seven," I said. "Let me go change."

Roger pumped his fist and said, "Yes."

I said hi to Mom and Dad, who were already dressing to go out, told them what I was doing, and closed the door to my room.

I changed from my khakis and blue Oxford with the Heinen's logo on it into a bright red shirt to cheer myself up, try anyway, some well-worn white painter's pants, and old Top-Siders, the right sole held to the shoe with duct tape.

"Well, look at Mr. Artsy Fartsy," Johnny said as I climbed into the back seat of Roger's Buick Skylark. Johnny, who never veered from starched white button-downs, faded jeans, and Jack Purcell sneakers, embraced preppiness as if it were a kind of Platonic ideal. The look fit with his short blond hair, always neatly parted on the right above his light blue eyes.

"You'd have Brooks Brothers dress the entire country if you could," I said.

"Not a *bad* idea."

Roger laughed as he backed out of the driveway. "How would you tell anyone apart?"

"By innate personality," Johnny said. "The idea that you need to express yourself through your clothing is ridiculous."

"Isn't that exactly what you're doing by dressing preppy?" Roger asked. "Clothes can't *help* but reflect our personality."

"Exactly. Which is why your school dress code is a good thing—it puts everybody on the same plane to shine or not based on who they are, not by what they wear."

This was always the big reason students at US, University School, lobbied the school to relax its dress code, which it never did. We still had to wear a coat and tie to morning assembly and to lunch. Otherwise, no jeans, T-shirts, or sneakers, which meant the standard attire was corduroys and Oxford-cloth shirts, and either L.L.Bean Bluchers, Top-Siders, or Wallabees.

Roger had been the first person to befriend me when I arrived at US in seventh grade. He had dark curly hair and a lightning white smile, which he used like a tool. I hadn't wanted to leave all my friends who went to public school to go to a stuck-up private school, an all-boys school no less. I think the only reason they let me in was because my dad had graduated from the school a million years ago. I certainly wasn't very good at the school part. Luckily, it was harder to get kicked out once you were in. I grew a full six inches in eighth grade and became one of the best athletes in my class. US cared about its sports teams, so I was pretty sure they wouldn't kick me out for crummy grades now that I was going to be a junior starting varsity in three sports.

Johnny was also my best friend, had been so since first grade at Fernway Elementary. I'd introduced him to Roger and now they were almost better friends than I was with either of them.

"You're the conformist," I said to Johnny.

"Who's going to go further?" Johnny said.

Johnny was always up to no good, but he never got caught on account of looking so clean-cut and innocent. He once broke into the local A&P through an air duct and stole five beef tenderloins and a case of beer, then he had a bunch of us over for a barbecue when his parents were out of town.

Roger was our Dale Carnegie and wanted to be president of the school by the time he was a senior.

Roger drove to the drive-through line at McDonald's. Odd.

"Aren't we going in?" I asked.

"Nope. What do you want?"

"Nothing, thanks. I'm making dinner at home."

Johnny turned in the passenger seat to face me. "If you *were* going to have something, what would it be?"

"You know I'm not a fan of Mickey D's."

"Stop being a snob."

"I'm not a snob. I like Chick-fil-A." Chick-fil-A at Beachwood Place mall did something to that chicken that I couldn't suss out no matter how much I ate. Best chicken sandwich anywhere.

"Humor me. If I held a gun to your head, what would you order?"

"I suppose a Big Mac. I'm curious about the 'special sauce.'"

Roger ordered quarter pounders for himself and Johnny, then added, "Oh, and two all-beef patties, special sauce, lettuce, cheese, pickles, onions on a sesame seed bun."

"And one Big Mac," said an annoyed voice through the staticky speaker.

"And three Cokes and three large fries."

"Roger, I don't *want* a Big Mac."

He ignored me. Something was up. We always ate inside unless we were going somewhere. Roger paid for all of us with his father's credit card and handed the drinks and white bag of food to Johnny.

"Whoa whoa whoa," I said, when he took a left onto Chagrin Boulevard. "Where are we going?"

"You, my friend, are *not* spending another Saturday night moping at home," Johnny said, and turned to fan three tickets so I could see. "Lawn seats to Jefferson Starship."

"Oh, *man*, no," I said. "Please, *no*." I was not exactly Mr. Spontaneous. I liked a plan: grilled steak and *The Love Boat*.

Blossom Music Center, the big outdoor amphitheater where most of the summer rock concerts were held, was a forty-five-minute drive from where I lived, Shaker Heights, Ohio, a twenty-minute drive from downtown Cleveland. Downtown Cleveland, in the so-called Rust Belt, could be grim, especially in February, but it was ringed by old, leafy suburbs with smooth curving streets. Beyond these, driving past farmland and into a national park, was Blossom, and the crowds were so big that you parked in fields where it took forever to find your car and get out of the parking lot after the show. So what I was really worried about now was that I wouldn't be home till one in the morning.

"My parents are going to *freak* if they get home and I'm not there. Why didn't you let me leave a note at least?"

"If we'd have told you where we were going, would you be sitting where you are now?"

"Of course not."

"Exactly."

"But what about my parents? At least let me find a pay phone. Shit, do either of you have a dime?" Then I realized they'd probably left already, and I never asked them where they went, so I had no way to reach them. "Seriously, guys. I've never done this before. They'll probably call the police when they get home and I'm not there."

Johnny, casual as could be, said, "You really don't give us *any* credit, do you?" He began to dig through the food as Roger took the I-271 on-ramp. "I called your father and told him what we were doing."

"And he said okay?"

"Okay? He was delighted, *delighted*, that we were getting you out of the house. It's been three frigging weeks, Theo." He handed me my Big Mac, fries, and Coke and said, "Eat up."

Admitting that I had no alternative, I leaned back to let the summer wind blow through my hair.

Of course I started thinking about Heather. I spent seven months of sophomore year not even getting to second base, and suddenly she's sneaking around with Jeptha Crowley, a super-rich kid who wore his blazer all day long, to classes and everything, which was just weird. What did I do wrong? Why did she suddenly like someone else?

Getting dumped was the worst feeling in the world. It made you feel so alone—no one could possibly understand how bad it was unless they'd already been through it. I mean she still filled my thoughts; her actual image floated through my mind every day. She was impossibly cute with bright red hair, huge blue eyes, a pert little nose, pale, plump lips.

Johnny had found a shop downtown in Cleveland's Terminal Tower, the big building at the center of the city, that made fake IDs.

The fake IDs allowed us to stop at a convenience store on the way to Blossom for three six-packs of Michelob, Roger's beer of choice, and a gallon of milk.

Johnny cracked a beer and Roger said, "Dude, not in the car—if we get stopped we're screwed. There are cops all over the place. They pull people over for no reason when there's a show."

"Stop being such a worrywart." He handed the beer to me, and I said, "I'll wait till we're parked."

"Oh, please, save me!" Johnny said, and sat back to drink his beer.

We hit the entrance and followed the slow line of cars being directed into a nearby field to park. People played music, threw Frisbees, and kept hacky sacks aloft. Johnny dumped the milk in the grass and emptied the remaining beer into the plastic jug. Blossom had a no-hard-containers rule but we could smuggle in plastic. I didn't drink during football season, but the two-a-day practices, which really began my school year, didn't start till mid-August, which meant I had six weeks to drink beer and feel sorry for myself.

Once we were through the turnstiles and into Blossom proper—what a perfect name; appropriately *thematic*, the air rich with the blossoming summer—it was like entering a celebration in a grassy bowl surrounded on all sides by a forest of maples and oaks. It felt like a street fair along the periphery at the top of the lawn where concessions, beer, and snacks were sold. The vast lawn sloped down a hundred yards to the amphitheater, built especially for the Cleveland Orchestra and famous for its acoustics. It looked like a giant brown-shingled shell.

The grade of the slope was perfect—not so gradual that the people in front of you got in the way and not so steep that people's blankets slid down into the blanket in front. We were early enough to get a good spot on the lawn, in the center, but not with one of the support beams in the way of the stage, and not too far from the broad concrete walkway that circumscribed the amphitheater and the seats there.

Roger spotted Kim and Alison, in our grade at Hathaway Brown, the all-girls school. Roger, who was on his way to being a politician or motivational speaker, was friends with everybody and shouted out to them. "Sit here. We'll make room."

"Really?" Kim said. "We've got two more coming."

"The more the better! Who's coming?"

"Sarah, and she's bringing a friend from Shaker."

Johnny, who went to Shaker Heights High, said, "Who?"

"Neither of us have met her." Both girls stood, scanning the crowd for their friend. The more time went by, the harder it was to find your friends as the big lawn filled up.

"Boo!" Sarah shouted. She'd come up from behind. Both Kim and Alison screamed (why do girls scream?), and threw their arms around Sarah. Sarah was always a lot of fun and had cool parents who let big groups of us hang out at her house and around the pool, with grilled cheese sandwiches and root beer floats.

"Oh my God!" she cried when she saw Roger and me. Roger jumped up and gave her a hug. She was a senior and they'd been friends forever, both of them "lifers" at their respective schools, enrolled since kindergarten. And when I saw the girl behind her, for some reason I stood, too. "Hey, everyone, this is my friend Julia Bevilacqua."

"Hiya!" she said, giving a single wave, her palm moving from due east to due west in one smooth motion, followed by a tentative tilt of the head. Candidate-for-president Roger all but leaped at her and said, "I'm Roger Schmitt!" holding out his hand.

Julia chuckled, said, "Hi, Roger Schmitt. I'm Julia." They shook.

"And this is my good buddy Theo," he said, presenting me with a flourish. I nodded, said hi. "And this is my good buddy Johnny." Again the flourish.

Julia shook her index finger at Johnny and squinted behind her large, round wire-rimmed glasses. She had long straight hair that was so blond it was nearly white. The round spectacles gave her a studious look. But the flowing flowered shirt, a V-neck that laced and tied loosely, ragged jeans with hand-sewn patches, and cowboy boots told another story.

He said, "I go to Shaker. You're a year ahead of me."

"I thought I'd seen you before."

The girls settled in. So she was going to be a senior, I thought.

Alison or Kim had brought an actual picnic basket and both were setting out a cheese board with three cheeses, grapes, and water crackers on their blanket. Girls were, will always be, mysterious in so many ways. Even *I* wouldn't have thought of that.

"Oh my God, that's so adorable," Julia said, looking at the basket.

"It's *practical*," Alison said, looking away, haughty.

"No, really!" Julia said, sitting on the edge of the blanket. I resumed my spot before Roger could take it, which he would have tried to do, as my edge of the blanket was next to where Julia sat.

Kim squeezed white wine from a wineskin into four plastic cups and passed them around. "I only brought four cups but you can have some if you want," she said to us.

"Thanks for offering," Roger said, sitting beside me and holding up a milk jug half full of foamy warm beer. Guys—we could be so embarrassing sometimes.

Julia had a leather pouchlike purse, slung round her neck and arm. She pulled out a pack of Marlboro Reds and a Zippo lighter. She took a first long drag, blew smoke into the air, and sighed. Then, as if forgetting herself—or because we were all staring at her, exotic creature that she was—she apologized and asked me if I'd like one.

"Thanks," I said. "Don't smoke." At least half the girls in our grade smoked. I thought it was an affectation, ridiculous, but maybe that was because my dad smoked, and I'd spent too many hours trapped in a smoke-filled car.

She leaned over to Roger and Johnny, the pack open with two cigarettes pulled out. Johnny held up a palm, but Roger said, "I'll have one, thanks." I gave Roger a look which he ignored. Roger did *not* smoke either.

He leaned across me as Julia lit his cigarette. God, she smelled nice, even with the cigarette smoke. I stared at Roger until he looked at me. "What? I felt like one." He puffed. He wasn't even inhaling—afraid he'd start coughing probably.

He turned to Johnny and whispered, "Know her?"

Johnny shook his head. "Not much. Hangs with the hippies, Deadheads."

The warm-up band had finished, and Jefferson Starship was beginning to take the stage to a cheering crowd. The lawn was a sea of people now, almost no green visible from one side to the other, a massive patchwork of blankets.

Johnny took a slug of beer and passed it down the line.

"What is that?" Julia asked when it came to me.

"Beer," I said, and took a slug. "Warm. Flat. Beer."

Julia smiled and said, "Here, wash the taste away," and handed me her wine.

I smiled back and took some.

"I presume you go to US?" she asked.

"You presume correctly."

Roger leaned over and said, "Julia, our friend needs serious cheering up."

She cocked her head at me.

"His girlfriend dumped him, and he refuses to get over it."

I closed my eyes and shook my head, wishing they hadn't brought this up. I mean, this is basically saying I'm a loser.

"More like took a dump *on* him," Johnny added.

Julia put her hand on my knee. "Oh no. I'm so sorry."

"Thanks."

"No, really." She kept her hand on my knee, forcing me to look at her. "It hurts."

She really meant it. As if she'd been through it herself (which was hard to believe—she was so beautiful). "Thank you," I said.

She took a last drag on her cigarette, stubbed it out, and put the butt in a small brown bag the girls were using for trash. She took another sip of wine and asked, "Recently?"

"Yeah," I said.

Johnny snorted and said, "If three weeks is recently."

"Oh, you gotta get back on that horse," Julia said. "Any dates at all?"

I shook my head.

"Well it's time you start," she said. She threw back her whole glass of wine, set the cup down, and turned to me. I looked down. She pulled my chin toward her, stared at me hard and serious, almost as if she were mad at me. She took the back of my head and drew me to her, put her lips to mine, one . . . two . . . three, and released me. "There! Consider yourself started!" And she grinned.

At that moment the band launched into its opener. Julia and Alison were evidently fans as they looked to each other, screamed, and bolted down the hill toward the amphitheater, bounding between the baskets and blankets. You could see the band better there and you had room to dance.

I turned to Roger and Johnny. Their mouths hung open. I turned to Sarah and Kim.

Kim said, "I think that means she's got a good feeling about you."

Sarah said, "Don't get your hopes up. She's got a boyfriend. Like a serious, long-term boyfriend."

I located Julia in the throng, just at the edge of the grass. Julia and Sarah were dancing ecstatically within the pulsating crowd. But the way Julia danced wasn't like anything I'd ever seen, certainly not at any dance I'd actually been to. It was utterly and jubilantly uninhibited. It was as if she were imitating water, but somehow weirdly in sync with the chords of the song at the same time, mesmerizing.

"Goodbye, Heather Johnson," I heard Johnny say, also watching her. "Hel-*loooo*, Julia Bevilacqua."

2

Roger dropped me off first. Johnny, who had pretty much fin-ished off the nasty beer himself, had fallen asleep in the back seat so it was a long, quiet ride home, our ears faintly ringing from the music. The most important thing we talked about was how to spell *Bevilacqua* so I could look her up in the phone book.

"See ya, good buddy Theo!" Roger said.

"See ya, Roger," I said. "Hey, Roger." I leaned into the pas-senger window. "Thanks. I'd never have done that if you'd given me a choice."

"I know. It's good to have our friend back."

I entered through the back door into the darkened kitchen. It was nearly 1:00 a.m., but I'd seen the light on in Dad's study. I got a glass of ice water and went to let him know I was back. I tried to make plenty of noise because sometimes he'd be so deep into a book that he'd jump out of his skin if I surprised him.

My dad, Robert Claverback, *Bob*, well, he was my dad, so I loved him, but if he'd sat me down and confessed that he was not my actual father, it wouldn't have surprised me. He still looked exactly the way he looked when I was born in the sixties—hair cropped super short, nerdy black glasses, stick thin. I had four inches on him in height. He read a lot of history books. And he had a thing for vintage cars—was always making me join him at the Western Reserve Historical Society, which had cars from all eras. And he himself kept a maroon 1965 Mustang in the garage, which he almost never used. He just washed it a lot.

By day, he was a wealth management advisor at the Cleveland Trust, or AmeriTrust as they just started calling it, the big bank downtown.

He didn't like playing catch, either baseball or football. And he was the only father I knew who didn't care about the Cleveland Browns. He was ten years older than Mom and seemed older than most of my friends' parents.

I found him in the den, seated by himself with a scotch on the rocks, a Lucky Strike in the ashtray, and a big fat book in his lap.

He was so engrossed I had to repeat, "I *said*, I'm home!"

He started, looking up from his book. "How was the concert?" he asked.

"Great. How was your party?"

"Ah, same old, same old." He wasn't the most social guy. He took a long drag on his cigarette, exhaled. I waved my hand in front of my face.

"I know, I know. I'll quit one of these days."

"I'm going to bed."

"Don't forget the lawn tomorrow."

"I know." This was a pain because we had a pretty big lawn.

"Okay. Good night, Skeezix."

Things like *that*. Who uses the word *Skeezix*? He was so embarrassing. "'Night, Dad."

I climbed into bed having hatched my plan. On the ride home Roger and I decided it had to be *Bevalaqua* or *Bevilaquois*, because we were in French together, and the name sounded French. Johnny knew seniors at Shaker and said he could find the spelling and probably even where Julia lived.

The morning light felt like a cracked whip, waking me. Mom. She stomped through my room, loudly furling the blinds.

"It's eleven o'clock, for crying out loud," she said.

"I was up late."

"Well, congratulations. You've wasted half the day."

Mom was already dressed in her tennis whites and had pulled her dark hair into a ponytail. We belonged to the Hunt Club, and Mom and Dad had a standing Sunday tennis match with the Watsons all summer long. Bill Watson was another lawyer at my mom's firm. She practiced antitrust and arbitration law or something like that—I could never quite follow it when she described it to me. It was one of the biggest firms in the city. But I didn't know if my mom's job made her a workaholic, or if she was a workaholic by nature and simply found the right job for her temperament.

The only other mom I knew who worked was Stan Elwood's mom, but she was divorced, so I figured she had to. Mom loved to work. She was a feminist. She was so impressed by Billie Jean King, she and my dad flew to Houston to watch King beat Bobby Riggs in the Battle of the Sexes tennis match. And when she married my dad, she kept her name—Kate Jones—which at the time was like proclaiming yourself to be an actual witch. Mom didn't care.

"I suppose Kate Claverback has a ring, but it just wasn't my *name*," she told me when I asked why.

I was lucky she had a job, otherwise *I* would have been her job, and she would have crushed me. I also liked that she didn't dye the gray out of her hair even though she was just in her early forties. I knew she was still beautiful because friends would tell me so—"Theo, your mom is *hot*"—which was kind of weird.

Before the storm cloud that was my mother left my room, she paused, hands on hips to stare at the new poster of Nastassja Kinski, naked but for a massive boa constrictor, above my bed. I loved it.

Mom released a huff and weather-stormed out. I let myself wake up slowly knowing they'd soon be gone. All three windows were open, and the air was summer fresh and the perfect temperature for just one sheet. I could see a clear blue sky above the leafy trees. I stayed in bed just to enjoy the air. A perfect summer morning.

I went down to the kitchen and called Johnny. He wasn't up. He often went back to sleep after his paper route.

I hadn't eaten since the Big Mac—normally I ravaged the fridge upon returning home from a concert—so now I was really starving. Happily, we had some Jimmy Dean sausage links in the fridge, and we always had eggs, so I fried those up. With Mom and Dad playing tennis at the club, I'd have the day to myself.

By the time I'd finished cutting the lawn, Johnny had called with the info I needed: an accurate spelling of Julia's last name and confirmation of street address, *and* the name of the boyfriend, one Bennett Van Horn, a senior at *my* school, an overachiever on all levels, and definitely in the cool crowd.

There was only one Bevilacqua in the phone book, so I had her number and father's name (Darren). The phone book was a fat dictionary-size paperback with every single household's phone number in it, the entire city of Cleveland. It would have taken an hour just to get through half the *B*s.

I could always count on Johnny for intel.

Julia lived on the poorer side of our suburbs, not literally on the other side of the tracks but pretty close. Her house was small, boxy, ragged around the edges—peeling yellow paint, a bent gutter over what I would later learn was Julia's bedroom, a driveway with weeds growing through the cracks.

We'd only talked a little during last night's concert, between songs, but I knew she was smart, that she asked a lot of questions about me, and she had the most beautiful smile with very large white teeth.

I took the stone steps to her front door. Strangely, I wasn't nervous or shy. I knew she had a boyfriend so I wasn't *after* anything. I wasn't planning to ask her out. I had two-a-day football practices coming up so that would be taking up most of my time starting in August, and once school began it was all about football and trying not to get kicked out of school because of grades and hanging with my buddies on the team. I guess you could say I had a certain misguided self-confidence from what I knew other people thought of me. An athlete, not much of a student, but basically a good reputation. Didn't get into trouble. I was neither good-looking nor bad-looking. I'd evaluate the mirror as I rubbed some zit cream into an annoying spot. Short brown hair, brown eyes, average lips and chin. It was the nose that took me down. I had a nose of no distinction whatsoever. I loved other people's noses. Noses made a face. My own nose was just kind of lumpy.

Given this idle rambling in my brain, which wouldn't stop making up stories, and the fact that I'd been standing in front of Julia's front door for at least two minutes, my gift, a book, in hand, I think I was, I guess, a little more nervous than I wanted to admit.

A short but powerfully built man opened the door, completely bald, with a lumpy nose not unlike mine, and no expression I could read. Darren Bevilacqua.

I asked if Julia was home.

He asked who he could tell her was calling. And not in a friendly way. Suspicious.

I said my name.

And just like that, astonishingly, there she was, right in front of me on the other side of the screen door. I felt surprised at seeing her, like spotting a wild animal out of its element.

"I don't know if I should have expected this or not," Julia said. But she smiled so I figured it was not going to be a disaster. "How did you find out where I lived?"

"A friend. Johnny—you met him last night."

"Hmm," she said, but I couldn't tell if it was a *hmm*-impressed or a *hmm*-creepy.

Which is maybe why suddenly I got *really* nervous. She was right *here*. I don't know what I was expecting. What was I doing here?

"I wanted to give you something," I said. She looked at the book in my hand. "Do you have a minute to talk?"

She turned and said, "Daddy, I'll be out on the front steps."

He said, "Not an inch beyond."

Whoa. Julia rolled her eyes and closed the heavy front door behind her. She sat cross-legged facing me. I sat on the steps and faced the street. I could look at her when I spoke but then turn away when necessary, because at four on a midsummer afternoon, she was even more beautiful than I remembered from last night. She was taller than I remembered. Her white-blond hair was full and tangled, parted haphazardly just off-center. She tucked her hair behind each ear. Her eyes, enlarged behind the John Lennon spectacles, were light brown, flecked with gold. She had a no-nonsense, straightforward nose, pale lips, and a spicy-floral scent that almost made me tip over when I sat.

"Great concert last night," I said.

"Oh my God, so great."

"What time did you get home?"

"Late. The line to get out was so long a bunch of us hung out playing Frisbee until the lot emptied out. Usually that's fine. I can sneak in, but Dad was awake. Curfew is twelve on weekends, ten on weekdays, unless I'm working."

"Even in summer?"

"Yep. But he woke up, which he never does, saw that it was after midnight, and waited up until two thirty. He was *pissed*. So, I'm grounded for a week."

"Meaning?"

"Can't leave the house except for work. And no talking on the phone."

"No talking on the phone? Wow. Strict."

"You have no idea," she said, looking away.

"Are you allowed to receive mail?"

"Mail?"

"Yeah. Letters."

"I suppose. It's never come up."

"You get grounded a lot then?"

"I guess you could say that." She looked away from me and said, "I gotta get outta here."

"What do you mean?"

"Just what I said. I'm saving my money. I'm getting a scholarship to some school far away from here, and the day I graduate high school, I . . . am . . . *gone*."

I had no idea what to say next. Was she serious? She seemed suddenly so much older than me.

When I didn't talk, she said, "So! What. In the fuck. Are you doing here?"

It wasn't mean or aggressive—didn't feel that way. I just looked at her, her eyes, her lips, her smile, her nose, breathed her in, then looked back to the street.

"I totally shouldn't have kissed you," she said.

I turned to her and said, "Oh, no, you totally should have."

"Let me rephrase. I shouldn't be surprised that you're here."

"I'm not here for that," I jumped in.

"For what?"

"To ask you out. I'm not looking for a girlfriend. Too painful. I know you've got a boyfriend. And my guess is that you're not the sort to date football players."

"Or youngsters," she said. She punched my shoulder to say, *kidding*. "So what else do you know?"

"*His* name is Bennett Van Horn, a senior at *my* school. I *know* Ben. I know that you go to Shaker and will be a senior this September. I know that you love Jefferson Starship."

"Well, really I love Jefferson Airplane and Grace Slick, but they broke up in the sixties."

"I don't know them."

"Yes you do. 'White Rabbit.' 'Somebody to Love.'"

"They opened with that last night," I said.

"Right, those are Grace Slick songs from Airplane."

"Okay, I know you like Jefferson Airplane. And presumably other bands from the sixties, judging from this and the way you dress. And I know that you smoke."

She made a shushing face.

24

I whispered, "And now I know your dad doesn't know it."

"He'd kill me," she whispered back. Then, in a normal voice, "Okay, I'm impressed. So then why *are* you here?"

"Well, first," I said, staring into those huge brown eyes because I wanted her to know that I meant it. "I really liked talking with you last night, and I would like to be your friend." I took a breath, looked into the street, then looked back to her. "I've been miserable for weeks, and you, well, you and Roger and Johnny, changed it. I was happy last night for the first time in so long, and I woke up this morning *still* happy. It was like the first good morning I've had all summer. I was just lying in bed, staring out the window at the blue sky and feeling the air, and I realized, *Hey, I'm not depressed anymore.* Like a fever broke. So I wanted to give you something that made *me* happy with hopes that it might make you happy. Do you read?"

"Um, well, yeah. And I'm gonna have time on my hands right now."

"It's this," I said, giving her the paperback. "Please tell me you haven't read it."

"*The Great Gatsby,*" she said. "Well, not exactly. We were supposed to sophomore year, but I only learned enough to pass the test."

"Are you good at school?"

"If you mean grade-wise, yes. I *only* get As."

"Really? Without reading the book?"

"Tenth-grade English was pathetically easy."

"Okay, well, I read it for English last spring and it made me feel euphoric. It was the first time reading a book that I felt like I was completely inside this world. That's never happened to me before. I don't know why, but it did. The writing is so beautiful.

And so I wanted to give it to you to . . . well, I felt I needed to give it to you to say thank you. So here, with thanks. It's a weird, sad love story. Read it or don't, just keep it. There won't be a quiz on Monday, promise."

She laughed. (I'd made her laugh!)

"I see there's an unusual bookmark," she said, taking the book.

When I'd turned the corner of her block, at Fernway and Warrington, I found a cluster of daisies, so how could I not? It was a sign.

"Ah, one of the characters, as I recall," she said.

"Do you believe that things happen for a reason?" I asked. "Or do you think that it's all just chaos and randomness? And we don't mean a thing. Dust in the wind and all that."

She seemed to scrutinize me. "What grade are *you* in?"

"I'll be a junior this fall."

She seemed to think about that. "I believe that it's a little bit of both, some things for a reason, but mostly it's just chaos. And I guess, if you're smart, you figure out which is which."

I turned to her and smiled.

"Unless you're talking about luck," she said. "Was that what you meant by things happening for a reason?"

I said, "Maybe?"

"Because luck is a different bag altogether."

"How so?"

"Sometimes you get lucky and sometimes you don't. But what I *know* is, if you *do* get lucky, it's because you made it yourself. *That* I believe in."

"Not so," I said. "Remember I told you Johnny and Roger kidnapped me last night?"

"Yeah."

"I was taken against my will to that concert, and I was really lucky to meet you."

She laughed, throwing her head back. "You are so flirting with me!"

"Not! *Swear.*" (I was. I totally was. When she said that, I realized I'd been lying to myself.)

The door opened and Mr. Bevilacqua loomed, as if he'd heard.

"I think I gotta go," she said.

We stood and I said to Mr. Bevilacqua, "I'm Theo Claverback, sir."

He gave me a quick glance, said, "You told me. I'm Darren Bevilacqua, Julia's father," then pushed the screen door open and said, "Julia?"

"One more second?"

He allowed the screen door to close but left the front door open.

"Thanks for the book, Theo. It was sweet of you. No one's ever given me a book before. Except, like, my aunt."

"If you read it, I hope you like it. Seriously, if you get to one sentence that doesn't make you want to read the next sentence, throw the book away."

"Deal."

I walked down the central paved walkway to the sidewalk. She said, "Hey," and I turned.

"Next time, give a girl some warning. I didn't even have time to brush my hair!"

3

Maybe I took the long way home because all I could think about was that she'd said "next time." There was going to be a next time. Or maybe it was the universe telling me it was indeed *all* randomness and chaos.

Whatever the reason, I walked away from Fernway Road, the way I'd come and should have returned. Either way it was quite a walk. Instead I carried on down Warrington, which brought me to Van Aken Boulevard. This was a genuine boulevard, meaning it had two lanes of traffic running west toward downtown four miles away, two lanes of traffic running east through the suburbs and beyond, to what was country and farmland. My old camp, Red Raider, was out there—summer idylls after the long school bus ride out, hiking and camping, river walks hunting crayfish under rocks, mud fights, swimming, games of tug-of-war and red rover. And in between these four lanes a broad median of lawn split by the tracks along which yellow, tubular cars ran, powered by overhead cables, which we called the Rapid, short for the Rapid Transit.

I started to jog. It wasn't a decision. My legs just went on their own because I felt so light. I thought about Julia's face and the way she smelled. How I wanted her to read *The Great Gatsby*. My Daisy. Bad girl Daisy, which I have to say, was exciting. She smoked and drank and got grounded regularly but was still a straight-A student.

The route I'd chosen took me past the churchyard, on the other side of the Rapid tracks, where Nick Thomas had put together a touch football game. I don't think any one of us had been inside the church beyond the tracks, but we'd spent hours and hours since fourth or fifth grade, when we were allowed to be off on our own, on the lawn next to it, a long, broad expanse of soft grass, treeless but for one craggy sycamore, which marked the fifty-yard line for football games.

Nick saw me in the distance as I reached the Kenmore Rapid stop and shouted, "Hey! Theo! We're short one player!"

These were all Shaker Heights High guys, all people I'd gone to Fernway Elementary School with but now only saw at the occasional party. It was a perfect summer day; I had nowhere I had to be, so I crossed the tracks.

I floated across the eastbound lanes and when I was on grass but still pretty far from the gang, Nick punted the football to me. The kick was short. I ran to it. The ball bounced high. I had to jump to catch it. When I came down, my left leg broke.

Just like that.

I pushed myself up onto my elbows. My left thigh was bent in the middle, with the rest of the leg, knee included, going in an impossible direction—as if it wanted to take me somewhere else. I remember saying as loud as I was able, "Something's wrong." I heard laughter and shouting and when I didn't get up, Nick jogged to me. "What's the matter?" he said. Then, when he got to me, he said, "Holy shit," and covered his mouth.

Nick lived closest to the church, right across the street in a big house on Van Aken. When he saw my leg, he bolted for home, where he told his parents, who called 911. Through a series of phone calls, they were able to reach the Hunt Club. Someone there was able to locate my parents on the tennis courts.

I had been in shock or maybe passed out because I don't remember the ride to the hospital or much of anything until I was in a room in the ER, and even that remains fuzzy. I'm sure I'd been given plenty of painkillers. I was in full skeletal traction to keep me still and pressure off my leg. My parents had appeared magically. I'd been X-rayed. I came to when I heard the words "lose the leg."

"No!" I said.

Mom put her hand on my forehead. I saw tears on her cheeks. Dad just appeared stunned. They looked really strange, still in their tennis whites, in a hospital room. Kind of like one of those dreams that's neither good nor bad, just so weird that you know it's just a dream while you're dreaming it. The problem was that it wasn't a dream.

"It's rare, I've only seen one other in twenty years," the man in blue scrubs explained. "In all likelihood it's benign and we can make a definitive repair today. But I won't know until I can get in there, have a look, take a biopsy. I'm obligated to make you aware of the worst-case scenario and possible risks involved with the surgery."

"The worst being?" Mom asked.

"Osteosarcoma." The guy said it like it was obvious, like Mom asked a question so obvious he shouldn't have needed to answer it. "We've got a room and we're prepping it now."

"I don't want him to be in pain," Mom said to the man in scrubs.

All I could think about was my leg. I liked my leg. I kind of needed my leg. If my nose was my worst feature, my legs were the best: long, strong, and perfectly proportioned. I was a fast runner, especially for my height, six three, and while I couldn't shoot a basket to save my life, I started on the basketball team because I was the best rebounder, could vault so high. What would I do without a leg? I needed *both* of them.

It's morning, I thought, coming awake. *Where am I?* I saw Mom and Dad asleep in chairs. Slowly but steadily, the events of yesterday solidified in my mind. I knew where I was, and my stomach turned over. My heart immediately raced. I heard my own breathing. Terrified, I moved my hand down to where my leg should be.

I exhaled hard. My leg was there.

I slept until they eased me off the serious pain medication and gave me stuff that didn't work, because my leg hurt like *hell*. I still had a drip in my arm, but it wasn't enough. I finally became myself late in the day. The summer light was beginning to dim, and I saw only Dad in the chair, reading.

"Dad?" I said.

"Theo," he said, bolting to his feet. "Thank God. How do you feel?" He came to the bed.

"What day is it?"

"It's Monday, son."

"I have my leg," I said.

"Yes, you do, and you're going to keep it."

"Why wouldn't I keep it?"

"The biopsy came back negative. Once they were in surgery they could see that it was a benign bone cyst that had been growing in your femur. They said you'd probably had it a long time, maybe born with it."

"Bone cyst?"

"You should rest more."

"No," I said, still groggy but too anxious to sleep. "Tell me. I need to know."

"A little hole in your bone, filled with fluid. They usually go away, but yours kept growing and growing as your bone got longer. What they didn't know for sure was if it was cancer or not. Osteosarcoma. Mom and I knew about it because Senator Kennedy's son had it. It was all over the news a few years ago. He lived but they amputated his leg."

It slowly dawned on me. Mom and Dad had been waiting to find out if I was going to wind up in a cancer ward with a stump where my left leg was supposed to be.

"Okay, I'm ready for the bad news," I said.

"There's no more bad news, Theo. The worst has happened, and they fixed it. They filled the hole with bone graft, realigned the femur, and screwed a plate into it with six screws, three on either side of the break. Except for your broken femur, you are super healthy. All your weight lifting and running and your—your *youth*. You're going to be *fine*."

I tried to sit up, but it felt like someone had punched a knife into my thigh, and I shouted from the pain. He sat gently on the edge of my bed. He put his arms around me, and his scratchy face next to mine.

"Dad, what's wrong?"

"Oh, Theo," he said. "I thought I was going to lose you. I guess I kept it all bottled up until now. It had never before occurred to me that I could lose you." He looked ready to start crying—which is kind of scary since I'd never seen him cry in my life—but he went to the sink that was in the room, pulled out paper towels from the dispenser, wiped his face, and blew his nose. He put his glasses back on.

He pulled a chair close so that he could be near enough to hold my hand as he spoke. He took two deep breaths and let them out before he continued.

"Theo, it's going to take a long time till you're better. You're going to be laid up for at least two months. They don't know, it depends. They're keeping you here for several days. You'll need some physical therapy to teach you how to move. You won't be able to put any pressure on your left leg for quite a while. After a couple months maybe you might be able to use a cane, they said. You're going to lose strength in that leg because you won't have used it for weeks. You might have a permanent limp, they don't know."

Two months, I thought suddenly. It was nearly July. I'd miss two-a-day practices in August. "Two months and then I should be good. I can start practicing with the team, right?"

He held my hand. "No sports for a year, at least."

"Dad, no!" I said. I covered my eyes with my arm.

"They'll have to see how you heal. They don't expect it to affect growth because it's not near a growth plate, but Theo. They said maybe *never*, at least not with a high-contact sport like football. I'm sorry."

I'd just been going to Blossom and mowing the lawn a couple days ago. Suddenly everything was changed. I'd never even considered the possibility that life could change so fast.

"Dad, is it my birthday? I'm sixteen today?"

"Yes, son."

When your entire life changes, and "entire life" includes everything that is and will be, your whole future, when that changes absolutely, it only follows that the way you think about that life changes. I could live without basketball and baseball—they were just hobbies I was good at till football came around.

And yet it wasn't up to me. The doctors said I should never play football again. There was talk of my staying back a grade if I couldn't get back to school in time. I went to a competitive school, and my parents really wanted me to go to a good college—they'd talked before about holding me back a grade. I knew they'd hold me back if they thought it increased my chances of getting into a good college. If I were held back a year, I would lose my friends to a higher grade and then completely when they went off to college and I didn't. And I couldn't write a letter to Julia and walk it to her house, as I'd planned, hoping to see her again. Would I *ever* see her again? I'd only just met her. It all came to me in a single comprehensive vision, my whole world changed. I was scared. I smeared the tears on my face with both hands.

Dad said, "Try to sleep some more, Theo. I'll be right here."

4

I spent a week in the hospital. The nurses were mainly managing the twelve-inch incision along the side of my left leg to make sure it healed properly. And I also had to do a couple hours a day of physical therapy. How to get in and out of bed. What not to do. Lessons in how to use crutches. Even though both halves of my femur were completely secured and immobile, they didn't want me to put even a feather's weight on my left leg while the bone graft took and the bone itself started to heal, for at least two weeks. Also the pain was intense—I had no intention of putting *any* weight on that leg.

I started watching Julia Child and Graham Kerr. I'd always liked to cook because I loved to eat. It was a means to an end. I'm not sure what it was about *watching* people cook food, but it was calming. There was never anything good on in the afternoon, which is why I'd turned the channel to the PBS station and found Julia Child's show, *The French Chef,* which was followed by Graham Kerr's *The Galloping Gourmet.* Maybe I liked these shows because the hospital food was so bad and I was always so hungry, but these two, Julia Child especially, made me want to cook what they were cooking. Also, I didn't think about myself when I watched them cook. I studied how she minced an onion. How she diced a potato. How she sautéed them till they were soft, then added a few well-beaten eggs.

I loved it when she tried to flip a whole big skilletful of food, as she did with a giant potato pancake—"when you flip the whole mass, you have to have the *courage* of your *convictions*," she trilled—then she zooped it into the air and half of the potato landed on the stove.

"Well, that didn't go very well!" she said, scooping potato off the stovetop and plopping it back in the pan. She looked up at the camera and said, "You see, I didn't have the *courage* the way I should have." She made you feel like she was talking to you personally. She wasn't embarrassed, didn't try to cover it up, or make it seem worse than it was. "You can always pick it up and put it back in the pan. Who's going to see?" Here was an optimistic realist. I liked that. You could eat your mistakes, and no one would ever know. I had to have *convictions* and also the *courage* to back them up. And I badly wanted that potato pancake.

The hospital delivered me home in a quiet ambulance, and two burly guys hauled me upstairs to my room on a stretcher. I was basically going to live in the hospital gown in my bed for the next two weeks. I was exhausted from the move. But once everything was settled and the delivery men left, I surveyed my room. My parents had reconfigured it. The big double bed used to be in the corner, but that would have forced me to get out on the left side, now my bad side. The headboard was now in the center of the long wall, and I faced the two windows looking into the neighbor's back lawn. They'd moved the toy chest with the stereo and speakers to the left side of the bed, near enough to reach, figuring I'd want to be able to play music. On the right side of the bed was what they called a commode. Basically a plastic bedpan set in a cheap metal chair. This would save me the long trip of fifteen feet to my bathroom. Humiliating.

"Can I get you a glass of milk or ice water?" Mom asked, pulling a sheet over me.

"No."

"Are you hungry?"

"No." I sat propped on pillows, arms folded across my chest.

"Are you sure, honey?" She felt my forehead, pushed my bangs back. I shook my head away. Now that the bed had been moved ninety degrees and into the center of the room, I lay directly beneath the Nastassja poster. I had to look across the room at the Browns' posters on the wall, Brian Sipe and Greg Pruitt.

"Please take those down," I said.

"Honey, they're part of your room, and you love them."

"Please take them down."

She frowned.

"And I'm not using that thing." I tilted my head toward the commode.

"Don't be silly. We don't mind."

"It's disgusting."

"It won't be any worse than cleaning out the kitty litter." I shook my head. She said, "We all go to the bathroom."

"I am not using that *shit* pan!" I pulled it out of the metal chair and flung it as hard as I could into my closet door, then shouted out as the pain stabbed my thigh like a knife.

"*Theo!*" she said in her cross voice. She was about to say more, so I said, "Fuck you!"

I waited. She was going to be *pissed*. I'd never said anything like this before to either of my parents. But she only closed her eyes, and her neck went limp. Then when she didn't get mad, I started to cry. "I'm sorry, Mom," I blubbered, covering my face. "I'm so sorry."

She sat on my bed, carefully, wiped my cheeks after I'd stopped crying.

"My darling boy," she said. "Your life is not over. It's beginning. This is just a big pause. Will your life *change* when the pause is over? Of course. Of *course* it will. But *you* decide how it will change. *You* choose."

Dad was leaning against the doorjamb. And this is when he said it, that thing that I'm still trying to understand if it's true or not. "You know, Theo," he said, "some ancient societies believed that the gods have to take something away from you, something precious and vital, in order to give you more of something else."

We negotiated a compromise. Dad was able to rent a wheelchair from a medical supply company that afternoon. He and Mom agreed to help me into that, and I'd wheel myself to the bathroom when I had to use the toilet. But if I just had to pee, I was to use the commode, especially if I woke in the middle of the night.

The next day, the evening of my first full day at home, a Tuesday, my parents surprised me with a small party of sorts, inviting Johnny and Roger for dinner and cake in my room. My mom had the clever idea of serving beef fondue, which was one of my favorites. You cook your own beef and vegetables in a pot of hot oil, and Mom and Dad both made delicious sauces to go with it.

"Since we can't be together in the kitchen, I thought we'd bring the kitchen to you," she said.

Johnny gave me some albums by the Ramones and the Dead Boys. He was always trying to get me to like punk and New Wave music. Roger got me a matching coffee mug and T-shirt, both of which read "Cleveland: You gotta be tough."

Mom made my favorite cake, an angel food cake with whipped cream sprinkled with crushed Heath Bars.

And then Dad gave me a card, his and mom's gift. I figured it was money that, as usual, I'd put in my savings account. But when I opened it, I found a key taped inside. I didn't even read the card because I knew that key. It was the key to Dad's 1965 Mustang.

"But, Dad, you love that car."

"That's why I want you to have it."

"Oh my God," I said. I looked at Johnny and Roger, who both mouthed, "Whoa."

I honestly couldn't believe it. I'd thought he'd loved that car more than anything.

"I'll take really good care of it, Dad."

"I know you will."

Johnny and Roger helped my parents clean up (Roger even stayed to do the dishes with my dad). Mom came up to check on me to see if there was anything I needed. I said no, that I was tired, and asked her to close the door.

With the lights off, I could start crying, and as it got heavier, I put my pillow over my face so my parents wouldn't hear. My sixteenth birthday. I just couldn't seem to stop crying, or maybe I just didn't want to.

5

The next day, the new normal began, spending every hour in my bed. My parents had to go back to work, so I was by myself until they returned, which would be at 6:25 (Dad) and 6:40 (Mom), almost unfailingly. They doled out as many pain pills as they could, Tylenol with codeine, which was never enough that first week. Sometimes the pain in my leg woke me in the middle of the night, a dull throbbing ache that seemed to radiate out of the center of my bone, and I couldn't go back to sleep. One day bled into another so that I hardly knew what day it was until it was the weekend when Mom and Dad weren't at work.

They'd put the coffee table from the living room beside the bed and loaded it with food during the week when they were at work—bread and sandwich meat and peanut butter and milk in ice in a cooler, a pitcher of water, Pop-Tarts, pretzels, my favorite candy, Now and Laters.

What I remember most is the boredom. You'd think I'd have been able to plow through my summer reading: *1984*, *A Tale of Two Cities*, and *The Grapes of Wrath*, with nothing to do other than lie on my back. But I couldn't concentrate. My mind just kept drifting. And I just didn't care about anything in the books. I didn't really care about anything. I went from angry to depressed back to angry again. I tried not to think about what my friends were doing. Making money at summer jobs, going to parties and concerts, or just hanging out around Sarah's pool on an ordinary summer afternoon, eating those great grilled cheeses and drinking root beer floats her mother made.

Nothing would be ordinary anymore.

Dad had bought a small TV and put it on, ironically, a TV table, one of the little foldout tables in the den for when we wanted to watch television during dinner. I had to sit up and stretch to turn the channel, which hurt, but the doctor said any movement I could stand was good as long as I didn't put any weight on my leg. If I only watched TV all day long, I felt crummy, so I allowed myself a morning game show, *Let's Make a Deal*, and I got hooked on the soap opera *All My Children* at one, then *The French Chef* and *The Galloping Gourmet* starting at four.

I was watching Julia Child when *Julia* Julia knocked on our back door and called out, "Hello?" I couldn't believe it. Then she entered the house and called out again, "Hello?"

"Hello?" I called back tentatively. I didn't want to hope too much—it was too much to believe.

"Theo?"

It *was* her. "Up here," I said. My heart hammered against my ribs.

And then, unbelievably, she stood in my doorway, dressed in a long flowered skirt, cowboy boots, a pale chamois shirt, bangles on her wrists, her beautiful hair flowing over her shoulders, my book in her hand.

"I hope you don't *mind*," she said.

"Are you kidding?" I pushed myself up, catching a whiff of myself and realizing how awful I must look. And smell. Thank goodness it was summer and the windows were open.

"Is it okay, being in your room? I mean what if one of your parents comes home?"

"They won't be home till after six. They'd be glad you're here. It's so crushingly boring."

"You're watching a cooking show?"

"Oh, um, no. I mean it just happened to come on." I turned the TV off and said, "How did you find me?"

"I bumped into your friend Johnny at the Record Exchange. He told me what happened. I'm so sorry, Theo. He said you wouldn't mind the company and that I should just let myself in."

"You should give a guy some warning. I didn't even have time to brush my hair."

She laughed. I scratched my head with both hands and pushed my hair back. It had to be super oily.

"I didn't have your number," she said.

Julia observed the room, intensely, as if she were trying to memorize it. All of it. The overhead light, my dresser and desk, the Nastassja Kinski poster. The wheelchair and commode (thank God Dad cleaned it before he left for work). She pushed open the door to the bathroom, turned the light on, then off. "Wow, you have your own *bathroom*?" she said.

She walked to the desk and touched the wall next to it where there were two pale rectangles of bright painted wall, where the Browns' posters had been.

"What used to be here?"

"Kid stuff," I said.

"Hmm," she said.

"You don't have to return the book. I meant for you to keep it."

"I wasn't sure, so I thought I'd bring it. I read it. You were right."

42

"Did you like it?"

"The language is so beautiful."

She made herself comfortable in the yellow swivel chair by the radiator. She spun around once completely, then pressed her knees together and leaned forward. "I loved all the little details, like the shaving cream on that guy's face. And the way he describes light. And how tawdry Wilson's garage was. What a brute Tom Buchanan was. And the eyeglasses theme. Owl eyes!"

"And the valley of ashes. That was a real place."

"Really? I loved the whole time period. It was so exotic. I didn't love Daisy."

"Why not?"

"Kind of vapid. Weak."

"I hadn't thought of her that way."

"Because you're a guy."

"What's that mean?"

"It doesn't bug you when women are portrayed as weak."

"I didn't think of her as weak. Just a girl."

"'The best a girl can be is a fool?' What she said when her daughter was born?"

I guessed Julia was right.

"'They were reckless people,'" she said, quoting from the book.

"And the green light!" I said. I'd written my paper on this, the theme of the green light. My parents almost fell over when I showed them the paper with an A at the top. My first ever A on an English paper.

"I do think love will make you do things like that," Julia said. "That whole world Gatsby created for her. He definitely had me in the end. So sad." Julia had the cutest way of tucking her long hair behind her ears when she spoke.

Julia spotted the milk crate by the bed filled with albums. She went to it, sat cross-legged, and flipped through them all. "Hmm. AC/DC. Meatloaf. Supertramp. Kiss. Journey. Kansas." Another tic I was beginning to notice was the way, when she was thinking, she pursed her lips to the left, as if trying to kiss someone to her left without moving her head.

"What?" I asked.

"Not really my kind of thing."

"What is your kind of thing?"

"Grateful Dead, Joni Mitchell, Carol King. Crosby, Stills, Nash and Young." She pulled out an old album my mom had wanted me to listen to by the weirdly named Simon and Garfunkel, and I wanted to say it wasn't mine. But Julia said, "Especially the Young part. Neil is the visionary." She opened the Simon and Garfunkel album. "Oh, cool, they've got the lyrics. These are great."

"I don't really know them. I've heard of them?"

"Well, you should know them," she said. She stood and for no apparent reason, she performed a pirouette. A wave of her spicy sweet scent wafted over me.

"Are you a dancer?"

"I used to take ballet, but that was ages ago. They say taking ballet is good for football players. You're on the team, right?"

"Was," I said, looking away. "No sports for a year and no hard contact sports. Maybe ever."

She sat on the edge of my bed and gently squeezed my left foot through the covers. I explained what had happened and what the doctors had said about sports.

"Oh my God, it's that bad? I'm so sorry. That's terrible." It was then that she noticed the two shelves above where my bed had been. "Oh, wow." And she stood to get a better look at a dozen or so trophies I'd won over the years. Several were from Little League, but the ones I was proudest of were the Punt, Pass, and Kick competitions, where we'd compete individually. I'd once made it to Canton and the Football Hall of Fame, the competition where two people in each age group went on to compete during halftime of a Browns game. I never made it to the stadium.

I don't know why I even let myself think about these things.

"How about golf or tennis?" she asked. "Your school has those teams, no?"

"Yeah. But I've never been much for those sports. It would be pretty hard to pick them up as a senior, even if the doctors said it was okay."

"You'll find something."

"Doubt it."

"Don't be so negative."

"Hard not to when I can't even get out of bed."

"Well, you're not doing yourself any good, thinking like that."

I wanted to tell her something I'd been obsessing over. Who was I now? Who was I going to be? But this scared me, and I didn't want her to see that.

I guess I waited too long to say something else because she glanced at her watch, which meant she was going to leave. I wished I hadn't been such a downer.

"I gotta get to work," she said.

"Where do you work?"

"Restaurant Margaux? On Larchmere?"

"Heard of it."

"You should get your parents to take you. Expensive but delicious."

"What do you do?"

"I'm a server. I used to be a back waiter, for like a year—back waiters drop the bread, refill waters, clear tables—but I was promoted at the beginning of the summer. Tips are *so* much better."

It dawned on me that it was completely possible that her being here was a one-time deal, to return the book. "Hey, is there any chance you could let me hear some of the bands you mentioned?" I asked.

She smiled her perfect beautiful natural smile and said, "Sure, that would be fun."

"Call me? That way I can at least take a washcloth bath. I must have terrible BO."

She laughed. "You don't!" My heart actually felt lighter for a few seconds when she laughed.

"There's a notepad on my desk. Write down my number."

She did, then tucked the piece of paper into *The Great Gatsby*. "It's going to be a few days, though."

"Because of Bennett?"

"I forgot, you *know* him, don't you?"

"Everyone knows him."

"He's on an eight-week trek through Southeast Asia with his parents. Won't be back till the start of school."

"Really?" I said with what I hoped wasn't too much gladness. This was *seriously* good news.

"Just really busy, that's all. See ya."

"Julia? You are so . . . wonderful for coming over. Thank you."

"You were sweet to give me this book, and I wanted to talk to you about it." Her gaze caught on the wheelchair and commode. "I'm so sorry about what happened. I can't imagine. I'll call you."

And just like that, she was gone.

6

Julia returned four days later, a collection of albums in her arms. She even called ahead of time so that I had a chance to, as Mom would have it, "freshen up."

"Okay, today you get a lesson in the Grateful Dead," she announced, striding into my room, setting the albums on my desk, and sitting in the yellow chair to remove her boots. She wore the same frayed and patched jeans she'd worn to the concert, and a flowered blouse. She picked up the first album and showed it to me. It had a cool painting of a skeleton playing a violin. *Blues For Allah*, it said.

I'd heard of the band, but it always had sinister connotations for me. I was wrong. It had the great guitar that I loved, but it was more refined than say the Ted Nugent album that I'd been listening to earlier. Julia said, "Hmm," as she returned that album to its cover and put on *Blues For Allah*.

We listened to the first two songs, "Help on the Way/ Slipknot!" and "Franklin's Tower," which was cool for the way one song blended into the next.

"So," Julia said, rising to turn the volume down as the next instrumental song came on. "What do you think?"

"I like it," I said, and I meant it. Though she could have brought the Mormon Tabernacle Choir and I'd have felt the same, I think.

"Yay!" she said.

"How did you find them?"

"My sister."

"You have a sister?"

"Two. Jeanie got me into the Dead. She's the oldest. She's married now, lives in Cleveland Heights. She's great. So is her husband, Joe. She's, like, my best friend. He's a nurse at the VA and drives a Harley. Janice is two years older than me, she goes to Cleveland State and still lives at home to save money. We don't get along."

"Why not."

"She's just a bitch. Any chance she gets to rat me out to Daddy, she will."

"What about your mom, what does she do?"

Julia's demeanor changed immediately. I saw something I hadn't seen before—a hardness that surprised me. It was kind of like her face turned to stone. "She died."

I pushed myself up in bed and said, "Oh my God, I'm sorry. How old were you?"

"Eleven." Julia shrugged and said, "It is what it is."

"How did she die?"

Julia paused a long time, staring at her lap, then stuck out her chin as if to defy the facts, I thought. "Breast cancer," she said.

"You must miss her."

"Yeah. A lot."

There was a long silence. We listened to the music.

"I bet she was beautiful," I said.

Julia said, "What?"

"Your mom. I bet she was beautiful."

Julia looked down, smiled softly, and said, "Jeanie says I look just like her. And sound like her."

"Tell me more."

"I remember her reading to me. I was the youngest. *Runaway Bunny*. Dr. Seuss." Julia closed her eyes for a moment. "You know, it's the inconsequential things that I really remember. Like standing at her side and looking up at her as she made us tuna fish sandwiches."

The stylus rose at the end of the album and returned itself to its cradle.

"I want to know everything about you," I said.

She stood abruptly and lifted another album. "*Workingman's Dead*. Your indoctrination continues."

We were still listening to the Grateful Dead when Dad got home from work. As soon as he called out "Hey, Theo, I'm home," Julia bolted to her feet. I said, "What?"—afraid she was leaving. When she saw I wasn't freaking out, she asked, "It's okay for me to be here?"

"Why wouldn't it be okay?"

Dad always came up to see me immediately. When he walked through the open door, Julia was still standing and he said, "Hello?"

"Dad, this is my friend Julia."

She strode directly to him and extended her hand. "Julia Bevilacqua. Pleased to meet you."

"And pleased to meet *you*." I could tell Dad was surprised by this girl.

She gave him a definitive handshake. Dad nodded his approval. "I am thrilled Theo has some company."

It's fair to say that Julia got me through those first few weeks when I could barely leave my bed. It wasn't just the couple times a week she was physically there, it was also the hope, every day, that today would be the day she'd visit. It took all my self-control not to call her every minute of the day.

I tried to keep a regular schedule. I watched the same shows at the same time. I failed to read my summer reading. Instead I became obsessed with a book mom gave me. Mom saw me watching *The French Chef* and gave me Julia Child's book *Mastering the Art of French Cooking*. "Lord knows I'll never use it," she said. With this book and her show, I couldn't wait to try some of her recipes.

After three and a half weeks, we returned to the doctor. I was pretty comfortable on crutches by now. I had a lot of power in my arms, and this helped. The doctor was surprised by how well I was recovering. The wound looked great, he said, and he was able to remove the stitches, so I didn't have to come back for another three weeks to get more X-rays and an evaluation, perhaps even graduate to a cane.

Back home, liberated from my bedroom and inspired by Julia on TV, her book, and literal hunger and boredom, I figured out how to position myself at the counter, on crutches, so that I could cut and chop. It was tiring and my armpits hurt because I had to put all my weight on them. If I used just one crutch under my left arm, I could transfer cut ingredients, all in their separate bowls, from counter to stovetop. It was all a matter of being organized. I had to be organized so that I could tell Dad, before he left for work, exactly what pots and pans, bowls and utensils to dig out from the cupboards that otherwise took me forever to get.

This was how I was able to cook for my Julia. More than a month after the break, early August, I worked up the nerve to call her and ask her to come over. I'd been messing about in the kitchen for a couple weeks by then. Cooking was fun, and when I finished I had something delicious to eat. Usually.

Mom especially was thrilled that I'd even begun to cook our dinner. She hated cooking and you could tell this from the food. Dinner was usually meat cooked in some kind of Campbell's soup, Minute Rice, and frozen vegetables. If I'd known I could cook better than her, I'd have started cooking our dinner a long time ago.

Dad, who continued to be astonished that I could make dinner, had gone to the library for me and gotten me *James Beard's American Cookery*, the second volume of Julia Child's *Mastering the Art of French Cooking*, and a number of books on different types of cuisines.

I decided to make Julia a Spanish tortilla, a kind of omelet with diced potato and onion. I'd tried the recipe the week before and it was exceptional. A lot of it could be done ahead of time, and it was easy to make so I wasn't likely to screw it up and embarrass myself in front of her.

I took a bath and got downstairs at about noon. Dad had set out what I'd asked for. Four Pyrex bowls, one each for the eggs, the onion, the potato, and one to put scraps in (potato peels, onion skin, eggshells) so that I didn't have to make unnecessary trips to the trash by the back door. A Teflon pan for the Spanish tortilla and a roasting pan for the roast pork I'd planned on making for dinner.

I had an hour to get everything set for Julia. Peel and dice the potato and onion. There are helpful illustrations in the cookbooks for how to do this, making a kind of grid on the face of the onion so that when I sliced it, the onion fell to the cutting board in a dice. I found that if I positioned the cutting board just right I could support myself on the crutches, and by leaning my hips into the counter I could use my hands and arms fully. I did everything I needed at the counter—peel and dice the onions and put them in one bowl; crack six eggs into another bowl and whisk them, adding salt and pepper; and last, because they'd turn brown if they sat, peel and dice the potatoes—I could then transfer each component to the stove top. For this I'd have to hop because I couldn't carry a bowl *and* use crutches.

When the diced onion was sizzling and sweet in the pan, it occurred to me how different it was to be cooking for Julia rather than just for myself or my parents. I had butterflies in my stomach like I did just before a game. I was always nervous until the sound of that first kickoff—a different gear engaged, and I was totally, almost thoughtlessly in the game. I wanted everything to be perfect for her. I knew I'd be nervous until she was here and I was actually cooking with her.

When the potatoes and onions were done, I took them off the burner and turned the oven on. I crutched to the den and cued up *Blues For Allah* on the stereo so that it would be ready when she arrived. Which was now—she was *early*. She drove a Volkswagen Beetle. Its muffler was shot, but she couldn't afford to replace it. I heard her even before she turned into our drive.

I could move pretty fast by now by taking long strides with the crutches. I wanted to be there to open the door for her—she'd never seen me downstairs and had taken to just walking in. I heard her call out, "Hello?" She stepped through the back door as I raced toward her. My left crutch hit a wet spot and slid out from under my arm and I went crashing to the floor at her feet right beside the kitchen island.

"Theo!"

I rolled over onto my back trying not to groan from the pain.

"Happens all the time," I lied.

"Oh, Theo," she said, more softly. She set the albums she'd brought on the counter and knelt beside me in the middle of the kitchen. I needed a moment to recover. The pain in my leg was pretty bad.

She put her hand lightly on my chest. "What can I do?"

"Don't move." I put my hand on her hand to keep it there. "Just give me a second."

This was really embarrassing but the trade-off of her touch made the pain worth it. She was kind of leaning over me and her hair swung near my face, and I breathed the scent in through my nose. Her hair smelled like springtime—whatever she washed it with, I wanted some.

"Are you all right? You didn't rebreak anything, did you?"

"I don't think so." I felt my left thigh gently. I'd put on my white painter's pants and the red shirt, which I'd been wearing when I first met her, hoping it would be good luck. "Just hurts. I think it's the way the muscles are growing around the metal plates holding the bone together."

"Thank goodness. I would have felt responsible."

"It's my own fault. About an hour ago, I dropped an ice cube. It's hard to pick stuff up, so I ignored it. Now it's punishing me."

After the silence grew awkward, I said, "Okay." I let go of her hand. I sat up, rolled over, and pushed myself up to my knees with all the weight on my right knee. I extended my left arm. "If you could get under me and lift."

"Lift."

"Kind of be my left leg until I'm upright." With my right arm using the middle of the crutch to support my right side, I rose. When I was up, and Julia retrieved the other crutch for me, I growled, putting all my weight on the crutches, and said, "God! Things that were so simple are so difficult now!"

"*Hey*, shhh," she said. I was breathing hard from the effort of standing. She looked up at me. Her eyes were so big and brown behind her glasses. She put her hand on my cheek. "This is *temporary*. And you're already downstairs, and whipping through the house from the looks of it. Be patient."

"I've never been very patient," I said.

She chuckled. "That was quite an entrance you made," she said.

"I must have looked like a cartoon."

She said, "Just don't stop falling for me."

Even clueless me knew that was a flirt and I kind of froze. She knew it, too, but she simply gave me a little curl of her lips and tipped her head.

"I brought you girl music today," she said. "I feel like poetry."

"Girl music."

"Yeah." She took the albums from the counter to display them. "Joni Mitchell. Carole King. James Taylor."

"James Taylor is girl music?"

"Yeah, girls like it. Don't worry, so will you."

"Do you want to put one on?"

"No, let's listen to the end of this side first." She held her long arms high in the air and swayed to the music. The song was moving from a slow beat of a bass guitar into a high-pitched *bing* from Jerry Garcia's clean, clear lead guitar and "Franklin's Tower." I'd

54

been listening to it obsessively. It was so much more elegant than the hard rock I always listened to. And, of course, the music was inseparable from thoughts of Julia herself.

She danced and swayed. She twirled. Her billowy white shirt echoed her sway, her jeans, her bare feet.

"What's this?" she said, noticing the bowls of partly cooked food on the stove.

"Lunch," I said.

"You're *cooking*?"

"I told you to come hungry."

"I thought you were being metaphorical. You're going to cook? Like, food?"

"Attempt to. But if it's bad, please lie."

"I doubt I'll have to. The only food at our house comes frozen in aluminum trays."

"Are you hungry?"

"I'm always hungry!"

I grinned. Most of the girls at Hathaway Brown "watched" their weight, drank can after can of Tab, the diet soda pop, which they kept in the pocket of their tweed skirts. Julia wasn't heavy, but she was definitely tall and fleshy, in a particularly gorgeous way, in a way that said "I am who I am." I found that really attractive. Her confidence and ease. But then, I found everything about her to be that way.

"Good. Let's go then." I crutched to the stove.

"What can I do to help?"

"One thing I'm really bad at on crutches is carrying things. Can you set the table?"

"*That* is something I know how to do."

"Oh, that's right. Sorry to make you work!"

"Not work when I'm one of the eaters. This will be a pleasure." She turned and opened the first cupboard door, which was where the plates were, as if she already knew. I turned on the large front burner, which would take several minutes to glow orange. Only when it was hot could I put the pan on, otherwise I couldn't gauge how hot the pan was. I'd already burned too much food starting the pan on a cold electric burner. I turned the oven knob to broil.

"Let's eat on the porch," I said. Julia had put the plates on the table in the breakfast nook. "Off the living room. It's nice out there." Mom, Dad, and I always ate most meals there in summer. Julia gathered all the silverware, paper napkins, and plates.

"What have you been doing?" I asked when she finally came back.

"Just looking around. You've got a really nice house."

"Really?"

"Um, yes. Your living room looks like it should have velvet roping around it."

"Mom's kind of a neat freak. And we almost never use that room. Just on holidays and when my parents have dinner parties."

I had everything I needed within reach, even the curly parsley for garnish (Mom told me this helped to keep the breath fresh, which I certainly wanted to do). And so I began to cook, explaining that I was preparing a Spanish tortilla. I melted some butter in the pan. When it was bubbling and almost all melted, I added the onion and potato and stirred them with a wooden spoon. They were already cooked, so I only needed to heat them. I gave the eggs one last whisk and poured them into the pan, setting the bowls on the counter to my right as I finished with them. Julia immediately rinsed them in the sink. I lowered the temperature of the burner and carefully pulled a rubber spatula around the edges to make sure the egg didn't stick.

Once, half of it stuck to the pan when I upended it onto a plate—still good to eat, it just didn't look good. Another time, I way overcooked the egg, and while sticking wasn't an issue, it was too brown and tough on the bottom.

I liked that, in cooking, you could eat your mistakes. Also, you always got a little better every time you cooked—unlike math, which I could study forever and never retain anything. I really wanted this dish to be perfect for her, so it was super important this time to make sure it didn't stick *and* that I didn't overcook it. Or, God forbid, burn it. That's one thing you couldn't fix *or* eat—burned. But also I didn't want the eggs to be runny when I turned it out. It was all incredibly delicate.

I transferred my left crutch to my right armpit so that both crutches were together. I then held on to the middle support, my left foot not even touching the floor, and hopped back once, opened the oven door, slid the pan onto the top rack under the broiler, and shut the door.

When I was back on both crutches to wait for the eggs to finish, Julia said, "Whoa. That was good."

"Practice," I said.

"I'm impressed."

"It should be done in, like, a minute."

"What should we drink?"

"I don't know, milk?" I felt silly the moment I said it, I don't know why. I always drank milk with food.

"Milk?"

"Water?"

"Do your parents have any white wine?"

I paused. I knew we did have wine because Mom usually had a big glass of it when she got home from work. But Julia was suggesting *we* drink it. "Yeah, I think so. In the fridge."

Julia looked. "Excellent, two big bottles." She pulled the opened bottle out. It was almost full. "Chablis," she read. "Perfect. Chef always recommends white wine with eggs."

"Chef?"

"Chef Jackson, my boss."

I'd had beer, of course, and had tried sips of my dad's evening martini, which was nasty. On special occasions, I would get a small glass of red wine, which burned my throat. Mom and Dad thought it very European of them to have me tasting wine. But it had never really affected me. I wasn't a big drinker like some of the other guys on the team. It was also against school rules, and I could be kicked off the team, maybe even expelled. I just never thought of drinking wine. For lunch.

Julia quickly found wineglasses, and she departed with the wine. I did my maneuver to check the eggs, supporting myself with my right hand and, reaching into the oven with my left, oven-mitted hand, pulled the pan out. I shook the pan gently. The eggs were still wavy, meaning they needed more time. I'd learned that you wanted a gentle jiggle, not waves, and if it didn't jiggle at all, it was overcooked. I took down a dinner plate.

Julia returned to the kitchen just as I pulled the pan out again and got the perfect jiggle. *Yes*, I said to myself. Julia was staring at me. I felt like I was performing—I suppose I was, and I liked it. I set the pan on a cool burner and dragged the spatula around the edge and even under the bottom a little. Now that it was cooked right, stickage was my main concern. I handed Julia my crutches. I needed full use of my arms. Standing on one leg, I put the plate over the pan, which was just larger than the pan. Quickly and with the courage of my conviction, as Julia Child taught me, I flipped the pan over. I didn't lift the pan immediately, I just peeked under. "I think it worked."

I lifted the pan, and the omelet came off cleanly, a perfect golden brown with pale flecks of potato and onion.

"Oh my God, it's beautiful," she said.

"We'll need a knife to serve this with," I said. Julia retrieved one and took the plate.

"Wait," I said, and I reached for a small dish of parsley sprigs and arranged them delicately around the tortilla.

"Nice," Julia said. "To the porch?"

"Yes!"

I'd done it. I turned off the broiler and made sure the burners were off and followed Julia onto the screened-in porch.

This was the best place in the house in summer. Abundant droopy deep green ferns were hung on the walls, and on the floor were pots of geraniums. All the cushions had brightly colored floral prints, like you'd see out at the Hunt Club. The iron table had a glass top and black plastic placemats. It could get wet out here on windy, rainy days. But on warm dry days like today, it was shady and cool, the leaves from the surrounding shrubbery brushing up against the screens. A quiet late July afternoon.

"You've even lit candles!" I said.

"Of course," she said. "Gotta have candles."

I leaned my crutches in the corner and sat. Julia sat. I cut the tortilla into three wedges and served her one. I added some parsley to her plate. When I'd done the same for me, I saw that Julia was staring at her plate as if there were something wrong.

"What's the matter?" I asked.

"It's just so beautiful."

Julia put her face close to the tortilla and inhaled. She lifted her wineglass and said, "Thank you, Theo." I touched my glass to hers. I didn't say anything and could feel my face flush.

Julia took a big gulp of wine, then tasted the tortilla. "Oh, man," she said, chewing. "This is great. I can't believe you *made* this."

I could tell from the way it cut that it was cooked *perfectly*. I wanted to shout yes and pump my fist but contained myself.

"You really like doing this," she said.

"I guess so."

Can a Spanish tortilla redirect your life? This one did.

I split the third wedge of the tortilla and served us when we'd finished the first two. Julia poured more wine. I was starting to see why people liked wine. It enhanced the flavors of the food and made my thoughts light and happy, not nervous at all to be around Julia.

When she'd finished her plate, Julia left to flip the album and returned with her purse. "Okay if I smoke?" she asked.

"Sure." I pointed to the ashtray.

She lit a cigarette with the snappy Zippo and blew smoke toward the ceiling, head back so I could see the entirety of her long, pale neck, and said, "Oh my God, that was so good. I could eat that every single day."

"Thanks for letting me cook for you."

"Are you kidding me?"

"No. You have no idea how boring it is here. I never leave this place. Sometimes I think I'll go crazy. Just being inside my own head all day."

"What's in your head?"

60

"Stuff, just all kinds of stuff." Like, well, *you*.

"You should work at my restaurant," she said, exhaling smoke and tapping her cigarette on the ashtray.

I reached for my crutches and held them up. "I'm on these for at least another month. Then I'll have to use a cane until I build enough muscle back up to even *walk* normally. Then if I can walk okay, school will be starting." I hated even thinking about this, how I'd never play football again. I couldn't even imagine what school would be like in the fall. Maybe that's why I liked cooking— it was a way not to think about my life.

"Um," she said, and held up her plate. "You did this, didn't you?"

"That's not exactly the same as having a job."

Julia leaned forward. "One of our cooks got deported this week, and Chef had to fire the dishwasher when he caught him stealing steaks, so Chef is short-handed. Half the stuff that needs doing you could do sitting down. He needs a prep cook."

"But I can't even walk."

"*Stop.*" Julia pointed her finger at me. "Don't ever tell yourself you can't *do* something."

"I can't get a job like this." I pointed at my leg.

"Hey," she said. "You're not allowed to say 'I can't.' What you're allowed to say, instead, what you're allowed to say to your- *self* is, 'I tried my hardest, but I did not succeed.' Not 'I can't so why even try?' You know why?"

"Why," I said. It came out as a pout, which I didn't mean to show her.

"Half the time, you won't need to say that sentence. Because half the time you'll succeed."

She actually lifted my chin off my chest with two fingers until I was looking her in the eye. And in a fake voice imitating me, she said, "Ooooh, I can't cook. I'm damaged goods. My life is over."

"I can *cook*," I said.

"And you know why you could? Because wanting made it so."

Wanting made it so, I thought. Can simply wanting, if it's strong enough, make impossible things happen? Like wanting Julia?

"You are . . . really amazing, Julia."

"I know," she said, smiling. She took a drag on her cigarette and said, "More wine?"

"Sure," I said.

She refilled our glasses. We'd almost finished the bottle. I wondered if Mom would notice.

Julia was so close, her lips so pink and full. My heart was pounding. I didn't want to be crushed, but I wanted to lean in, I wanted so badly to kiss her. And as I slowly, slowly tilted toward her, she didn't move back. I leaned forward a little more. She didn't move. *Don't say can't*, I thought, and as I began to actually make the move to kiss her, the back door slammed and Mom called, *"Theo?!"*

My *mom*!

"Oh shit," Julia said, sitting up straight and stabbing her cigarette out, waving her hand quickly through the smoke.

I pressed the air down with my hands and said, "Act *casual*." She enlarged her eyes comically and I couldn't help but giggle.

"Theo?!" Mom called again. She *never* came home in the afternoon. But then she'd always had that spooky Mom sense.

I heard her take the stairs so I called out, as casually as I could, "We're on the porch, Mom." I took a breath and waited.

Mom appeared like the prow of a ship emerging slowly through a dark mist.

"What . . . is going *on* here?" she asked.

"Mom, this is Julia."

Julia, who was already standing, held out her hand. Mom gave it a weak shake and said, "Julia."

"Mrs. Claverback," she returned.

Mom didn't correct her as she usually did. Instead she surveyed the table.

"Julia's been so great about visiting and loaning me albums, I wanted to make her lunch."

"With wine? Since when do you drink *wine?*"

After giving the table a once-over, she gave Julia the same.

"Are you at Hathaway Brown?"

"I'll be a senior at Shaker this fall."

Mom's mouth tightened and she made an (almost) imperceptible "Hm." I felt my toes curl.

"I should be going," Julia said.

I thought, *please, no!*

Julia reached for her purse.

"No," Mom said. "Finish." She paused and looked at the table, then to me. She lifted the bottle from the table and studied the inch or so remaining. "How much did you *have?*"

"Just like a glass . . . maybe two?"

She gave me a skeptical look. "I've got to get to a meeting out in Solon." She turned to Julia and said, "Good to meet you, Julia," in a way that gave me no idea what she was really thinking.

Julia and I finished our glasses of wine, mainly talking about how lucky we'd been that Mom hadn't flipped. I knew she hadn't known *what* to do, she was so surprised. But the mood had changed irrevocably. The chance to kiss her was gone.

Julia did all the cleaning up as we listened to the second side of Joni Mitchell's *Blue*, which Julia called a masterpiece.

When she left, I put on side one of the album to listen to again. I lay down on the couch in the living room, and the next thing I knew, Dad was shaking me awake.

Dad was mad that we had to order pizza since I'd fallen asleep and never got the pork roast in the oven as I'd promised. Mom and Dad now did all the bussing and cleaning up after dinner, and I left to get Julia's albums from the den and take them to my room. Mom hadn't brought up Julia or the reason I'd fallen asleep and failed to prepare dinner. But I knew it was only because there hadn't been time to talk with Dad about it first. They always discussed an issue before they came at me as a United Front. Like when I failed earth science in ninth grade—that was bad. I knew she'd wait till she was alone with Dad. On my way up the stairs, I paused to listen. I could hear them in the kitchen. Cleanup was fast since there were few dishes, and I could picture just where they were, both leaning against adjacent kitchen counters, Dad having a second martini, Mom a second glass of wine, her arms crossed.

"And she was *smoking*."

"A lot of kids smoke," Dad said.

"She *was* polite, I'll give her that."

"I thought so, too."

"She just seems to be so much *older* than Theo. I don't know if she's a good influence."

"Spending time with Theo when he's stuck at home and depressed? I'd say that's a good influence."

"Getting him drunk and encouraging him to smoke?"

"Kate, you don't know that."

"By her example."

"And he cooked for her. Cooking for a pretty girl when otherwise he'd be lying around watching television, I'd say that's pretty good. All his friends have jobs and what can they do with Theo? He can't *do* anything."

"She goes to Shaker."

"Don't be a snob, Kate."

"I'm not being a snob. I just want him associating with . . . the right kind of friends."

"Oh please."

"Well, have a talk with him. Make sure his head is on straight with this girl."

"And say what?"

"Just make sure he tells us in advance what he's doing. I don't want him to all of a sudden start sneaking around."

Dad laughed and said, "How's he going to sneak around on crutches?"

"He's not going to be on crutches forever."

"And thank God for that."

They were quiet for a while.

Dad said, "I'll talk to him," and I began my laborious way up to my room.

The phone was right next to my bed, so I was able to pick it up before the first ring finished.

"Hey," Julia whispered.

"Julia?"

"Sorry for calling so late. I would have hung up if your parents answered."

"That's okay. I'm up. I was just waiting for the *Tonight Show* to come on."

"I couldn't wait to tell you. Chef agreed to see you. About a job."

"Did you tell him about my leg?"

"He said there's always work to be done. But there's one thing. You'll probably have to work for free until he can see you can do the work."

"Anything to get out of this house! But there's another thing: How am I going to get there?"

"I'll drive you, silly."

"Julia, this is so cool."

"Hey, did anything happen because of today?"

"Dad just asked me a few questions and told me I had to let them know ahead of time when I was having people over, and that I'm not to drink alcohol unless they're present."

"That's it?"

"My dad's been really cool since I broke my leg. We've talked more in the past month than we have, like, in my whole life. Mom's the hard-ass. But I think it's because she doesn't want me feeling sorry for myself. Dad's the opposite."

"Your dad, that's right, the *car*. Jesus."

"I can't even drive it. If I could only get my license." I was dying to be able to drive that car. "He said we could start practicing now that I'm more mobile. I can get in and out of the car and I don't need my left leg at all to drive. I don't know if I could drive your car."

"When your leg's better you'll have to let me teach you how to drive a stick."

"That would be cool."

"Okay." She went back to a whisper. "I hear my dad walking around upstairs. I gotta go. I'll pick you up at three forty-five."

"Should I wear a coat and tie?"

Julia laughed. "You're interviewing for back of the house, not front."

"Back of the house?"

"The kitchen. You'll learn. Daddy's coming down, gotta go. Thanks for lunch, Theo." And quickly, but gently, she replaced the phone in its cradle.

7

Julia parked on Larchmere Boulevard, a dicey mix of houses, brick storefronts, antique stores, bookstores, a barber shop, a tavern. Right on the edge of a bad part of town I didn't know well. She pointed to a Victorian house, green siding with maroon trim, across the street.

"This is it," she said.

"It's in a house?"

"Yeah, converted. You'll see."

A sign hanging from a lamppost by the sidewalk read simply, Margaux. I followed Julia along a brick pathway that should have been a driveway but was part raised garden and part walkway. Six tables were on what would have been a front lawn, set on fine white gravel within a boundary of shrubs. Broad stone steps led to a deep porch and a large wood front door with leaded glass.

I could move pretty fast on crutches now and so was a little ahead of Julia on the path beside the house when we turned into the backyard. It looked like a normal backyard, a garage, two picnic tables, shady, all of it surrounded by a chain-link fence. Closer to the house was an enormous white cloud of smoke. As if he had been conjured, a man appeared from within. A tall, slender figure in a plain white T-shirt, black pants, and black clogs.

He had wild brown hair that fell in loose coils, golden brown in the afternoon light, his eyes dark below a heavy brow. He was almost beautiful but for a long nose with a knobby bridge, and it bent slightly to the left. He had a gap between his large front teeth. This was the chef? I didn't know what I'd expected—someone fat and old, wearing a tall hat. This guy was young—more hippie than chef. I crutched toward him, Julia beside me.

"Chef, this is the friend, Theo, I was telling you about?"

I held my hand out. "Chef," I said loudly. Julia had told me to just call him Chef and nothing else. We shook. He looked me over. He bared his teeth, grinding the top teeth back and forth over the bottom teeth. Then he turned back to a big, rusted drum, opened the lid, and was again engulfed in smoke. It smelled so good, I said, "What's that?"

With a long set of tongs he lifted a huge rectangle of meat, displayed it, and flipped it, slapping it down on the grate. "Bacon," he said. At the far end of the kettle drum, he stirred the coals, closed it, and adjusted a central vent.

"Bacon?" I asked. The only bacon I'd ever seen came in strips in a yellow package.

He looked me over again, as if he couldn't believe I was standing there. He shook his head again. He said to Julia, "Show him around, then introduce him to Paul. Paul will set him up."

"Oui, Chef," she said.

To me he said, "We're clear, this is just a *stahj*, correct?"

I knew exactly what to say! "Oui, Chef!"

"Come on," Julia said. I followed.

"What's a *stahj*?" I asked.

"Short for *stagiaire*. Which I think is French for you work for free."

69

She led me up back steps through a small foyer through a kitchen and into the house, which had four large rooms that had been turned into ornate dining rooms with tables covered in white cloth. "You should meet Clive first. He's the maître d'."

Clive was an older man in a dark suit, more my dad's age than the chef's age. He had rust-colored hair and a pencil mustache. He stood at a stand next to the front door, studying a reservation book with a number two pencil. "Hey, Clive, this is my friend Theo. He's trying out in the kitchen."

Clive had a British accent. "This should be interesting."

"Want to see the upstairs?" she asked me.

"Sure." Stairs were still something of an ordeal, but I made a point of trying not to say no to anything just because I was on crutches.

We passed a guy and a girl wearing vests and ties, polishing wineglasses at one of the tables. "Who's the gimp," said the guy.

"Hey, Tony," Julia said, rolling her eyes.

There were two staircases, one off the front hall and one in the back near the kitchen. Julia took me to the former. "Up the front staircase and down the back. That way there are no traffic jams. Though the guests get in the way." The second floor had five more rooms, also with white tablecloths, now being set with silver and glasses and plates by two more people in vests and ties. We'd interrupted an exchange. One woman, with a pinched face and dark curly hair, stuffed a plastic bag into her pocket while the other, older and with red hair, counted bills before pocketing them.

"You're late," said the redhead when she looked up at us.

"Hey, Jules," said the other.

"Am not, Jackie," she said to the redhead. "I'm in charge of the new guy."

70

"He's *working* here?" she asked.

"*Staging* in the kitchen."

"You've got to be kidding," Jackie said.

To me, Julia said, "I'm working up here tonight, which is a bummer."

"Why?" I asked, then whispered in her ear. "Because you're working with her?"

Julia laughed, throwing her head back. I was in kind of a continuous swoon around her.

Julia pulled at my elbow and whispered back, "She's not so bad once you get to know her." Then in a normal voice she explained. "It's a lot of stairs all night long. Long nights, but keeps me in shape." She swatted her hip. "I gotta go change."

"What's in there?" I said, nodding at a door with a small sign with the word Private written in script.

Julia said, "Chef lives on the third floor."

"Have you ever seen it?"

"Are you kidding? Chef likes to be alone. I gotta change. I'll meet you in the kitchen. Chef Paul's the short white guy. He was behind the stove when we went through."

When I swung my way to go back toward the stairs we'd come up, she said, "Uh uh uh."

"Right," I said, pivoting on my right crutch, "front stairway is the up stairway." She followed me down the stairs, pointed to Paul, and disappeared down more steps to the basement.

The restaurant already felt busy, though it wasn't even open. A lot of people rushing about in the "front of the house" who completely ignored me—as if guys on crutches were a normal part of

71

the restaurant—and I was glad for it. Some were polishing wine-glasses, holding them up to the window, others stroked cloths over the silverware. I made my way back through the warren of Victorian rooms to the kitchen by smell—an aroma that I'd never smelled before, something savory but also sweet. When I entered the kitchen from the dining room, it was like going from cool springtime into the rainforest, so hot and steamy and smokey. The day wasn't that hot, even though we were well into August.

Against the back wall loomed a giant range. I'd never seen a stove this big either. I counted ten burners, above which was a shelf and a long steel hood. And at the far end, unbelievably, was a grill, with flames shooting up. Indoors. In front of it stretched a long stainless-steel table.

There were two cooks at the range, a Black guy who was la-dling a thin batter into six pans on the stove simultaneously, and next to him, a woman who was working some kind of metal con-traption I'd never seen, running peeled potatoes over it, and the cutter produced not thin slices of potato but long oval waffle shapes, which was pretty cool. How did that work? It was mes-merizing, but not as much as the woman herself. She had a tattoo of a snake on her neck, black hair with a shock of white hair like a lightning bolt in the middle and shaved close on the sides, above ears rimmed with silver rings and two skull earrings. I'd never seen a woman with a tattoo. She was short but broad as a fullback and moving so fast I worried she was going to lose a finger.

One chef sat in the corner on a stool by a wall-mounted phone, receiver cradled against his shoulder, a clipboard and a pen in hand—Paul, I presumed. Behind him there was a room with steam coming out of it. An older Black man wearing a black rubber apron and rubber gloves emerged carrying big sheet trays and a stack of pots and skillets, which he set next to the scary woman with the tattoos. "Clean but hot!" he said.

"Thanks, George," said the woman without looking up.

I stood in the doorway of what would have been a large mudroom, back when this was a house, by the back door. A long butcher block table sat before windows that looked into the kitchen. The two windows were wide open so you could hear what was going on in the kitchen. Next to the butcher block was metal shelving with boxes and bags and cans and bottles—pasta, tomatoes, oils, sugar, flour. A man carrying three large boxes pushed past me and set them on the long table opposite the stove where the guy was sliding thin pancakes, which I realized were crepes (I'd read about those from Julia Child), onto a stack. The delivery man turned to me and said, "Can somebody sign for these?"

"What?" I said. But Chef appeared through the door, carrying a sheet tray with the slab of meat he'd been smoking. Everything was double the size of any of the trays and pots and pans I was used to. Chef put the meat down next to the boxes and took the lid off the top box. He pulled out a bunch of asparagus and examined it. Then pulled out another, and another. "I can't use these. They're slimy."

"I'm just delivering."

Chef held up a bunch, pulled out a stalk. Its shaft was mushy and brown. "Eat it," Chef said to the delivery man.

"C'mon, Chef, this my last delivery."

"Eat it!"

The delivery man wasn't about to eat it. He just quickly picked up the boxes. Chef slammed the bunch in his hand into a trash bin like he was dunking a basket.

"Tell Ansel if he sends me shit one more time, I'll find someone else." Chef dragged his hands through his long, ropy curls. "God*dammit*."

The delivery guy couldn't get out fast enough.

Chef said, "You just learned how to get decent asparagus.

"Paul," he said to the guy still on the phone. "The asparagus were shit. Do we have enough peas for service?"

Without looking up, Paul, still on the phone, gave a thumbs-up. Chef disappeared through a door leading to the basement.

I felt the tension in the kitchen getting higher, like someone was slowly turning a knob. Chef reappeared, racing up the stairs. "Here," he said to me. I followed him into the mudroom. It was nice and cool out there and I had a clear view into the kitchen. Chef set down a wooden crate, on top of which was a long pan with a huge fish buried in ice. He took the tray with the fish, revealing a crateful of thick pea pods and said, "You just got your first job. Can you work standing?"

"Yes, Chef."

"Good. You can work here. Shuck these. *Fast*."

"How many do you need?" The crate of pea pods was huge.

Chef looked at me like I was an idiot. "*All* of them."

He left with his fish on ice. I was already afraid of the chef and now he thought I was an idiot.

Julia appeared to check on me. Gone were the blousy shirt and long skirt. She wore a black vest, a white button-down shirt, and a black tie. Below she wore a full white apron that went down to what were now not cowboy boots, but black loafers. Her hair was pulled back into a tight ponytail. She looked transformed, older. I almost wouldn't have recognized her.

"Hey," she said, grabbing my elbow. "I'm really behind in my side work. We're going to get slammed early. That's Chef Paul on the phone. Have you talked to him?"

"No."

"Introduce yourself. He knows who you are. Do whatever he tells you. Just try to stay out of people's way. Are you good?"

"Chef told me to shuck these peas." She was about to race off, so I said, "Julia."

"What do you need?" She was annoyed in an urgent kind of way.

"Something to put the peas in. Like a bowl or something."

Exasperated, she went to the metal shelving and grabbed a silver bowl.

I said, "Two bowls!" I knew I'd need something for the pods, too—at home I always had a trash bowl to save trips to the garbage.

She spun two silver bowls onto the butcher block next to the crate of peas and hustled back to the dining room. *Okay, not a great start*, I thought. I opened the box, which was filled with enormous fat pods. I picked one up and squeezed. It opened along its seam. There were eight perfect peas, each with its own little connector to the pod itself. Wow. Peas. *These* are peas. I'd seen peas, of course. They were in my Swanson's chicken pot pie. Mom sometimes dumped a frozen rectangular block of Birds Eye peas and carrots out of a box into boiling water. I hated peas, and I hated mushy carrots. Roger's mom served canned peas, which were even worse. But these peas looked like bright green berries.

I ate one. That wasn't a pea. It was delicious. Sweet. I ate another. It was crunchy and fresh. I ate all of them.

"Those peas are on the menu, not fucking staff meal," I heard the chef say. He was on the other side of the window, cutting the fish. He wasn't even looking at me. Spooky.

"Sorry, Chef!" Thankfully the peas were easy to shuck. They were practically bursting open. Chef came out and looked in my bowl and at the crate. "Okay, you've got to go faster than that. Jesus. I needed these five minutes ago."

"Sorry, Chef, I'm going as fast as I can." Chef didn't say anything else. He violently grabbed a handful of peas, slipped his thumb into one and bulleted out the entire pod. Then another. Then another. He shucked five pods when I'd done one.

"I don't think you're *going* as *fast* as you *can*," he said. And he left.

"Yes, Chef." Thank God he was gone. He may have been an asshole, but you can bet I finished off those peas lickety-split.

Strangely, everything calmed down after that. No one was cooking anymore. Three giant pans of food were set out on the table across from the range. All the waiters stood in line with plates for the food.

"Hey," Julia said, poking her head in. "Get family meal if you want to eat."

"I gotta finish these peas."

"Just as well," she said. "Family meal has sucked since we lost Nando."

I was starving but I figured Chef would probably kick me out of his kitchen if I abandoned the peas now. Some of the waiters leaned against walls in the kitchen, silently eating. Others had taken their food to the dining room. The two cooks, the Black guy and the woman with the snake tattoo, were eating side by side, leaning against the range, shaking their heads. The woman threw her half-finished dinner into the garbage.

The next time I looked up, all the food was gone, and there were only the four cooks in the kitchen, all of them wiping down the steel tables and the stove, as if the night was already over. I heard a vacuum cleaner moving fast in the dining room.

Chef called out, "Fifteen minutes!"

Everyone who was in the kitchen shouted, "Fifteen minutes!" That was a sound I knew. To end every huddle the quarterback would say, "On three. Ready . . . break!" And we'd all clap once, simultaneously.

When the cooks had wiped everything down, they huddled around the long stainless-steel table in front of the range, with Chef on the opposite side, Paul beside him. He had what looked like a menu in his hand and a pencil. He was clearly going over it with the other cooks—like calling out the plays in a football huddle. The woman leaned on her elbows, studying the paper, and pointed at something. Chef pulled a pencil from behind his ear and drew something on the paper. The woman nodded and gave him a thumbs-up. It *was* like diagramming a play.

The exact moment I finished the last pod, Paul was there. Seeing the crate was empty he said, "Beautiful." And disappeared with the peas, returning with a silver bowl filled with small red onions.

"Do you have knives?"

"No, Chef."

The sense of tension in the kitchen started to increase again, as stacks of plates were delivered to the central steel table, the Pass. Servers filled the bottom shelves with plates and bowls. All the cooks set up a series of small rectangular pans in inserts attached to their side of the table. The Black guy, named Reggie, hefted a big pan filled with water and four cylindrical vessels, and slid it to the back burners. He put a ladle in each of the vessels and gave them each a stir. Sauces, I guessed. The woman with the tattoos, whose name was Amanda, kept squatting and setting small pans into slots at her station. I realized there were refrigerators underneath the table and all the cooks had an array of small pans in inserts in front of their stations.

Paul weaved between them with huge stacks of skillets, which he put on the range's shelves above the burners, then set neat stacks of white towels at each station.

Chef was at one of the burners with a giant skillet, jumping my peas chef style with, it looked like, carrots and something else in the pan—they must have gone a foot in the air before falling, amazingly, into the center of the pan. He took a great glob of butter on a big spoon and slapped it into the pan. He reached into a small dish, holding his hand high over the skillet, and released salt with a swirl. He flipped the peas again, took a spoon out of a steel canister, tasted them, nodded.

Paul appeared with a giant knife, a small knife, and more huge pans, one filled with enormous onions, and on top of this, a pan filled with the biggest carrots I'd ever seen and several bunches of celery. "You can use my knives for now. We have some utility knives downstairs as well. I'm Paul, by the way." We shook. His pale blue eyes were bloodshot, but he gave off a friendly, mellow vibe, not scary like Chef. "Large dice on the mirepoix," he said, slapping his hand on the carrots and celery. "It's for stock later tonight so get to it when you can. I need these shallots minced first."

And he was gone. Mirepoix? I was afraid to ask.

I picked up one of the small red onions—so these were shallots. Julia Child used them all over the place. I cut off the root end and began peeling the first one. And Paul was back. He took his knife from me, lifted a shallot, cut the end off, halved it, ripped the skin off, made a cross hatch the way Julia did. Only his were super tiny and I could barely follow his movements. In seconds he'd reduced the shallot to a small pile. "This is a small dice right here. These need to be minced, very very *very* fine. Okay?" He minced for a couple seconds so I could see how he did it. It was just as it was in Julia's book. Only faster.

He handed the knife back to me. I took the shallot I'd started and cut it in half. Paul shook his head with a sigh. He took the knife from me again. "Here's how you hold a knife." He didn't grip the handle the way I did, the way you hold a hammer; instead, he pinched the blade of the knife with his thumb and index finger so that only his back fingers curled around the knife handle.

He handed me the knife and I imitated his grip. It felt funny but I saw why it worked. When you held the blade and grip, as opposed to just the grip, you worked the blade, not the handle.

"Complete control of your knife at all times," Paul said. "Got it? When you've done the shallots, call me, I'll show you how I want the mirepoix."

Mirepoix, I thought—looking at the carrots, onion, and celery as I cut into a shallot—and sliced off the tip of my middle finger. "Ah!" I shouted, sticking the finger in my mouth and tasting iron. Nobody heard. I could tell it wasn't too bad, just a little divot I'd cut off, but it bled like crazy. There was a rag on the shelves with the bowls, and I wrapped it around my finger. I was too scared Paul would see I'd cut myself two seconds after I picked up a knife. I'd never used a knife so sharp. Holding the towel around my finger made it really hard to cut the shallot but I didn't want to get blood all over it.

I heard Chef shout, "Ordering! Two steaks mid-rare, one bass, one salmon, three frisées." And every chef called back what the chef said. "Ordering!" he said again. "Three steaks, two mid-rare, one mid-well! One lamb! Three pastas! Two pâtés!"

And again the chefs called back the order: Amanda shouted, "Three steaks, two mid-rare, one mid-well!" Reggie shouted, "One lamb mid-rare," as he dipped down and pulled out a rack of lamb, put it on a small platter, and seasoned it with salt and pepper. And Paul shouted, "Three pastas! Two pâtés!" The action was heating up fast—obviously the restaurant was open for business.

I wanted to watch, but I had to focus on the shallots. Paul shouted, "Off the line!" to come check on me. I showed him the shallots. "More," he said. "Very fine." Then he turned back. "Did you cut yourself?"

I guess he noticed I held my left hand behind my back so he didn't see. I showed him my hand with the bloody rag wrapped around my middle finger. "I'm fine, it's almost stopped." Paul resumed his spot at the range next to the other cooks.

I kept on mincing, holding the tip of the blade with my cut hand (it wouldn't stop bleeding), and rocking the blade through the shallot on the pivot of the tip as fast as I could. Each time Paul came back he said, "More." How much more fine could they get?

I only said, "More?" once because I didn't believe you could make the onion smaller. But the way he said, "Yeah," made it clear to me I was not to question.

I kept mincing and mincing. Now my right hand was killing me, and I saw I'd gotten a blister at the base of my index finger, where the knuckle held the edge of the knife.

"More."

And I kept on. I wanted to see what all the food looked like—dishes were flying out of the kitchen faster than I could believe—but I had to work on the damned shallots.

"There we go," Paul said at last. They looked almost like a paste. He pulled a plastic scraper from his back pocket and lifted my minced shallots into a small pan. *Thank God*, I thought. Paul hustled down the line spooning my shallots into pans at each chef's station.

They were going to be using my shallot—I couldn't believe it. That I just cut. That was so cool. I felt elated. The blister had popped a while ago and my right hand was now bleeding as well. I found another rag to tie around that hand.

When I returned to my workbench, I found a small oval tray, pewter colored and beat up. On it was an immaculate silver spoon containing my peas, carrot diced to the exact size of the peas, and filaments of green on top. I looked at Chef through the window. He nodded once. He must have put them there. I tasted.

It was like seeing a new color that had never been there before. I'd had Mom's frozen peas and carrots at least once a week for my whole life. What I'd just eaten was not that. It was fresh and delicious, buttery, creamy, and fresh—was that mint on top?

I stood in the doorway to watch for a bit. Paul, Reggie, and the tattooed Amanda moved from stove to the steel table and back to pans on the stove. She really did move like a fullback. The three at the range didn't move fast so much as move continuously. Paul commandeered four burners and, beside the range, another steel table where he put together salads and pâtés while Reggie next to him ladled sauce onto a plate. He worked four burners but also dipped into the oven. When Reggie finished a plate, he set it before Chef and announced what it was—lamb shank or halibut up. Chef drew a towel around the rim of the plate and put some garnish on it. He glanced at one of the many tickets to his left and said, "Amanda, waiting on a steak and a salmon."

Without looking away from what she was doing, she said, "Thirty seconds, Chef." She worked the grill, stopping to throw logs into the fire below. She stood, poked her index finger into five or six steaks smoking on the grill. As she plated a salmon, she said, "Paul, I'm ready to go on that eight-top."

"Picking up the eight-top, Chef," Paul said, setting out four plates exactly as Amanda did the same thing. It was a weird kind of choreography. Kind of like when a pulling right guard, instead of shooting forward when the ball is snapped, goes behind the center to take out the defensive tackle on the other side of the line, bang, *surprise*. Everyone seemed to be aware of where the others were without even looking. In a matter of minutes—minutes, I couldn't believe it—Chef was wiping down eight plates of the most beautiful food I'd ever seen and calling, "Runners! Table twelve." And the plates were gone as fast as they appeared. Julia looked so damn good in that long white apron and vest and tie, breezing in to hand a ticket to Chef, who before reading it said, "Can you get these to table twenty-five?"

"Yes, Chef," she said, and, with a large plate on her left forearm and two more plates in each hand, she swished out the Out door. She was actually going to the front of the house, literally the front of this house, climbing the stairs and delivering the food to table twenty-five, without dropping that plate balanced on her arm.

Unbelievably, new plates already filled the Pass as more and more tickets got slammed onto a spike there.

I had to rest every now and then, sitting against the windowsill behind me. But each time I did, Chef glared at me as if he could sense my relief at resting and forbade it. I'd stand and get back to the vegetables. Paul broke from the line when he could to demo how he wanted the mirepoix cut, which were indeed, the onions, carrot, and celery. He also put the biggest pot I'd ever seen down at my side, filled with potatoes in water that needed peeling. I'd seen all the beautiful waffle chips Amanda fried all night and the mashed potatoes served with the lamb. Already I was trying to memorize plates the way I'd memorized Coach Lambert's play diagrams.

Every now and then I left my piles of vegetables to watch the action, which came not steadily, but rather in surges. A clock on the wall read 7:50 as Julia and two others arrived, saying, "Order in." Chef picked up the three tickets and read them off. "Ordering. Three halibut, three shanks, and a pasta." Reggie called back three halibut and three shanks, and Paul called back pasta.

Chef read, "Ordering! Four halibut, one frisée." And I saw Reggie shaking his head as he called back, "Halibut!" and at the same time, still cooking, Amanda shook her head, but she was chuckling.

Chef read, "Ordering." And he paused. Until Reggie stopped cooking and turned to Chef who said, "Six halibut."

"What the fuck?" Reggie said. I didn't know what was going on here, but whatever it was, Reggie did not seem to be enjoying himself.

"That's thirteen halibut ordered, seventeen halibut all day," Chef said.

Chef leaned over the counter and pulled one of Reggie's pans out of its insert. "Do you have more mushrooms below?"

Reggie, salting a row of fish fillets, said, "No, Chef."

"Why do you lie to yourself?"

"Because I didn't think all of Cleveland wanted to eat halibut tonight."

"Why do you *lie* to yourself?"

Reggie kept moving as if he and Chef weren't having a conversation.

Chef dragged his hands through his hair. "Paul, take the Pass."

"Yes, Chef!"

I knew to get looking busy and went to peel potatoes, but before I'd finished one, Chef slid a tray of large, round mushrooms with long, tough stems in front of me. He said, "Stemmed. Julienned." And he was gone.

Paul must have seen the terror in my eyes, because he quickly reached into one of Reggie's inserts and pulled out a thin, long slice of mushroom. All I needed to know.

I don't want to brag or anything, but I plowed through those mushrooms in a way I'd never cut anything. Superfast but careful not to cut any more fingers. The reason I could suddenly move so fast had nothing to do with skill. I was terrified.

I kept hearing Chef ordering, firing, and picking up halibut.

As soon as I had a big pile of mushroom strips I put them on the sheet tray. I couldn't carry anything on crutches, so I put my crutches aside and, tray in both hands, I hopped on my right leg out to the line and handed them to Paul who put them in Reggie's insert. Reggie paused just for a moment to look at the ceiling, then at me, mouth the words "Thank you," and he was back at it.

I don't know how to explain the feeling I had other than to say I was euphoric. Like intercepting a pass and taking it into the end zone. You're not thinking about it as it's happening—it's all instinct until it's over and you realize what you've done. I know it was just a pile of mushrooms, but it felt huge.

8

"So? Tell all!" Julia said, making a U-turn on Larchmere in her noisy little Bug. She was back in her normal clothes, hair once again free flowing. Both our windows were down. The night was warm and leafy and quiet. "Amanda said it was like having their own three-legged dog, you hopping around in the kitchen!"

"She called me Tripod. I hope it doesn't stick."

"She meant it to be funny. But seriously, what did Chef say, anything?"

"He just said, 'Am I going to see you tomorrow?' What does that mean?"

"Yay! It means he likes you, dummy!"

I tried to keep from smiling. "There was a piece of meat, pinkish with a thick layer of glistening fat running through, that bacon he was cooking when we arrived. Chef gave me a slice. It was *unbelievable.*"

"Chef is letting you taste his food? He must *really* like you . . . So how did *you* like it? The work."

"Julia, it was a-*mazing.*"

We were stopped at a light. She reached for my right hand to have a look at the raw divot on my index finger knuckle. "That's a nasty one."

"Not as bad as my armpits. I must have blisters there, too."

Julia laughed.

"All those plates of food, the pace, pressure. And the language. I don't even understand it, like 'all day' and 'on the fly.' It was like being in a movie! Even you. You were like a different *character* with your vest and tie and hair pulled back."

"Not really my style."

"No, you looked great."

She put her hand on my knee and shook it gently, then downshifted to turn onto my street. She rolled smoothly into my driveway.

"Thank you so much."

"No problemo," she said, smiling with those big fat white teeth.

She turned the car off and pulled the emergency brake up.

She reached below her seat and produced two plastic containers filled with ice and handed me one. From the purse in her lap, she pulled out a pint bottle.

"Southern Comfort? You like?"

"Sure," I said, wondering what exactly it was.

"Gimme your deli."

"My what?"

"Your cup. That's a pint deli. FYI."

She poured a generous portion of the bottle into my cup. Filled hers. She said, "Cheers. To your first day in the kitchen."

We touched the delis and drank. Embarrassingly, I started coughing immediately and said, "What *is* this?"

"This is your first shift drink."

"Huh?"

"Servers get a shift drink at the end of their shift. But we're underage, so Chef doesn't want us drinking on premises."

I took another sip. This one went down smoothly, and it tasted sweet and good. I took another sip. "This is good."

"You earned it."

"This feels *really* good," I said. I put my head back and exhaled. "I'm just so keyed up, I don't think I'll be able to sleep."

"Just wait till you hit the bed. You're going to be exhausted."

I turned in my seat to face her. "Julia," I said. She tilted her head, not sure what to expect. "Why are you doing this for me?"

As if it was obvious, she said, "Because I like you, silly, and you're cute."

I took a big slug of the drink—the whiskey felt warm, turning the adrenaline into relaxation.

"I'm um. I'm kinda crazy about you."

I regretted this immediately.

But she was the one who did it. She leaned in and kissed me. Just as she had the first time. She had the softest lips. She pulled away, then I kissed her back just like that. I didn't even think about it. It felt completely natural. And I kissed her again. And again. My whole body was suddenly humming, my heart racing, like there was an actual current in her lips.

Then I just stared into her eyes.

As if she were reading my mind, she said, "Like I said. I like you. And you're cute."

"But what about your boyfriend?"

"Well, he took off for the summer. And, well. Like the song says, 'If you can't be with the one you love . . .'"

She'd played me this song. We both knew the line that came next. I set my deli on the floor, and we were kissing again, but not just kissing, seriously making out. I couldn't get enough of her. I wanted to devour her. And be devoured.

She pulled away, and reluctantly I let her. She took a breath, placed a palm on her chest, and said, "My," to the windshield.

"That's how I feel, too," I said. And then we were kissing again, but more. She tugged my lip gently with her teeth, the tips of our tongues just touching. Exploring each other's mouths. I wanted more and more. I wanted it never to end.

But finally she said, "I've got to go."

"I understand."

I finished my Southern Comfort.

"Just put it on the floor, I'll bring it back to work tomorrow. A little earlier tomorrow, okay? Like three?"

"Yes."

She drew fingers across my cheek, leaned in again, kissed me, and said, "Good night, Theo."

"Hey, can you call me when you get home?" I asked.

"Maybe, if Daddy's asleep. But I'll wake your parents."

"I'll pick up fast."

"Okay, if I *can* call you, I'll call exactly at midnight. Twenty minutes. Okay?"

"Till then." I crossed my fingers. I kissed her again. I tilted out of the car onto my right leg as Julia grabbed my crutches from the back and handed them to me.

"Midnight," I said.

"If I can," she whispered back.

She could and did, calling exactly at midnight. We talked till just before 2:00 a.m. Till she couldn't keep her eyes open. I could. I wasn't tired at all. My whole body was thrumming and aching and feeling too alive and in love to sleep. I was in love. *This* was love. I didn't see how I could wait till tomorrow to see her. And more. I couldn't wait to get back in the kitchen.

9

"Look at the rich boy, peeling potatoes."

I turned to find Jackie, the redhead, entering the mudroom with a bundle of table linens wrapped in plastic.

"How's it feel?"

I honestly didn't know what to say—was it a real question? "Like peeling potatoes?" was all I could think to say.

It was my third day at the restaurant, and I could already feel a routine engaging. I'd start by mincing shallots because all of the cooks needed a ton of minced shallots. Then I'd peel ten pounds of potatoes for Amanda. She used what she called a mandolin to cut those cool waffle chips, which she fried to order, and stacked five, one on top of the other, on the plate for the *steak frites*. Then I'd ask Paul, Reggie, and Amanda what they needed for their mise en place, which they just called *meez*. There were only so many questions I felt I could ask without appearing stupid or inept.

For instance, the day before, I was in the kitchen when Paul took half of Reggie's chopped parsley and put it in a little container called a ninth pan (I didn't ask), and Reggie said, "Dude, hands out of my fucking meez."

It looked like parsley to me, so I said, "What's meez?"

Jackie happened to be passing through the kitchen, heard my question, and said, "Oh my God," and snorted. Jackie was tall, but she seemed even taller than me. She had a frizzy perm, parted in the middle, cool blue eyes, and a distinctive nose, long and narrow with a small cleft at the end. She would have been pretty if she didn't have a bulbous jowl and double chin. And a kind of perpetual sneer in her upper lip. Roger always said that we make our own faces, which didn't make any sense to me until I got to know Jackie.

Reggie told me, "Meez, *mise en place*, your station setup. All these ninth pans." These were small, deep pans that fit into inserts at his station. "But also the sauté pans, my sauces, my stack of nice fluffy side towels. Everything I need to get the job done. That's my meez, my man." He turned to Paul, who was making a pasta sauce with a lot of Reggie's parsley in it, and spoke slowly. "Which is . . . *inviolable*." He took the time to enunciate each syllable. Paul ignored him.

Using a side towel, Reggie grabbed the sauté pan on the burner and launched a mess of white beans a foot into the air; they landed in the dead center of the pan, which he swirled for good measure.

This was how I learned the language—by watching and listening. I would try to use the new words—"Do you need help with your mise en place, shallots, parsley?" I would ask—because when I used these special terms, I felt more like a member of the kitchen.

Until Jackie said what she did.

"Bitch," Julia proclaimed when I drew her aside to ask why she'd called me rich boy. "She's just mean. Don't listen to her."

"But why does she think that?"

"Because you go to a private school. You live on a ritzy street in Shaker Heights. That's rich to her." When I didn't respond, she took my chin and shook it till I looked at her. "Hey," she said, "don't let assholes get you down. Most of the girls think you're hunky. Tony, too. Especially Tony, come to think of it."

"Who's Tony?"

"Shortish guy? Dark, curly hair."

"Hm."

Paul asked me to tear up half a loaf of white bread for a stuffing he was making, or farce, as he called it. We kept the bagged loaves of white bread next to the pasta and rice in the mudroom, my prep area. I was rushing and I did kind of what I'd do at home. I ripped the bag open and three seconds later handed Paul the bread, torn and in a small bowl with some milk, like he'd asked for. Hours later, while I was picking thyme for Chef, I heard Chef, standing in the center of the kitchen, call out, "Who opened this bread?"

I couldn't believe it. I'm not sure why he cared. But he did and it wasn't good. I put my crutches under me and entered the kitchen from the mudroom. He held the bag, which had the big gash I'd ripped in it, just above the intact yellow twist-tie. The bag could have been a dead rabbit.

"I did, Chef."

He took a longish moment to look me in the eye, then removed the yellow twist tie and opened the bag the way it was intended to be opened, very slowly and theatrically. And he handed it to me. I took it back to my station. Everyone was pretending to be busy and not notice but I could see them smirking.

As I had the previous two nights, I stayed late, cleaning while I waited for Julia, till it was just me and Chef scrubbing things down.

And for the third night in a row, we were too late to spend enough time in my driveway. A few fervent kisses, and she was gone. The initial adrenaline and excitement I felt after a night's service had diminished, and I was pretty tired now, too. A good tired, like you feel after a particularly intense workout.

By Saturday I had a routine. And routine was critical because it allowed you to get more done in less time, which meant two things. I could keep asking for more and more things to do and learn. Paul taught me how to make tomato concassé, for instance, a fancy name for chopped tomatoes. The tomatoes had to be peeled first, which meant dunking them in boiling water, then transferring them to ice and water to loosen the skin. Or as he put it, "Blanch and shock the tomatoes." That was cool, learning this stuff. And, second, because I could get more done, I could spend more time watching the action in the kitchen and trying to learn the food. The cooks didn't seem to care that I was a "rich boy." I guess as long as I minced their shallots and parsley and cut all the mirepoix for the stock and peeled potatoes and anything else they told me to do, it didn't matter who I was.

Saturday was special, too, because when Julia and I arrived at the restaurant, and I began to gather the stuff I'd need, Paul handed me a white chef's jacket. "Chef says you should be wearing a jacket. Keep it clean, okay?"

I felt like I'd earned something, even though I hadn't. Chef just didn't want some kid in jeans and a T-shirt working in his kitchen. Chef was into everything French and attention to detail, which included how his staff looked. I was proud, anyway, buttoning it up, smoothing it out, examining the sleeves and carefully rolling up the cuffs.

And before I knew it, I was cleaning the kitchen at the end of my first Saturday night—my first four days. They had zipped by, but because so much had happened and I'd learned so much and met so many people, Wednesday seemed like weeks ago.

Julia appeared in street clothes after what had been a busy but steady Saturday night and said, "Ready?"

I took off my jacket, folded it neatly, and left it on my cutting block. I'd kept it pretty clean.

Chef, who had materialized out of nowhere behind me, said, "Theo, can I talk to you a minute?"

I almost slid off my crutches. He rarely addressed me except to yell at me when I was doing something wrong. He didn't yell with his voice, he did it with his actions, like with the bag of bread.

I straightened, pivoted on my left crutch, and said, "Yes, Chef."

"I got this," he said. He lifted my jacket, held it by the shoulders to scrutinize it. *What now?* I thought. This couldn't be good. Chef pushed out his lower lip and nodded before balling up the jacket and tossing it into a laundry bin in the corner I hadn't noticed before, filled with jackets, aprons, and side towels.

"Theo, both Paul and Clive said I was crazy to let someone into the kitchen with crutches. I just figured what the hell. But, Theo." Chef let out a sigh.

Julia quickly said, "I'll wait in the car," and hustled through the mudroom door.

Five minutes later, I left the mudroom where I'd spent most of the past week, taking the steps slowly down into the backyard. The chain-link fencing around the backyard was lit with Christmas lights all year long because the chef hated chain-link and this made them festive at night. The backyard was spacious, but a city ordinance prevented Chef from putting tables out there. So he used it for smoking meats. Two picnic tables gave the staff a place to hang outside. Beyond this was a two-car garage, now used to store broken equipment, old stoves, and, weirdly, a beat-up broken-down Model T, which I knew about from visiting the car museum with Dad. It was in bad shape and smelled of gasoline.

I paused to take in the night. Crickets were out in full force. The moon behind the trees cast pale light and shadows. A warm breeze rustled the leaves. The air itself felt potent.

I crutched down the long walkway that used to be a driveway but was now a narrow path between the side of the house and a long, raised garden where Chef grew lettuces and herbs. I could see Julia across the street leaning against her old Bug smoking and looking beautiful and mysterious under a streetlight. Her beauty came off her like sound waves you could actually feel.

I swung myself slowly toward her, but I stopped for a moment when I got to the front yard area, covered in white gravel, all the tables and chairs chained up on the front porch. I imagined all the night's guests, as Chef called them, fattening themselves on Dover sole and chocolate tarts. This was beautiful, too. The night was so quiet I could hear the buzz of the streetlights.

"Hey!" Julia called. "You coming or not? Whaddhe *say*?"

I crossed the sidewalk in front of the house and crossed the street. Even though she was just dressed in a way-too-big-for-her men's white dress shirt and jeans, she looked especially fine—the streetlight put a rim of light around her. Stray strands of her hair lit up white.

"What?" she said, grinding her cigarette out with her boot.

"He said, 'I can't believe I'm actually saying this, but if you want a job, it's yours.'"

"Oh my God," Julia said, covering her mouth with both hands.

"I really hope I didn't make a mistake," I said.

"What do you mean?"

"I accepted."

Julia screamed. Like girls do. It was short and loud. What girls don't normally do, though, is throw up their arms, shake their butt, do a jig, spin, and throw their arms around me.

"I knew it! I *knew* this would happen. I knew you could do it."

She kissed me. I kissed her back. If I hadn't been on crutches I'd have fallen over. I couldn't shake the feeling that something really good had just happened, or rather was in the middle of happening.

"What's the matter?" she said, stepping back but holding on to my shoulders.

"School starts in a month. I only *have* the job if I give my word that I'll stay for a year. I don't know if my parents will *let* me."

One of the things I loved most about Cleveland were the trees. There were so many, at least here on the city's east side and the old suburbs. Old huge trees. This industrial city had once been among the biggest in the country, home of J. D. Rockefeller and Standard Oil, but before that it was called the Forest City, and somehow, the people who carved out these suburbs around the streetcar lines more than a hundred years ago left an abundance of them. Tall and full, making a canopy over the streets, and dense around the small lakes, the Shaker Lakes, that dotted the neighborhood, repositories for the brooks that ultimately fed into our Great Lake, Lake Erie.

Until my leg broke, I walked pretty much everywhere. Johnny was a twenty-minute walk from my house, so I'd often find myself returning from his house at midnight on foot. All the grand houses would be dark, and the streetlights lit the maple leaves to a shade of green that you couldn't replicate. Nothing could be that green. Unless you saw those same leaves in early spring, when the green was almost electric. In my opinion, trees were the best argument for God. My parents were Protestants, technically, because of their parents. My dad said he was agnostic, but too matter-of-factly. "Let's face it," he'd say if the subject of religion came up, "no one knows for sure, correct? So how is there any other logical position?"

This annoyed me. It was a cop-out. I wanted him to make up his mind. Where did everything come from? Like trees. Maybe I'm weird, I don't know. But when you breathe this air . . .

"You're not weird!" Julia said. "I love your thoughts."

"I didn't know I was speaking out loud."

She laughed (and my heart fluttered). She said, "I love the trees, too."

If I'd told my old teammates that I loved trees, they'd have guffawed, or wrestled me to the ground in a pileup and pounded my thigh to give me a charley horse.

"Okay, so. What's the big deal?" She shifted into third gear along Shaker Boulevard. "I work after school and still get everything done. I haven't gotten a B since seventh grade."

I leaned as far back as I could and let the sweet night air pour over me. Nothing seemed real. Julia turned right onto Attleboro, where the trees were especially tall and dense above the streetlights.

"Yeah, well, you're smart," I told her.

"You're smart, you just don't know it."

"How am I going to do it? Work from three thirty till ten during the week after going to school all day?"

"Same as I do. You get it done. You've got Saturday morning, all day Sunday, and Monday after school. Besides, what else are you going to do?"

"Wait a minute, where are you going?"

Instead of taking a left on South Woodland, she'd taken a right.

"Not ready to go home. We need to celebrate."

"What about your dad?"

"He knows Saturday nights can go late, so he never waits up. And I got more Southern Comfort from my sister Jeanie." She patted her purse. "But I didn't bring any ice, so we'll have to do shots."

I'd seen people do shots at parties, and most of them wound up in the bathroom or the bushes. On the other hand, that shift drink we'd had a few days ago was awfully nice.

"Shots," I said.

"Don't worry, we're not getting shit-faced. Moderation in all things."

"Ooooh-kay," I said.

"Especially moderation."

"Ha," I said.

She turned right onto West Park Boulevard and soon we were in a darkened parking area along one of the Shaker Lakes. She cranked the safety break up and cut the engine, removed the key. She reached across to the glove compartment, unlocked it with a separate key, and rummaged for what turned out to be a shot glass as several parking tickets spilled out.

Picking them up, I said, "God, what if your dad went through your glove compartment?"

"I keep it locked. Besides, he would never do that."

"How do you know?"

"Because he doesn't have a key! I keep my diary in there as well."

"Why?"

"Because when I was thirteen, I caught him going through my drawers. So this became the only place in my life that's completely private, my glove compartment."

I pushed my hand into the debris, and under a crumpled registration and a pack of cigarettes was a small leather-bound book. "Can I read?"

"No!" she said, snatched it from me, shoved it back in the compartment, and closed it. She dug through her purse and pulled out the bottle. "You first," she said, handing me a full shot.

Normally I would have paused to think about this, but Julia had yet to steer me wrong, so I closed my eyes and threw it back. It was sweet and didn't burn too much. Julia did the same, first holding the glass to me, saying, "To you, Theodore, and your new job."

No one, no one, called me Theodore. I'd never liked my full given name, but the way Julia said it, with a heavy emphasis on the *Theee*, sounded oddly appealing.

"Like I said, I don't know if my parents will let me."

"Won't know until you *tell* them." She poured herself another shot, drank, dragged the back of her hand across her mouth. "Notice I said *tell*, not *ask*." She handed me a full shot glass. After the second one, my anxiety about taking this job faded as the excitement of having this job became real. Maybe I really could do this.

"And think about it. Fall is going to be hard for you, not being able to play football. Or any sports. You'll go *crazy*. What will you do—be a team mascot? That's the line you take with your parents. They'll understand that."

"I know my mom. She's going to say I can use the extra time to study. To work harder."

"So make them a deal. If your grades get worse, you'll quit. But they won't. They'll get better. I'll help."

She uncapped the bottle and said, "Another?"

I paused just long enough to take in her face yet again. "Of course."

I kissed her, my lips still wet with the Southern Comfort. We would kiss each night before she dropped me off, but not long because there was always the ticking clock. Not so here, in the darkness, far from both our homes.

I could never get enough of her. I wanted to physically merge with her, be inside her head, be her lips. The skin of her back was warm and smooth. The smell of her hair. I hadn't been thinking at all, just lips to lips, but she pulled gently away, kissed my cheek, and whispered, "It unfastens in the front."

I kept kissing her, though now part of me was outside myself, thinking. I'd been rubbing the back of her bra. It took a moment to understand and then respond. This was happening. To be touching her body, her generous flesh.

And soon she had put her hand on me. And perhaps twenty seconds later I gasped—I couldn't believe what just happened. She kissed my neck and said, "Shh," softly in my ear.

I swallowed hard, still trembling. I couldn't believe I just came.

"Am I the first girl to make you do that?"

"Uh-huh," I managed, and leaned back in my seat, head back, eyes closed. She snuggled into me and rubbed my chest.

"I'm especially honored, then."

"I just want you to know that I wanted that to go on forever."

She kissed my neck and said, "I didn't even have time to un-buckle your belt."

I groaned involuntarily—this opened a whole new line of possibilities I hadn't even considered.

"Okay," Julia said, "one more, then I'd better be getting home."

We each did another shot. I felt happily buzzed. I was liking this Southern Comfort. Julia started the car and I said, "Wait, are you okay to drive?"

She turned to me, almost angrily, it seemed. She stared at me hard. "When my hands are on this steering wheel, I am deadly serious. You'll need to know this. Cars *kill* people. Always, always follow the rules, street rules. You have to take them *very* seriously. Okay?"

I nodded quickly, chastened.

She flipped the tape, put the car in reverse, and we left the lot. Julia never went even a smidge over the speed limit and came to complete full stops at stop signs.

Before leaving the car, I asked her if I could see her tomorrow.

"Sundays are family days. I don't know what we're doing but we always do something together, the four of us."

"How about Monday? *Caddyshack* is playing at the Vogue. The Saucy Crepe is right next door." I'd used the entire ride home to mastermind this, a real date.

"Deal," she said. "Now go."

She knew I'd never go if she didn't tell me to. I kissed her three times, then began my awkward, hopping exit out of her car. I had to get off these damned crutches.

I leaned through the window and said, "I'm going to do my best to resist calling you tomorrow, but I will call you Monday, okay?"

"Thee-odore," she said with a smile. "Okay."

One of the random things that went through my mind this past dizzying summer was that it had been just a little more than a month since Roger went the opposite direction of the one I expected on Chagrin Boulevard to take us out to Blossom and changed my life. And tonight Julia had gone the opposite direction and changed my life again. I took the wrong way home and my life changed. I wondered if going the wrong way might be a good life strategy from time to time.

I whispered good night to Mom and Dad, but they were both snoring by the time I got in. I undressed, put the crutches beside the bed, against the wall, and fell into bed. My mind still buzzed. I put my hands behind my head and stared at the ceiling in the dark, smiling, thinking about what had just happened.

How weird was it that twenty-four hours before my leg snapped in two, fate had put Julia Bevilacqua in my path. Was my leg foreordained? Well, of course, to some extent—it was going to go sometime. But why then, literally hours after making friends with Julia? Chance? I couldn't shake the sense that it might *not* have been random. That it was part of a plan specifically for me. A course I was meant to embrace rather than passively follow.

I relived what had happened in the Shaker Lakes parking lot, maybe three or four times. Or five or six, until I fell asleep.

10

Midweek, last week of August and the last week of summer vacation. It had been less than twelve hours since Julia broke up with me, and I didn't feel like sitting around in my own head waiting to go to work, so I decided to go to the restaurant early. Four hours early. This was my fourth week at the restaurant, but the first time Julia and I hadn't arrived together. Since getting my license, I'd driven us. I should have called her. I know I know I know.

Strange to find the kitchen so clean and cool and quiet, as if it were still sleeping after the previous night's busy service. The hood above the range, which hummed like an engine all night, had yet to be turned on, so the kitchen was weirdly quiet. Nothing going on there except a big vat of stock on the stove slowly simmering and filling the place with the smells of sweet vegetables and tomato and roasted veal bones. I found Chef in the dining room with a cup of coffee, scribbling on a legal pad. He was the only one here. I'd never been at the restaurant before noon. I didn't know it could feel so peaceful. I felt lucky to be here, to get out of my own thoughts.

"Hey, Chef."

He started at my unexpected appearance, pushed the ropes of hair out of his face, and raised his eyebrows.

"I just figured I'd get a jump on things. Don't worry, I won't clock in till my shift starts."

"Where's the cane?" he asked.

"I'm sick of that thing—I'm done with it." This was a last-minute decision when I parked out front. I'd been off my crutches for a while now. (I refused to take Julia to a movie and dinner on crutches—that had been my first crutchless outing, *Caddyshack* and dinner at the Saucy Crepe. But that had been more than two weeks ago.) And so I ditched the cane today just as I'd ditched the crutches. I figured if my leg started hurting, I could go get it. But I'd just have to put up with the pain till it went away, which the docs said would happen eventually. Though they warned that the nerve damage would likely blindside me every now and then. Not much they could do about that.

Also, working in a kitchen changed my relationship to pain. Once, Reggie handed me a sauté pan to take to the pot washer. He used his tongs to grab the pan itself and held the handle toward me, but kept his eyes focused on pans on the stove. I grabbed the pan and heard my skin sizzle. I dropped the pan and shouted, "Fuck!"

Reggie shook his head at me. "Sorry, man. But this is a *kitchen—expect* things to be hot."

After that, I stopped paying attention to burns. People burned themselves a lot—me more than most. My forearms, wrists, and hands were mottled with brown burn marks. Mainly reaching in and out of the oven. When you burn yourself enough you stop noticing it. I still had a huge scabbed-over burn at the base of my right thumb, and I have no memory of how I got it.

This didn't apply to Julia-pain though. That was a kind of global flu-like illness.

"I don't want you to make it worse," Chef said. "But no cane will make going up and down those stairs a lot easier." He picked up his pencil, and the ropes of hair obscured his face as he returned to the legal pad, working on a fall menu from the looks of it.

"Veal's ready to strain," he said.

"Oui, Chef."

I went down to the basement to grab a chef coat.

Until I got off the crutches, I had no idea where these stairs went—I'd only known that people would go down there and return with trays of food. Or servers would descend in jeans and come back up in vest and tie. Turns out that the basement was exactly as big as the rest of this big Victorian house. There was a whole other kitchen and prep area down there and a six-burner range directly below the main kitchen's stove, with a hood venting out through a window well. A second gleaming kitchen—hard to believe. There were large room-size refrigerators, "walk-ins," because you walk into them. What do you think you call a refrigerator that you *reach in* to get something? Right. Not exactly elegant, like the Rapid Transit, but practical, I suppose. Most of the perishable food was stored there.

There was another whole room for all the stuff that didn't need to be refrigerated. This was called dry storage. There was a separate room for pots and pans and containers, bowls and plastic tubs. Another room had a long rack with chef coats on them, as well as stacks of laundered table linens, napkins, side towels, pinstriped kitchen aprons, and the server aprons (white). I learned to squirrel away the XL chef coats, because the Ls were too tight around my chest and there were only four of them and Amanda needed an XL same as me.

By habit, I punched the time clock on my way out, even though I told Chef otherwise. I'd have to remember to not punch out tonight and explain to Maryann what happened. Maryann, the bookkeeper, worked three days a week in a cramped little room down there with an old-fashioned rolltop desk, shelves of ledgers, a safe, and stacks and stacks of papers and receipts all over the place.

Chef agreed to pay me four dollars an hour, almost a dollar more than minimum wage for five eight-hour days, no overtime, and I'd be paid in cash at the end of each Friday. Actually, I noticed that Reggie, Amanda, and Paul got checks and cash when they opened their Friday envelope. When I asked Paul why, he smiled and said, "Weekly bonus."

"How come I don't get a check?"

"It's all bonus work for you!" While I tried to figure this out, he said, "Nah, I think Chef figures you're young enough to be under the radar." I still looked confused, I guess, because Paul said, "Just be glad you don't have to report it."

It was a pretty cool basement, but except in the brightly lit, white-tiled kitchen, it was still dark and basement-like. A lot of stuff happened down there that I'd never realized till I didn't need crutches. Secret meetings. Whispered conversations. If you were to see two servers making out, that was where it would happen—such as Tony and Brandon. (Which was super weird because I'd never seen two guys actually kissing. I went to an all-boys school where no one was gay—at least I didn't *think* any were; the number one insult was calling someone gay.) Or if you were having a bad service and needed to collect yourself, you could find a place down there to be alone for a minute, and maybe someone else would be there because of their own bad day, which made days a little better for both.

I once came down five minutes before we opened to see Reggie sitting on a stool in the downstairs kitchen gripping his head with both hands, rocking back and forth, with a scarily blank expression.

"Reggie, what's wrong? Service is in five minutes."

He looked at me as if he was totally lost. "My crepes, something's wrong. They're not coming together. They're falling apart."

"Reggie, you gotta have crepes." The crepes were a huge seller—shredded chicken and wild mushrooms wrapped in a crepe, sauced with a chicken-and-black-truffle velouté. It was actually a clever way to sell leftover chicken supremes, Chef explained. Any chickens left over from the night before got picked clean and saved so that every other day those crepes were on the menu and the bones went into the chicken stock.

I ran upstairs and told Paul. Paul was the mellowest guy I'd ever known, always had a semi smile on his face, soft blue eyes, the whites always slightly pink, curly brown hair, pale lips. He was unfazed. "Tell Reg I got him."

It was as if Reggie were in a bad dream he couldn't get out of, but when he emerged from the depths of the basement, Paul had a stack of twenty crepes ready to go, with more on the way, and Reggie regained his groove.

As I got to know it better, I began to think of the basement as the restaurant's subconscious.

I filled a metal bowl with shallots, which needed mincing, found a plastic five-gallon tub and a large fine-mesh strainer, called a *chinois*—*sheen-wah*—for the veal stock. I limped up the stairs, straining a bit, but I would be able to get a lot more done without needing one arm for the cane anymore.

Everyone was usually already full steam into their day by the time I appeared, so I didn't really know them outside of service. Today I saw Paul pull up in a rusted Ford Pinto at 10:30, and park on the side street by the restaurant. He crossed the street to the restaurant's backyard with a *Plain Dealer* tucked under one arm, a cup of coffee and a paper bag in hand.

He went straight to the picnic table in back to read the paper with his donut and coffee. When he was done, he leaned against the table and, in the most relaxed fashion, enjoyed a cigarette, or I thought it was a cigarette until some of the smoke drifted into the mudroom where I was peeling potatoes.

Amanda arrived as I was hauling trash out to what was once the garage. Amanda parked her Harley here as well. She rumbled past me, in her black leather jacket and wind-whipped bicolored hair. "Tripod! Where's the cane? What are you doing here so early?" She popped the kickstand down and got off the bike.

I put the black bag of garbage in the bin, closed it, and said, "You know, I really don't know. And I'm done with the cane, so you can call me Theo."

"Grumpster today," she said. She pulled a pack of cigarettes from her jacket pocket. "Smoke?"

I took it. I figured what the hell. I couldn't feel worse.

She held the lighter for me, I inhaled and, of course, started coughing. Not too much, but it was a surprise, the acrid burning sensation.

"Tell me this is not your first cigarette."

"Okay, I won't tell you."

"Oh, man, Theo. I never would have offered." She lit one herself.

I scrutinized the cigarette, took another drag. This one made me feel pleasantly dizzy. I exhaled like a pro.

Just then I heard screaming from the street. I couldn't tell what it was, but it was a she and she was loud. I left the garage. I heard not only a woman shouting but the sound of wailing children. It was coming from a boat-size Lincoln Continental, more rusted than Paul's car and the back bumper, slightly askew, attached to the back with wire. Reggie emerged from the passenger side, looking beaten already. He walked around the front of the car. Through the open driver's-side window, the woman shouted. "You're not home by midnight you know where I'm coming looking for you!"

"Give us a kiss, babe."

"I am not foolin'!"

He leaned down, she kissed him, and the two kids in back quieted as well.

"Love you, babe."

She grudgingly said she loved him back and drove off.

We all joined Paul at the picnic table.

"What did you do?" I asked Reggie.

"Search me."

Paul chuckled and said, "Every morning."

"Not exactly a morning person, is she?" Amanda said.

"Not an evening person, either," Reggie said.

Paul laughed, Amanda laughed, and Reggie joined in, too. I listened to them talk, like I was one of them. We smoked our cigarettes. I felt lucky to be with them because while I was, they were in the foreground and Julia was in the background. And just being with other people helped.

By eleven all were dressed and prepping their stations for the night's service.

At 3:45, I was in my mudroom, picking a crate of green beans, when Julia appeared and said, "What the fuck?"

"Sorry, I should have called."

"I'm late. When you didn't show, I called Clive, who told me you were already *here*. My car wouldn't start, and I had to beg my asshole sister for a ride. So thanks a lot. What a shit move."

"You're the one who broke up with me."

"*What?*" she said. "I didn't 'break up' with you. We weren't even going out."

"What do you call what we've been doing all month?"

"A fun summer fling."

"A *fling?*" I couldn't believe it.

"I've been straight with you this whole time, Theo." I kept picking beans, not looking at her. The way my name came out of her mouth, it sounded sour. She said, "I'm late. Jesus." And she disappeared down the stairs to change. If you'd have asked me two seconds ago could I feel any lower, I'd have said impossible. Which was wrong. Now I was an asshole on top of everything.

I kept picking beans. Amanda came to the mudroom for five boxes of pasta.

"My advice?" She waited for me to turn to her. "Don't try to make up now. Apologize after service. Service gives the steam a chance to escape. She'll be a different person by the end of the night. I mean, I have no idea what you *did*, but that girl is *pissed*. So apologize and be genuine about it."

She gave me a meaty slap on the back that almost knocked me down and departed.

Everybody had heard. Reggie simply said, "I know how it feels, man."

And of course the gossip spread through the server ranks. My least favorite server, Jackie, the tall redhead who always rolled her eyes at me like I was an idiot, said, "I heard she ripped you a new one," and laughed.

I was behind Jackie in line for family meal. The family meal sucked as usual. Some kind of weird chicken chop suey over rice and peas, and as always, a salad of iceberg lettuce, tomatoes, and cucumbers with too much Italian dressing.

I usually ate standing at my cutting board in the mudroom as the kitchen got crowded with basically the entire restaurant staff filing through for food. But I could see Paul and Chef both with plates of food in hand, obviously talking about the food. Chef held the plate in one hand and pointed at it with the other like *it* was doing something wrong. Paul picked through his with a fork, not eating. Then Chef slammed the side of the plate against the inside of the trash bin. He must have really hated it, because Chef *never* wasted food.

I knew that Nando had been deported to Nicaragua earlier in the summer. People always sighed when his name came up. He was apparently a decent guy who did much of the prep that I now did, but he also was in charge of making family meal. Now it was up to George.

George was lightning fast with pots, but as Reggie said, "He couldn't cook his way out of a paper bag." Everyone seemed to get crabby when family meal was up.

I spotted Julia taking her empty family meal plate and silver to the dish station and hurried to catch her before she made it back to the dining room where I wouldn't be able to talk to her.

"What?" she said—not a question, a knife. She put her face right in mine. Daring me.

"I want to talk to you."

"I've got to work."

"Can I drive you home after service?"

"I got it, thanks."

"How will you get home?"

"Walk if I have to."

Jackie, dropping her plate at the dish station, said, "I can give you a lift." She addressed Julia but she was looking at me when she said it. Why did she hate me? I'd never done anything to her.

"Thanks, Jackie." Julia addressed Jackie, but glared at me when she said it.

"Theo," Chef called. "You get the pâtés out of the oven?"

"Yes, Chef!" I said, as always. But he saw me bolt for the basement door. I didn't make them, but I was in charge of getting them out of the oven when they got to be 130 degrees on the inside. The pâtés cooked in the downstairs range, and I'd forgotten about them because of the Julia business. Five big terrine molds in a big roasting pan filled with water in a 300-degree oven. A hundred portions of a four-dollar appetizer. If I fucked that up, Chef, who had to be a math savant, would have calculated the loss in one second.

I pounded down the wood stairs. Threw the oven door open so hard it closed back. I opened it more slowly. I grabbed two side towels out of my apron and pulled out the roasting pan, topped to the brim with water so that the five long rectangular terrine molds would cook gently. Because I was rushing, a wave of water washed over my right wrist. I screamed and dropped the whole pan on the open oven door, and it tipped over onto the floor, one end propped on the oven door. The topmost mold had rolled over the rest, tumbling out of the roasting pan, its lid falling off and the block of meat that was the pâté tumbling on the floor, juices spilling out around it.

I didn't even tend to my scalded hand. I needed to get the terrine molds still in the pan upright and keep the juices in so the meat could reabsorb those juices, as Chef had taught me. I lifted the roasting pan to right it, but it hurt like hell as one side towel was wet and heat went right through it. As I got four of them on the steel table next to the range, I heard Chef's heavy footsteps on the stairs. He stood over me as I stared down at the terrine mold on its side and the rectangular pâté on the floor in a pool of juice and fat. I quickly picked it up and put it next to the four pâtés I'd saved.

He was like a god, descending from the clouds to obliterate me. That's how he seemed to me. He looked at me, his long, ropy curls hanging in his face. Just looked. And it was like a giant hand squeezing my rib cage.

He pulled a small thermometer from a pocket on his sleeve and punched it into one of the good pâtés. A straight pâté needed to be 150 to 155 degrees. But these had a whole pork tenderloin inlay in the center, which only needed to get to 130 degrees. If it got to 140, it would quickly turn gray and dry. Things keep cooking after you take them out of the oven.

We stared at the thermometer's hand as it moved past 100, 120, 125, and the speed with which it was moving made my heart sink, 130. But then 132, 133, where it stopped.

"These are good. Put some weights in them and get them in the walk-in."

"And this?" I asked.

"I can't serve that. And you know what that means?"

"No, Chef," I said. It was cool enough to handle or at least my hands had got used to the burning.

"Theo, this whole pâté cost $7 to make. I can cut twenty portions of it and charge $4 a portion. So you just dropped $80 on the floor. That's, what, half a week's pay for you. You're lucky I don't have to worry about food cost too much."

I walked over to the sink and ran the pâté under scalding water. "It's still okay. I can wash it off."

"Maybe, but I can't serve it to customers."

"But it's so delicious, you can't throw it out."

"Save it for staff."

"I can make sandwiches. I mean, this is kind of like a fancy meat loaf, and I love a meat loaf sandwich."

He paused to think about this. "There's a Vietnamese sandwich that actually calls for pâté," Chef said. "Banh mi. I used to eat them in Paris. I'll help you figure it out."

"I think I may have read about those," I said.

"We should have plenty of cilantro in the garden."

I had no idea what cilantro was, but I was too afraid to ask.

"For now, get those into the walk-in."

He halted midway up the stairs. He said, "You think you *read* about it?"

"Yeah, my dad got me a book on international cooking from the library."

When he was gone I could at last run to the ice machine and jam my right hand into the ice and just hold it there. While I felt the relief of the cold I thought, *How did he know? He was doing a million things, but it was like a bell went off in his head, knowing that the pâtés were perfectly cooked. Spooky.*

Chef didn't stay pissed for long, not in the middle of a weirdly busy Wednesday, the week before Labor Day. And tonight Amanda was the one getting hammered. Everyone wanted steak. Amanda, her face beet red, her thick bicolored hair sticking to her sweaty forehead, did three-sixties right at her station trying to keep up.

"Amanda," Chef said, "your fire is low—feed your fire."

"Yes, Chef," she called back, but only stacked four steaks on top of one another on an oval pewter tray everyone called "sizzles," carried them to the Pass where four plates were already out, but sensing the waffle chips were getting too dark, she pulled the fry basket out of the oil.

"Ordering," Chef called, taking a ticket from Jackie who did a quick U-turn through the kitchen back to the dining room. "Two pastas, two halibuts, four steaks, two rare, one mid-rare, one well."

After all had called back the dishes they were responsible for, Chef shouted my name. I was peeling potatoes in the mudroom. We went through so many potatoes, this was a job that always needed doing.

I limped into the kitchen. "Yes, Chef."

"Throw some wood in Amanda's grill, then help her out. Be her chip guy—make sure she's got a steady supply of hot chips. Know how to season them?"

"Yes, Chef!" I'd watched Amanda cook hundreds of those chips. She'd dump them out of the fry basket into a silver bowl lined with paper towels–C-folds–and, holding the bowl in her left hand, she'd toss the chips into the air while, with her right held high above the bowl, she'd swirl salt out of her fingers so that it rained down evenly on the potatoes. Jumping them in the bowl this way shook excess oil off them, kept them crispy, and moved them around so they all got an equal amount of salt.

I threw some big fireplace-size logs into her grill—"Thanks, Theo," she said—then squeezed in between Amanda and Reggie. I was on the line! I saw that about ten chips were ready to come out. I grabbed the big bowl on the shelf above the fryer, shook the chips out into the bowl, seasoned them just like I'd seen Amanda do, flipping them in the air as I salted. I set the bowl down where Amanda plated her food.

Chef reached over the table and took a chip and ate. I held still—he was checking them for seasoning. He nodded once, then said, "Ordering!" and I fired twenty more chips as Amanda ladled her Bordelaise sauce over three steaks, then scooped out creamed spinach from the pot that sat on a cool part of her grill.

"One salmon, one burger mid-rare, two steaks mid-rare!"

Amanda shook her head because all these came off her station. Her grill had so much meat and fish on it there was almost no room to cook more food. But this had just been "ordered," not "fired," so she simply took the meat out of her reach-in, put them on sizzles, and slid the sizzles onto a shelf above the grill, just below the hood.

The food would temper there, warm up from the heat of the grill, and she could finish them faster this way.

"Need chips, Theo," she said calmly, though she wasn't moving calmly. I quickly grabbed the bowl, dumped the cooked chips out of the fry basket, seasoned them, and spun counterclockwise to set them down, but I turned just as Reggie was turning with a saucepan to finish the lamb, knocking the saucepan so that the sauce leaped out of the pan and onto the black rubber mats we worked on.

"Fuck, Theo."

"Sorry, Reggie."

He turned back to put more sauce in his pan to reheat it. He said, "Don't pay attention to where I am, pay attention to where I'm *gonna* be."

"Theo, *chips!*"

Upset, I moved too fast and carelessly, and set the bowl down for Amanda, but the four plates, steaks sauced next to the spinach, waiting only for the chips, were lined in a perfect row, and the way I put the bowl down, it shoved the first plate, which knocked into the next and I saw the last plate in the line, already close to the edge, get knocked as well. It tilted, then—everything turned slow motion—that plate tilted, tilted, I shouted *"No."* Amanda, who had been flipping meat waiting for the chips, turned just in time to see her beautifully plated steak crash on the tile floor, shards of china flying.

"Jesus *fucking* Christ, Theo," she said.

"Sorry."

"Fucking spaz," she said, dropping to her reach-in for another steak.

"Do you have another working to replace it so we can get this table out now?" Chef asked, setting a clean plate where the old one had fallen. Amanda jabbed a finger into each of the ten steaks currently being grilled. "Yes, Chef." George appeared with a broom and a dustpan, but first grabbed the steak for himself for an after-service snack in the pot room.

"Theo, off the line," Chef said.

"Chef?"

"You're done for the night. You can go home."

Julia entered the kitchen, said, "Order in," took in the scene, and departed.

"Chef?"

"Ordering!" Chef said.

I left the line without any further damage and went to sit on the windowsill in the mudroom. I was breathing hard. I took off my chef coat and threw it in the hamper. I didn't put my potatoes away. I didn't put anything away. I didn't think it was possible to be so angry. I walked out back in just my T-shirt, sat at a picnic table, put my head down. After I'd pounded my head against the wood four times, it started to hurt and I stopped. Anger faded into self-pity and self-loathing. Worst day ever.

I turned on the picnic bench to face the house, held my head in my hands. The sound of conversation and clinking silverware and china sounded distantly through the muggy night. My thoughts swirled. What was happening today? Amanda and Reggie hate me. Jackie hates me. Julia, Julia wasn't about to forgive me. What was I *doing*?

I don't know how long I'd been sitting there when I heard the back screen door smack shut and saw Amanda headed my way. I wiped my face as fast as I could. I didn't move until her black boots came into my view.

"Smoke?" she asked, holding a pack toward me with a cigarette pulled out. I looked at her, confused. Wasn't she pissed?

"Thanks?" I said, taking it.

She lit mine first then hers, sat next to me.

She took a deep drag and exhaled it loudly into the night. "Man, we just got . . . *crushed*."

"How's it now?"

"Calmer, just desserts, one last deuce mooning over themselves and not ordering."

"What happened in there?" I asked.

"Clive seated everyone at once, which meant everyone *ordered* at the same time. And everyone wanted salmon, steak, or the burger."

"I'm really sorry, Amanda."

"One of the good things about a kitchen is that when it's over, it's over, gone, don't look back. I mean you can't *keep* doing that shit or you *will* get fired. We all have bad days. And in restaurants, one bad move can cascade into a dozen."

I so needed that—I could have hugged her ankles. I wasn't hated. I looked at her profile—the thick, cool hair, tattooed neck, and, I noticed for the first time, a kind of cute, upturned, button nose. She was actually kind of pretty once you got past the scary stuff.

I took a deep drag, felt the pleasure of the nicotine rush. I immediately took another and leaned back. My second cigarette of the day.

"But I'm guessing your bad day has more to do with events outside the kitchen," Amanda said.

I nodded.

"Talk to me."

We sat shoulder to shoulder, both of us facing the house, Christmas lights twinkling on the fence surrounding us, the big branch of the oak tree rustling a few feet above our heads.

"Julia."

"Women are the worst." She sighed. "They're also the best, which is what makes it so hard." When I didn't speak Amanda asked, "What happened?"

"I told her I loved her last night."

"And?"

"She told me her boyfriend gets home on Friday."

"Ouch."

"I mean, I knew she had a boyfriend. And I knew he was coming home. I guess I thought I could change her mind."

"Have you slept with her?"

"No!"

"But you've been fooling around?" She laughed and said, "Theo, you just turned red as a pomegranate."

"Amanda, I am crazy in love with her. I stupidly thought she might feel the same way."

"The boyfriend is going to be a problem, then."

"And he goes to my school."

"That's gonna suck. What are you going to do?"

"I don't know."

"Win her heart the old-fashioned way. Steady determination and patience. That's how I got my wife, Alice."

"Wife?"

"Well, not legally, but spiritually. And we made a vow not to hide. Fuck these provincial bastards. Cleveland's got to wake up."

Wow, I thought. *Just wow.*

Amanda reached below the table for the old Maxwell House coffee can she, well, now I, used for an ashtray.

"Time to get cleaning," she said, standing and arching her back.

"Amanda? Thank you."

She shrugged. She said, "Want me to tell her you're out here?"

"Nah, I should go clean up my stuff, anyway. I'll find her."

I was peeling the last of the potatoes—Chef taught me always finish the job at hand before moving to the next, and never leave a task undone, that it will only put you behind tomorrow—when Chef appeared in the doorway. I didn't know if he was angry that I didn't go home, so I said, "Like I said, I'm doing those sandwiches tomorrow for family meal." I stared at the potato I was peeling, then added, "If that's all right."

He paused for a long time. I thought he might be firing me. But instead he said, "I'll put aside the leftover baguettes. You can use those for the bread."

Inner sigh of relief—not fired.

"You're making them for twenty people, right? See what's in the walk-in. I know there's a hotel pan full of rice George cooked earlier in the week."

"Okay . . ."

"You know, keep it Asian. Do a stir-fried rice of some sort—use up any veg that's on its way out. And an additional veg. And salad."

"Yes, Chef. I'll see you at ten, like today."

I stared at the potatoes, but I sensed him nod once, and then he was gone, and I didn't see him again. I did spot Julia lugging a plastic tub of dishes to the dish station. I met her as she left it.

"Julia?" She stopped. Stared at me blankly. "When you're done. Can you meet me at the picnic tables? Can we talk?"

She took her time responding. Of course, Jackie appeared, apparently for the sole purpose of scowling at me.

The mudroom door smacked shut behind Julia as she descended the steps, backlit and outlined in white, dressed in jeans and the same oversize shirt she'd worn the first night she'd let me unfasten her bra. I loved that shirt. I loved her patched jeans and boots. I loved her.

"I brought you a beer, figured you could use it."

"So you heard."

She chuckled and said, *"Oh yeah."*

We clinked beer bottles and drank.

"Good old POC," Julia said. "Pride of Cleveland."

"Does Chef know you have those?"

"He wasn't around so I took them."

"You stole them?"

"I put money on the bar, but Clive told me to just take 'em and drink 'em outside."

She pulled a pack of cigarettes from her purse and before she could put the pack away, I said, "Can I have one?"

"When did you start smoking?"

I realized it was just today, but it seemed days ago.

I'd been thinking this whole time waiting for her, figuring out what to say. The first words were easy and true.

"Julia, I'm sorry. I acted like a baby."

"That was passive-aggressive."

"What's passive-aggressive?"

"The opposite of aggressive, but achieving the same result." She swung one leg over the bench so that she faced me. "Aggressive is you do something to make someone angry. Passive-aggressive is when you *don't* do something to make them angry."

"Like not pick them up when you know they're expecting you."

"Right."

The back door smacked shut. I could tell from the tall silhouette and outline of red hair who it was. She stared at us for a few seconds, then called to Julia, "You sure?"

"Yeah, I'm good, Jackie. Thanks."

The day had finally begun to turn—Julia was going to let me take her home. Amanda had been right.

When Jackie had disappeared down the walkway, I spoke: "I meant what I said yesterday."

She shook her head and sighed.

"C'mon, Julia, you must feel something."

She was quiet for a while. "Of *course* I do, Theo. I've spent practically my whole summer with you. And yes, I've loved our nights at the Shaker Lakes."

She pulled my face toward her and kissed me on the lips. "That wasn't meaningless to me. But I'm still with Bennett. I've always told you that. And now he's coming home."

"Do you love him?"

She only paused a moment before saying, "I do."

I turned away, took a long swallow of POC.

"Of *course* I do . . . but."

"But?" I said.

"But we've been away from each other for what, like ten weeks now. Who knows? I don't know how we're going to feel. I don't know how he's going to feel about me. He hasn't written much. One postcard from Japan, one from Thailand." She blew a raspberry. "That was it until he called yesterday from New York."

She sighed and said, "We've been together for more than a year, shared a lot of experiences."

I stubbed my cigarette out and put it in the can.

"Can I ask you something?" I turned to look at her, saw that perfect profile, the pale lips and sweet nose and round gold frames shining.

"I guess you're going to."

"Are you a virgin?"

She looked at me a long time, presumably considering whether or not to tell me it's none of my business. But instead she said, "No. I'm not."

"Bennett," I said.

"Of course, Bennett."

I took this info rather well, all things considered. It didn't hurt the way I'd thought. I mean, I didn't like it, but it wasn't a surprise.

"It's the most special thing two people can do together," she said.

I'd never thought of it like that. I hadn't thought of it as anything other than this great big mystery, like a big, heavy door that you pushed through into a different world. That was the best I could do with my imagination. So I had my imagination and a stack of *Playboys* my dad kept on a deep shelf in his closet. Not hidden, but not readily accessible, either.

"So, are you going to talk to me?" she said.

"Just thinking. I'm not going to stop being friends with you."

"Better not."

"You saved my life, Julia. I mean, this was the worst summer of my life. Of my *life*. My whole future changed. If I hadn't met you at Blossom, I'd probably have maggots in my bed sores by now."

She laughed and said, "Stop." It never failed: When I said something that made her laugh, my heart lifted.

"No, seriously!" I said.

She put her hand on my thigh. I put my hand on her hand.

"I can't believe school starts *Tuesday*," she said.

"I *know*," I said. "Hey, are you doing anything Labor Day?"

"I am actually."

"Family?"

Long pause. "Bennett's parents are having a party to see all the people they've been away from all summer."

"Oh," I said. "Right."

She squeezed my hand till I looked at her. "I've asked for Saturday off, so I won't be at the restaurant."

"Bennett," I said for the second time that night.

"He's taking me to dinner."

I felt sick to my stomach suddenly. "And then?"

The sound of my voice, the tone, God did I hate myself for it.

"Theo. Don't."

I recovered quickly, saying, "Can I still bring you to work tomorrow?"

"You'd better, my car's broke!"

She set the bottles by the back door as we left the yard, then held my hand as we walked to my car, shining bright maroon beneath the streetlamp.

11

September 2, 1980, the first day of my junior year of high school, was clear, hot, and dry. August mugginess gives way to crisp air as Cleveland summer slides into fall—cold mornings, hot, dry afternoons. The air still smelled of summer as I followed a line of cars down University School's driveway, smooth blacktop that wound for a quarter mile to a modern multitiered brick building and parking lot surrounded by dense woods.

The fact that I was driving, and not arriving by school bus, felt adult, liberating. I noticed several people turn to see who was driving this cool, unfamiliar car. It didn't look like a rich-kids parking lot. Most of the cars were parental hand-me-downs, like Roger's old Buick Skylark. It was the parental drop-off line, with BMWs and Mercedes Benzes spitting out freshmen and sophomores, that described the economic makeup of the student body. But me, I had one of the coolest damn cars in the lot. A 1965 vintage maroon Mustang. I leaned back, one arm out the window, my right wrist atop the steering wheel. Taking it slow as heads turned. Too cool for school!

But also it was back to the grind. Eight a.m. arrival for 8:10 assembly. Only I wasn't the person I'd been when I'd left last June. In a previous universe, I've been coming to school for most of August for football practice, not getting my ass kicked in a restaurant kitchen. Two-a-days we called these practices, morning and afternoon with a break for weight lifting and lunch. Such heaven that was. My God, playing all day long. For me it was like camp. We roamed the empty lower level of the school, a broad, open, carpeted expanse, owning it, school without the classes. But I hadn't watched a single practice this year and I completely skipped last Saturday's opener. Julia let me know Bennett was taking her to the game, before their night out, so I wouldn't have gone even if I didn't have to work.

I'd crushed the banh mi sandwiches with a vegetable fried rice for family meal. I cheated a bit by driving to Cleveland's Chinatown. I wanted to succeed so badly, prove myself, make up for the embarrassment of the night before when I'd fucked up the line. I could sneak in some oyster sauce and fresh ginger, which I'd never heard of, water chestnuts, and bean sprouts, all of which I'd read about in Craig Claiborne's *The Chinese Cookbook*. Chef had quick-pickled some thinly cut carrots for me, and with the cilantro from the garden, julienned cucumber, and the toasted baguettes, the sandwiches were really good. With fried rice (from the Claiborne book), and a weird carrot-and-celery stir-fry I came up with—it was all we had in the walk-in—family meal was the best they'd had in a month. Even George thanked me, relieved to have the pressure lifted. I'd never thought of the burden he was under, everyone hating his food. He came up to me, still chewing, plate in hand, and said with a laugh, "Saved my ass!"

And Julia. I'd left the restaurant that day to pick her up at 2:45 and told her what I was doing and how nervous I was—I'd gotten to the restaurant at 9:00 a.m. (woke Chef up which I'd have to remember not to do again). I saw her across the kitchen while we were eating the banh mi and fried rice. She beelined for me, plate in hand, and said, "Fan, *fucking*, tastic!"

"Really?"

"I'd smooch you right here if there weren't so many people."

I'd tasted the sandwich, the rice, and the celery-carrot weirdness to make sure it wasn't inedible, but I was too nervous and exhausted to actually eat once I'd put family meal up at 4:45. I leaned against a worktable off to the side, just resting. The whole staff was there. Usually most servers ate in front. That day the kitchen was crowded.

Chef came up to me stone-faced. But then he grinned and held up his palm. I smacked it. He leaned against the worktable next to me. He was quiet for a while. I had to start cleaning up, but I wasn't going to leave with Chef right next to me.

"Well," he said. "You found your job. Or I should say, you *made* your job."

"Chef?"

He held his hand out to the kitchen, as if presenting it. "You sense it?"

I said, "Sense what?"

He said, "It feels like a *party* in here."

True, it was unusually crowded in the kitchen, with people chatting and going back for seconds on the rice until it was gone.

"That's the power of good food, Theo. That's what it's all about. Bottom line. It makes people happy." Even Chef seemed at ease, not smoldering and tense. "So, Theo. This is now your job."

"Chef?"

"Your job is to feed the staff. You're in charge of family meal. I still need you mincing shallots, picking thyme, peeling potatoes, cutting mirepoix for the stocks and sauces, all that. You'll have to pick up the speed on that. But your main job is family meal. You up to it?"

Terrified. "I don't know!"

"Wrong answer."

"Yes, Chef!"

"Good. I'll help you out, get you going. Don't overstress."

"But, Chef, I start school Tuesday, I won't be able to get here till three thirty."

Chef said, "That gives you an hour and fifteen minutes to get family meal up—then you can get on with your other work."

"An hour and fifteen to feed twenty people every day?" I said, astonished. Frankly. I mean, *what*?

"You've watched three people serve one hundred fifty people in three hours every night for the past month. How do you think that happens?"

"Hadn't gotten that far, Chef." And I really hadn't—I had no idea the restaurant served that many people. My God, with just Amanda, Reggie, and Paul doing the cooking? That's crazy. That's impossible.

"Preparation," he said. "Think about it. There is almost nothing I serve that wasn't cooked hours, or days, prior. Come five thirty, we're basically a heat-and-serve operation." I hadn't thought of *that*, either. "So basically you'll cook the whole family meal, or most of it, the day before. Then heat and serve, and just cook the raw protein when you get in."

"Protein?"

He chuckled at me. "Meat."

"Feeding the staff is my job?"

"I've seen it everywhere I've cooked," Chef said, looking out over his kitchen. "A happy staff is a better staff—they treat the guests better and they're less likely to leave. Which makes the restaurant better and more successful."

"Because of family meal?"

"Yep." He looked at me for the first time since we high-fived. "That, my friend, is the power of food."

Thing is, he didn't know the *real* reason I'd worked so hard on this family meal. It wasn't to make the staff happy or even to impress Chef. It was Julia. I wanted her to love it. And she did. She *really* did.

I pulled into a parking space at the back of the school's lot, already three-quarters full. I grabbed my brown corduroy blazer, maroon-and-black striped tie, and a canvas book bag. The bag would be heavy with books by the end of the day.

"Good buddy Theo!" I heard from behind.

Roger already had his jacket and tie on. He planned to run for class president, and he always said you have to look and act like what you want to become so you're ready when you do make it.

"Hey, Roger," I said.

"Feeling any better?"

"Worse."

"Theo, you gotta have a better outlook. You can't go all year like this."

"Thanks, Mr. Carnegie," I said. Roger was always touting the book *How to Win Friends and Influence People*.

"We start the summer with your bellyaching about Heather Heather Heather. Now it's going to be Julia Julia Julia."

"This is different."

"How so?"

"I love her."

"That's what you said about Heather!" he said.

"I had my head up my ass."

He sighed. I could tell I was bringing Mr. Positive down. So I said, "How's Sarah?"

Roger and Sarah had started actually dating this summer after ten years of being best friends. I was glad for him. Sarah was cool. Roger, Johnny, and I had spent yesterday, Labor Day, around the pool at the Hunt Club, eating burgers and onion rings, first time all summer I'd been able to relax like that. We took turns getting Johnny in as a guest. Johnny repaid the club by stealing beers for us.

Had to admire him. He pulled an apron out of a bin in the kitchen and pretended to be a new server and just delivered them to us. On a tray! No one blinked because it was too outrageous, and Johnny knew it. So it was with good food and my two best friends around a country club swimming pool that I unloaded everything that had happened over the past month—even, generally, the Shaker Lakes stuff—and where things stood.

"Did she even return your calls?" Roger asked me as we walked through the parking lot toward school.

"Yeah, she called," I told Roger as we marched toward school.

"Well, that's good at least. What did she say?"

"Basically that she and Bennett were fan, fucking, tastic."

"She didn't."

"Not exactly."

"Then there's hope!"

"You're impossible," I said.

He put his arm over my shoulder, which I was grateful for, and we entered the maw of the school and a crowd of four hundred boys interspersed with teachers refreshed from a summer away from us. It felt like a party or a concert, all the energy of the first day of school. I didn't used to mind the first day of school. But I realized today that it was only because at the end of the school day, I got to play football. That wasn't going to happen today, or ever again. And my persistent limp only served as a reminder of what I'd lost.

University School was not your ordinary high school, architecturally or otherwise. It was built of brick, and that is the end of the resemblance. The school opened in 1890 closer to downtown. Another campus was built in Shaker Heights—the one my dad graduated from. This new campus had been built in 1968, in woods beyond the old suburbs. Structurally, it was the high school equivalent of the split-level ranch we saw every day on *The Brady Bunch* reruns. And it was one of the few remaining all-boys schools in the country, most of which had gone coed during the last decade.

Roger and I parted in the sea of boys for our separate lockers.

I dropped my bag in the bottom of my locker. As I was knotting my tie, I noticed Jamie Scott leaning against his locker, staring at the knot he was trying to tie, swaying just a bit. Jamie, who was in my grade, looked like a California surfer, if surfers also wore argyle sweater vests. He was red in the face and laughing.

"Jamie?"

He looked up at me, still laughing, and said, "I am *so* high." And kept laughing.

"Jesus, Jamie," I said, helping him knot his tie. "You gotta quit laughing. Be cool."

I spotted Dave Becker, who was also in the stoner crowd. I hurried to him and said, "Dave, Jamie's totally stoned. Help get him to his seat." I hoped there was enough commotion that Dave could lead Jamie to his seat without running into any of the faculty.

As I took the few steps down from the locker area I bumped into Mr. Dalton, my nemesis last year in geometry.

"Mr. Claverback," he said.

"Good morning, sir," I said.

"I got switched to trig, so our friendship will continue."

Did he see me deflate?

"Let's make this a better math year than last year, okay?"

"Yes, Chef."

"What?"

"I mean, yes, Mr. Dalton."

I looked at my schedule. Trigonometry first period. Followed by chemistry. That was going to suck. Every. Day. English and history were in the afternoon. I wasn't better at these subjects but at least they were interesting. The bright light in my schedule, though, was that I had two free periods, one of them last period. Which meant I could talk to the dean of students to see if I could leave school early, which would give me forty-five extra minutes to get family meal up, which I was going to need.

12

I spent most of ninth period hanging out by myself on Monkey Island, the multiplatformed hanging out area, flipping through my new schoolbooks and writing a list of homework assignments. Everyone said junior year was both the hardest year and the most important, in terms of getting into college. What I, who was lucky to get Cs, would do now, without the prospect of an athletic scholarship, I had no idea. I figured I was going to have to get serious about school. But I wasn't hopeful.

I thumbed through the first three novels we'd be reading: *Invisible Man*, *Lucky Jim*, and *The Bell Jar*. All my other classes, like American history, trig, and chem, used big fat textbooks. For French we used both a textbook and a workbook. Overall, a decent first day of school. I liked most of my classmates. I'd been assigned to a good lunch table, and they'd served macaroni and beef, which was always good. First day of announcements at morning assembly went on so long, Jamie Scott was able to calm down enough to not be noticed and get kicked out of school.

I could have left for home as the throngs of boys hit their lockers and headed for the doors, underclassmen to school buses or to parents waiting in idling cars, but most had after-school sports or clubs to go to. I did not, but habits are hard to break, so I put my books in my locker and headed to the athletic wing.

I pushed through the door to the locker room and the smell hit me hard, the rank odor of sweat, grass, leather, and BO that made my soul relax.

The locker room roiled with kids, freshmen, sophomores, juniors, and seniors, dressing for their sport—football, soccer, and cross-country. Toward the end of the lockers was a smaller locker room given over to senior and junior starters on the football team. Where I would have had a locker. I could hear my old teammates shouting and laughing.

But when I entered, everyone stopped talking, just kept going about their business. A few people kept looking at Terry, the captain, who finally approached me, cleats clicking on the concrete floor.

He held out his hand and said, "Hey."

"Hey," I said.

Sam Marcus, a bruising white-haired defensive tackle, slammed his locker shut, lifted his helmet from the bench, and headed out, stopping to say, "Sorry about what happened, Theo."

A few more people passed me, giving me pats on the shoulder as they did.

Before I took any more air out of the room, I said, "Well, see you guys."

Terry said, "Hey, come out and watch practice."

"Yeah, maybe."

I noticed Trip McLeary and Tom Evans, both wiry defensive backs, seated together on the bench in front of their lockers. I could hear Tom whisper, "It's so sad, man."

As if I weren't even there.

"Well," I said, "have a good practice."

A smattering of "See ya, Theo"s and I left.

I couldn't help myself, though. The restaurant closed on the Tuesday after Labor Day to give staff, who had Mondays off, anyway, an actual post-summer holiday, so the only place I had to go was back to a big empty house. Roger was on the soccer team and likely already out on the fields, so I couldn't talk to him. I sat on Monkey Island till I knew everyone would be out of the locker room and off to the fields. I took another stroll through the now deserted lockers—the smell of it almost made me cry—then headed out the doors to the gravel road that led to the fields.

I couldn't remember the last time I actually walked this path around the lake. Every day we'd gather at the doors outside the athletic wing and jog out as a team, thirty pairs of cleats loudly clump-clumping on the gravel. Now I could think about the trees, still in summer fullness. Crickets buzzing in the afternoon heat. I passed the ravine to the right and could see the trout hatchery. This was my third year at the upper campus, and I'd never been in it. I'd passed it in a helmet and pads for two years without thinking.

I turned off the gravel road, onto a narrow dirt path, baked hard from summer heat, that led into a forest of impossibly tall trees. The air cooled as I moved through the short stretch of woods. It was so quiet here that the sound of a twig cracking resounded. Ten feet away, a large deer with white spots and a white tail nibbled low leaves. She was so peaceful, so lovely, I was afraid to move. She froze when she noticed me. I tried to be as still as possible. She looked at me and I looked at her, trying to will her to stay. But she quickly bounded deep into the woods, out of sight.

I emerged from the woods into the athletic field's parking lot and crossed it to the hill overlooking the football fields: varsity practice on the main field, and beyond, two other fields where JV and freshman teams practiced. These fields sloped down to an even larger expanse of fields where the soccer teams practiced.

I could hear Coach Lambert screaming. I saw him slam his clipboard into the turf. He was going to have a stroke one of these days. "Jarvis!" he yelled as the quarterback, Juan Espinoza, took the ball into the end zone. "The defensive back has the running back covered! You always stay on the quarterback!"

It was a classic mistake. Juan faked an option to the running back, and Jarvis went after the running back while Juan kept the ball, cut inside, and was in the clear for a touchdown. Sigh.

I didn't stay long. It was like standing outside a house where a great party was going on and you weren't invited. I didn't belong here anymore.

I hefted my canvas book bag, slammed my locker shut, and headed for the doors. But I heard my name called. It was Bennett Van Horn.

"Hey, man."

"Hey," I said.

Bennett was about a half foot shorter than I was, skinny, with soft brown hair that swooped across his eyebrows. He tucked much of his hair behind either ear and shook his bangs out of his face. He wore a blue pinstripe Oxford, khaki slacks, and Doc Martens, which was radical for this school and one of the many reasons why Bennett was cool.

"I hear you've been hanging out with Julia. She says you're really cool."

"Julia saved my life."

"Yeah, she told me about your leg. I just wanted to say how remarkable it is that you got a job at that restaurant. It's like the best in the city."

"Thanks, Bennett. What else am I going to do after school?"

"I think a lot of people would just kind of drop out if something like what happened to you happened to them."

I really wanted to dislike him. And just picturing him and Julia together made me angry—but I realized I didn't hate *him*. He was too nice a guy. And smart. But the thought of him even holding hands with Julia, let alone their kissing, or worse, made my stomach turn. I should have been angry with Julia for taking things so far last month. But I couldn't do that, either, because I loved her. Like, crazy. And I couldn't keep myself from believing that this was a good thing, no matter the pain, no matter what.

13

I parked across from Restaurant Margaux, grabbed my books, and stepped into the corner drugstore. I put a bottle of orange Crush on the counter and said to the elderly guy, casually, "Oh, and a pack of Marlboro Reds."

He gave me a look and said, "How old are you?"

"Eighteen," I said. I knew I was big enough to look at least eighteen, so the lie was easy.

He paused but said, "A dollar ten. Matches?"

"Yes, please," I said, pulling out a dollar and change.

I know it's silly, but I felt older leaving the drugstore with my first pack of cigarettes. I crossed the street and walked to the backyard of the restaurant. The kitchen lights were on, but I didn't want to bother Chef on his day off. I put my book bag on the picnic table. I hooked the bottle cap ridge on the edge of the table and pounded down to uncap the bottle, something I'd seen Reggie do. I sat, lit a cigarette, and pulled out my books.

After about forty-five minutes of chem homework, Chef spotted me from the mudroom. "Theo?" he called. I was pretty deep into writing out definitions of *ionic bond* and *covalent* and *anion* so I was glad for the interruption. "What are you doing here?"

"Homework," I said.

He turned to go back into the restaurant, and I called out, "Need a hand with anything?"

"Always," he called back.

Chef stood at the long stainless-steel table with his back to the range, a huge, heavy cutting board in front of him. To his left was a large sheet tray with dozens of chickens. To his right was a second sheet tray with the first of the chickens cut up, breasts lined next to each other, the legs lined up next to them and at the bottom of the sheet, assorted bones, skin, and fat.

Chef regarded my preppy attire longer than was necessary. "You might want to put an apron on. And grab a knife and a cutting board."

By the time I'd returned, apron on, from the basement, he'd moved to make room for me and my cutting board. I put a wet side towel down and set my cutting board on top of it; the towel kept the board from sliding.

"Know how to break down a chicken?" he asked.

"Umm . . ."

"Watch." He swiped his knife down either side of his steel. It was a different knife, more slender and curvy than my chef's knife. He saw me eyeing it, turned it from side to side so that I could see. "Boning knife," he said. He pressed the tip of the knife against the cutting board. The blade flexed. "This one's flexible. Know what they call a boning knife that doesn't bend?"

"No?"

"A stiff boner."

I didn't know what to say, other than, "Seriously?"

He chuckled. "Actually, yeah." I realized then he'd been hoping for a laugh. He was trying to be funny. But Chef was never funny. I guess when no one was around he could be himself. He'd been intimidating for so long, I didn't imagine laughing was an appropriate response to anything he said. "They come in handy, boning knives, but really you should be able to do anything with a chef's knife and a paring knife."

He put a fresh chicken on his board. "Okay," he said. "I like to take the wings off first, but leave this part on, the drumette. Next, you take the legs off." He sliced the skin between the breast and the leg, and bent the drumstick toward him with a *pop*. "And you just"—he pulled the knife along the backbone—"pull your knife along here. There's a little pocket in the backbone where the best muscle on the chicken is. The oyster. You want to capture the oyster." He did the same on the other side so that both legs were removed. "Now you take the breasts," he said, drawing the knife down the center of the chicken. "And you slide your knife down along the wishbone to the wing joint and . . . through the joint." He held the breast in his hand, the skin pale white, the little part of the wing still attached. "This is the supreme cut." He pronounced it su-*prem*.

"For the chicken supreme!" I said. This was on the menu, but I never knew where it came from. "Chicken Supreme with a Shallot Tarragon Jus." But now I felt stupid for saying it aloud.

He said, "Look at the college boy go."

With his chef's knife he cut the knob at the end of the wing off, just went right through the bone. Then he scraped the bone till it was clean and the wing meat was bunched up at the end. "To make it look pretty," he said. He held it in his palm for me to see. He set it in the line of supremes already cut. He cut the other half of the breast off the carcass. He ripped the rib cage off the backbone. He cut the bones into smaller pieces. "For stock," he said. He drew a leg to the center of his board, skin-side down. "See this line of fat, right where the thigh and drumstick come together?" There was a pale yellow line, demarcating the two pieces. "Slice right through it." And without using any pressure, as if the leg were butter, he slid his knife through the joint, and the drumstick and thigh separated. It looked like a magic trick.

"Can I try?"

"No. I got a lot of chickens to get through. And forty skate wings after that. But you're going to help. What do we do with the drumsticks and thighs?"

"Um, they're on the menu?"

"Nope. What's your official job?"

"Family meal."

"Bingo, they're yours—what are you going to do with them?"

"Um."

Chef held his hands out, waiting.

"My mom puts corn flakes on them and bakes them."

He wasn't happy with this response, but he wasn't dismissive, either. "I'm not really a fan of that. Also, you're getting here you said at three thirty, so you'll barely be able to get them cooked. I was thinking maybe a coq au vin."

I knew what that was. I'd read about it. No, I'd *seen* it! On Julia. She was mad about coq au vin.

"Chicken cooked in wine," I blurted.

"College boy, well done."

"I'm not in college."

"Headed there though. Should I call you the Prepper?"

143

I know there was not a single kid at my school who didn't hate, who wasn't *supremely* embarrassed, that our school's mascot was the Prepper.

"Please don't do that," I said.

"Okay. I need the breasts to be pretty, skin intact and joint attached, so I'm going to do those; you'll do the rest—legs, thighs, and stock. And when we're done, I'll show you how to do the coq au vin."

He looked over my shoulder toward the mudroom and said to himself, "Oh, hell."

I'd never heard Chef swear before. I turned. Two older men in dark suits, the short one in a hat, were staring at us through the window. They were older than Chef, more like my parents' age. They entered the kitchen. The tall one said, "Quinn."

I'd never heard him called that before. I knew his name was Jackson Quinn but only because there were framed newspaper and magazine articles near the bathrooms about Chef and the restaurant's opening. But he was only called Chef or Chef Jackson.

"Well, if it isn't the Hand," Chef said.

"Who's this?" the tall one said, staring at me.

"New hire." Pause. "He's all right."

The man was as tall as I was, and beefy. He held out his hands to Chef and smiled. "Happy to see me?"

Chef said to me, "Take the legs off all these," indicating the thirty chickens on the sheet tray. "Separate the legs and thighs, leave the breasts and wings alone. Got it?"

"Yes, Chef."

Chef went to the small hand sink against the dish room wall and washed his hands. He threw a towel over his shoulder, and the two men in suits followed Chef into the dining room, the short one carrying a briefcase.

I got to work on the first chicken, successfully removing the legs and then following that line of fat with my knife, and sure enough, my knife slipped right through the joint, separating the drumstick from the thigh. I grabbed the next chicken and spotted Chef's cool boning knife on his board. I wanted to try it. But I didn't know if I should. I thought I'd better ask Chef first. But when I saw them way in the front of the restaurant, at a small circular table covered with a tablecloth but not set for service, something made me pause. Maybe it was their murmuring tone. Or the fact that there were stacks of cash on the table. They all seemed to be focused on the bundles on the table and didn't notice me.

I pulled back out of sight but heard one of the men say, "Well, I guess you're just going to have to buy more chicken."

I decided this was not the best time to interrupt Chef just so I could try out his knife.

I returned to my chickens. After three birds I was getting the hang of it. I timed myself: fifteen seconds to take both legs off. Because there was always more to do in a kitchen than you had time for, I had to learn to use my time well and recognize how long something should take me, and push myself if it took longer than it should be taking.

I'd gotten only about half the chickens' legs off when Chef reentered the kitchen, several zippered pouches tucked in his arm like a football, and went straight to the basement. The tall man strolled in next, followed by the short guy with the briefcase who stood stiffly at the door to the mudroom, as if guarding it.

The tall man approached me, standing in front of the work-table until I looked up. He wore his hair slicked back, thick hair but receding high over each temple. "Jimmy Holliday," he said, and extended a hand so enormous I paused at the sight of it. The knuckles were dense with fur, and he wore a ring with a red stone on his pinky. The cuff was fastened with a cuff link. I'd seen my dad wear cuff links when he wore a tuxedo, but I didn't realize you used them on, like, a regular weekday.

He smiled at me. It wasn't a friendly smile, but it wasn't exactly an unfriendly smile, either. It was just more smile than the situation seemed to require.

I held both my hands out to show that they were smeared with chicken fat. But I extended my elbow, which was how Reggie and Paul greeted one another.

"Theo Claverback, sir."

His smile increased and he tapped his elbow against mine. "Love it!" he said. "Good to meet you, Theo."

Chef returned from the basement and handed Jimmy Holliday a piece of paper folded in thirds. Holliday slipped it into the inside pocket of his buttoned jacket.

"Have a good evening, gents," he said, and left the kitchen through the mudroom, followed by the man with the briefcase.

I kept moving through the chickens. Chef picked up his knife to begin taking the breasts off, and when he didn't say anything, I asked, "Who was that?"

"One of the investors." Chef kept his attention focused on the chicken.

"But I thought . . . ," I said, thinking maybe I'd got it wrong. Two weeks ago, there was a big to-do in the kitchen because the restaurant's owners—one was somebody high up at National City

Bank, the other a bigwig at Jones Day, Cleveland's most prestigious law firm—were coming in with their wives. They'd visited the kitchen after their meal, and I remembered that one of the wives was so drunk, she was making passes at Chef.

"Jimmy's what you call a silent partner."

I cut some more chicken. "You didn't seem happy to see him."

Chef looked over at my tray, pointing and counting the legs and thighs. "You got enough there to start the coq au vin. Go downstairs and grab a big rondeau, a slab of bacon, onions, carrots."

"Yes, Chef," I said. I wasn't sure what I was more curious about, who Jimmy Holliday was and what his business here had been or how to make a proper coq au vin.

I hustled down the steps to the basement to collect the goods. The pot room was across from the bookkeeper's office. I noticed those pouches lying out on her desk, illuminated by a desk lamp. I couldn't help it, I was curious. I unzipped the top one. Here was the money I'd seen on the table. Up close I noticed that they were bundles of bills secured by rubber bands. These were not nice crisp new bills straight from a bank. These were rough and wrinkled, well used. They were divided by bill size, and most of the bundles seemed to be twenties, but there were several bundles of hundreds as well.

I heard the door to the basement squeak open, so I zipped the pouch fast and hustled across the hallway into the pot room as Chef pounded down the wooden steps. I found the huge round pot with medium-high sides and brought it to the walk-in.

Someone had shoved a crate of cream onto the shelf where the bacon normally was. Chef would have been angry. All dairy went in one place, all produce in another, all proteins, stocks, sauces in their place. That way you didn't waste time digging through things. I loved the order and efficiency of this. I moved the create of cream to the back of the walk-in, next to the milk, half-and-half, and butter, and found the bacon, pushed up against the back of the walk-in shelf by whoever shoved the cream crate on the shelf (likely a waiter, as none of the cooks would do that). I put four large onions in the rondeau with the bacon and ten fat carrots.

I passed the office. The light had been turned off and the pouches were gone.

Back in the kitchen, Chef was working away at the chicken breasts, making perfect supremes and laying them carefully side by side, smoothing the skin as he did so, almost as if he were petting a delicate animal. He liked to touch the food, and I learned to like it, too.

I organized my station, washed and returned the cutting board, and set up to work next to Chef. He said only, "Cut the bacon into lardons, get them cooking. Then do a large dice on the onion and carrot, just like for stock."

I knew stock, and I knew that we did a lardon salad with a poached egg on top, so I knew the lardons, same size as a McDonald's fry, only shorter. I was proud I didn't have to ask him a question— whenever I asked him a question I should have known the answer to, he shook his head like he was sorry he hired me.

"A little bigger," he said. "This isn't for salad. You want nice big meaty chunks." I cut one bigger, he nodded, and I got to it.

Working in a quiet kitchen, especially when you weren't hustling for service, was relaxing and meditative. I focused on making my lardons all exactly the same size and let my mind wander.

But soon they wandered to Julia. Was she at Bennett's house? He at hers? Were they at the Shaker Lakes?

"So, Chef," I said to change my thoughts, "can I ask you something?"

"Maybe."

"Whenever you smell something, you tilt your head to the left. How come? Is that something you learned?"

"I can't smell out of the left side, so I lean the right side close to the food."

"What happened?"

"Broken."

"How?"

"Dad."

"Your father? Why?"

"I told him to fuck off, and he punched me in the nose."

Chef didn't look up from his cutting.

"Why did you tell him to fuck off?"

"Which time?"

"Which *time*?"

"Yeah, he broke it three times—which time do you want to know about?"

I was so shocked by this information, I didn't respond.

"It was different each time, except for the fact that each time he was drunk. And when he was drunk he'd ride me until I mouthed off and he had an excuse to break my nose."

"What did your mom do?"

"She wasn't around. Split when I was seven."

"Why?"

"Theo, I would love to ask her." He stopped cutting and looked at me. "I would *love* to ask her."

"Where is she?"

"I have no idea."

I'd finished the bacon. I lifted the cutting board and scraped the bacon into the rondeau and turned on the gas. Chef filled a pint deli with water and poured some of it over the bacon, explaining that the water would render the fat then cook off, leaving just the bacon and its fat.

"A lot of people don't flour the chicken before browning it," he continued. "I like the way it helps thicken the sauce and, of course, there's the smell." We were on to the coq au vin, having cooked the bacon, which had released a ton of fat. He tapped flour off the next thigh and put it into the fat, skin-side down. "Smell that." I did. It was one of the best things I'd ever smelled. He tilted his head and leaned close to the pot to breathe in. "Floured meat hitting bacon fat," he said. "Reason itself to braise." He handed me the big steel bowl filled with the chicken pieces in flour. "Get all these browned, just a nice color. Careful with the heat. Do not let the flour burn or we'll lose all the beautiful fat."

That was another thing—Chef always seemed to run counter to everything I knew. You're supposed to avoid fat. Or so I thought. To him, it was beautiful.

Chef carried the bowl of livers and the two big sheet trays of chicken down the stairs. He reappeared with a smaller sheet tray, "a half sheet," lined with brown paper towels from the dispenser above the sink. We both removed the browned legs from the rondeau to the half sheet.

"Now sweat the onion and carrot." He dumped the vegetables into the pan, where they sizzled and hissed. He took what seemed like an enormous amount of salt out of a ramekin and rained it all over the carrots and onion. "Season as you go," he said.

"Season as you go," I repeated.

As I stirred the vegetables, Chef uncorked three bottles of red wine.

He nestled the chicken back into the pan. "Now the wine, plonk, the cooking medium. Drinkable but cheap." He swirled the upended bottle, creating a whirlpool, and the wine didn't *glug glug* out of the bottle but came out as if the bottle were a hose. Another magic trick.

"So. This is a braise, Theo. Tough meat, floured and seared, then cooked low and slow in the oven in some kind of liquid. Combination cooking method, they call it in culinary school. When this comes up to a simmer, cover it loosely with foil and pop it into a three-hundred-degree oven."

"For how long?"

He stopped and leaned into my face and growled menacingly, "Till it's done."

This kind of scared me.

Chef chuckled and said, "Also something they tell you in culinary school. Couple hours should do it for this chicken."

The time, what time was it? I looked at the clock on the wall. "Chef, I told my parents I'd be home at six. And I've got homework."

Chef looked at the clock and said, "Six fifteen; you'd better get rolling."

"But—"

"No worries, Theo. I'm here for the night. I'll pull it when it's done. It'll be in the walk-in when you get here tomorrow. You can serve it with egg noodles and the usual salad. I'll show you how to adjust the consistency when you get here."

"Yes, Chef," I said. I knew better than to leave all my stuff out, so I hustled to clean the cutting board and wipe everything down. I untied my apron, tossed it in the hamper, and got my books.

"Theo."

"Yes, Chef."

"You're a good man. I'm glad to have you in the kitchen."

I tried not to smile, but could feel my face flush. "Thank you, Chef."

I moved toward the mudroom to leave, but Chef called out again. "And, Theo? Jimmy Holliday isn't someone you want to like you. If he's ever here and I'm not around, steer clear."

Was Bennett's house on my way home? Not really, but it was on South Park Boulevard, not far from where I lived. Julia's house was definitely not on the way. When I saw that her car was not in her driveway, it wasn't too much more out of the way to drive by Bennett's. Why why why? Why did I *do* this? I sat in my car in the street looking at Bennett's enormous house, set a hundred yards back from the street, behind a field of lawn smooth as a putting green, and there in the circular driveway was the car that I loved so much, that held so much power because it was Julia's and because of what we'd done in it. Julia.

I carried on—now forty-five minutes past when I said I'd be home—creating the most likely scenario in my head. Julia had arrived at Bennett's in the afternoon when his parents were gone. She and Bennett hung out in his room listening to the Grateful Dead and drinking wine and having sex. Obviously.

"Honestly, Theo, where have you been?"

Mom.

"I left a note."

"Which said you'd be home at six."

Mom had yet to look at me. She ducked into the freezer for a box of frozen green beans which she set by the stove. I could smell what was for dinner, not unusually but ironically, the chicken in corn flakes. This was a customary dinner on the days Linda, our housekeeper, cleaned. Linda often set up dinner so Mom or Dad could just pop it in the oven on arriving home. By the time Dad had finished his martini and a cigarette, and Mom had had a glass of wine, dinner would be ready.

"I was at the restaurant."

"*Really,*" she said. Not a question.

"Really."

"Well, I called and no one answered. Rang and rang and rang."

"We're closed today. Chef never answers the phone. Clive takes all the reservations."

She looked at me sideways and cleared her throat.

I let out a sigh and explained exactly what I'd done (I left out the buying cigarettes part).

"Hm," she said, drying her hands. "Dinner in thirty minutes."

"Jeez," I said, and went to my room. I couldn't leave my book bag lying around with a pack of cigarettes in it. Mom might go through my stuff—she wasn't super snoopy, but like I said, she had that weird mom-sense. I passed the porch where Dad read the *Plain Dealer.* The air was so still, a thin stream of smoke rose straight off the cigarette in a long unbroken stream. His martini glass sweated beside it.

"Hi, Dad," I said.

"Hey, Skeezix," he said, lowering the paper. Seriously but not ominously he said, "How was the first day back?"

"It was good," I said. I shook my head as I took the stairs to my room. I put on my favorite Neil Young album, *Time Fades Away*. Plugged in my headphones so I could play it loud, and I lay on my back on the floor staring at the ceiling. I didn't want to be here. I didn't want to be anywhere except the Margaux kitchen. It was the only place I could be that didn't hurt. And the only place I knew for certain I'd be near Julia.

But at the same time, I wanted to be here, comfortable in my room. I was beginning to realize this was pretty nice, from the plush carpet I lay on to a father who didn't break my nose and a mom who set the table after a long day of work and got dinner on. I rolled on my side and brought my knees to my chest. Just thinking. I didn't move until Mom called me for dinner.

14

I left school after eighth period and got to the restaurant the next day a little after three. Julia was late. I knew this because I felt like I was suffocating in the basement kitchen, my stomach knotted. What if she didn't show up? What if she quit to be with Bennett? What would I do? If she quit, I'd never see her at all.

The coq au vin in the walk-in, covered in plastic and labeled, was solid—I tapped it, hard as a Super Ball. I guessed it was supposed to be like this, but I was surprised. Why did it get so solid? I covered it with foil and put it in the oven.

I put two huge pots of water on to boil, one for four bags of egg noodles and one for four pounds of green beans, which I'd pick while the water boiled. I was emptying out a box of kosher salt into the bean water—Chef wanted tons of salt in vegetable water, said it should taste like the ocean. But the noodle water was different—*this* water simply had to taste seasoned, like a soup. And he wanted me to bring him water from each when I'd seasoned them properly.

Fingers covered my eyes from behind at the same moment I smelled the spicy floral scent. "Guess who," she whispered.

My whole soul uncoiled, and my lungs opened up. I turned and there she was. It felt like forever since I'd seen her, but really it had only been four days. Four incredibly long days. Without thinking I threw my arms around her and hugged her.

"Whoa," she said.

"Julia, I hope this doesn't sound weird, but I *missed* you." This was arguably an ill-advised strategy, to come at her this way. This wasn't exactly playing hard to get. But I couldn't help it. She opened me up.

"You. Silly." She squeezed the skin below my jaw.

"I'm serious," I said, doubling down.

"And I'm late," she said. "I gotta get changed."

But before she left, she gave me the smallest smile, just a little curl of the lips and a sideways glance. It was just enough to let me know she liked being missed. I think? That maybe she felt a little of what I felt. Or was I being an idiot, knowing that some girls didn't want things so easy? But hard-to-get wasn't me. My strategy, to counter this weakness, was to pretend not to care about Bennett, even embrace him. This might disarm her.

The few words with Julia, and knowing she'd be there all night, was all I needed to move through the second half of my day. This was really the first day of my new life, one that began with 8:10 assembly. English ended at 2:20, which meant, instead of remaining at school until 3:10 every day, I could get to the restaurant before 3:00. This would give me almost two hours to get family meal up—a protein, a starch, a veg, and a salad. Even if I weren't able to cook the main dish the day before, I'd still have a lot of time.

Chef bounded down the stairs, saying, "Ready to finish the coq au vin?" He had several hefty books under one arm.

"Yes, Chef!"

"I brought you some reading material. They're really important to me, so they don't leave the house, but you're free to peruse. This was my school textbook, *The New Pro Chef.* Use it for ideas for family meal—the recipes are solid." He set it on my worktable. "This here is *Larousse Gastronomique*, a food encyclopedia; you should find most terms you don't know here. And this is my inspiration." He held it before me with both hands.

The title read *Great Chefs of France*.

"It's not to use—you're not going to be doing any recipes out of it, but read it to know what the French are doing. Read it for ideas."

He grabbed a spoon out of a "bain"—a metal canister filled with water and spoons. Chef dipped it into the now steaming water, tasted, and said, "More salt." He tasted the other.

"That's for noodles," I said.

"That one's good. Cover these—they'll boil faster."

"I didn't see any lids."

Chef dipped below my worktable, pulled out two half sheet trays, and put them on top of the pots. "Gotta learn to improvise in a kitchen, Theo." He squatted at the open oven, pulled two white side towels out of his apron string, and hefted the heavy rondeau onto the top of the six-burner stove. He lit the flame below it.

"Wow," I said. "That was rock solid when I put it in the oven a half hour ago."

"Because of the gelatin."

"You put Jell-O in this?"

Chef chuckled. "No, knucklehead. Gelatin is what makes broth solid when cold. Here the gelatin comes from bone, skin, and cartilage. It's protein."

"I thought meat was protein." I knew I should just keep saying "Yes, Chef," but I was curious.

He gently stirred the massive pot of stew. "All food, everything we serve here, everything in your fridge at home is composed of three types of molecules. Proteins, fats, and carbohydrates. It's all in the way they come together that gives us infinite forms of food."

"What about water?" I asked. We were studying water in chemistry, or just getting into it.

"Well, if you don't have water you don't have anything, so I'm not sure that counts."

Chef vanished into the walk-in and returned with a big quart deli filled with something that looked like paste. Only when he dug into it with a spoon did I see how hard it was. He took out a big chunk, size of a tennis ball, and dropped it into the chicken stew.

"So, Theo. We've done everything perfectly here. We floured and browned the meat. We got nice color on the bacon, a nice crust on the chicken. We used the fat to cook the chicken and sweat the aromatics and flavor the sauce. Then we cooked the meat till it was perfectly tender. We tasted. We adjusted the flavor with a little more salt and pepper. Now we have one final thing to do."

He paused, maybe expecting me to know what it was? Um, not.

"Adjust the consistency. See this?" He lifted some sauce with a spoon and poured the sauce back in. "Too thin. We want it to coat the chicken pieces luxuriously, to coat the noodles you're serving it on, so that you naturally get plenty of this delicious sauce with each bite."

Chef had his big hair contained in a red bandanna tied in a triangle today, which meant he was having a busy cooking day, and these words sounded strange coming out of this face with the gap teeth, bandanna, and broken nose. But I found them utterly compelling.

"How do you do that?"

"With roux," he said, holding up the plastic container of the paste. "Flour and butter. Butter coats the granules of flour so they don't stick to each other, and the flour absorbs the liquid and swells up, thickening the sauce. Here, stir. Keep it moving until the roux is completely melted. Keep adding roux until you have the consistency you want. *Nappé*."

"Huh?"

"Look it up."

"What kind of molecules are in the roux?" I asked, thinking this might stump him.

He held the plastic container up as if it were a kind of beacon. "Wheat flour, so that's carbohydrate and protein, and the butter is the fat. You've got the culinary universe right here in a plastic deli!"

"Is there water in there?"

"No—we clarify the butter for the roux, cook the water out of it."

"Huh?"

"That's for next time. I gotta get back upstairs."

I stirred the sauce and chicken slowly and gently. The chicken had become so tender it would fall off the bone if I stirred harder. But nothing more was happening—the stew remained more like soup. But then, as it began to bubble, it really did get thicker. Chef was right. It became more opaque and, well, saucelike. I turned the flame to low and pushed the pot mostly off the flame, as I'd seen Reggie do with his sauces, and got to work picking beans for twenty people.

I loved picking beans. I loved doing all this stuff, chores that required doing the same thing over and over. You didn't have to think and could let your mind wander. And now that I knew Julia was polishing silver and filling saltshakers (I checked the schedule—she had the downstairs tonight, so she'd be in a good mood), my mind wandered.

I thought about those few nights in August when we'd parked at the Shaker Lakes, and Julia had led me into the spread of pine trees that bordered that side of the lake. The pine was so intense I could smell it in my imagination. And the bed of pine needles was so soft. We'd sit cross-legged facing each other in the dark. Julia's cigarette made her face glow when she inhaled. And we just talked.

About everything. Whether or not Ronald Reagan would beat President Carter. The Grateful Dead concert at Music Hall in December. Gossip about people we both knew, who was dating who, who had broken up. And one big event: Julia had recently accompanied a sort-of friend to an abortion clinic because this girl didn't have anyone else to go with her.

"Bennett likes to smoke pot," she told me one night, crickets in the background but silent other than that, not even passing cars. "I don't. It just makes me stupid."

"Me too!" I said, very glad she felt this way. I'd gotten high with Roger for the first and only time the previous spring, right after school let out. In the afternoon, before I had a dentist appointment downtown. It was really weird.

"Acid, on the other hand, is uh-mazing," Julia said.

"Really?" Acid sounded scary to me.

"Pot makes you stupid. Acid makes you aware of absolutely everything, all at once."

"At once? I don't know how I'd handle that."

"It's beautiful," she said, the contours of her face just visible, the smell of pine thick, the Southern Comfort . . . comforting. And she smiled at me so softly, I swooned inside. "In, like, a way you've never experienced."

"Once," I said, "I was at my grandma's on Sanibel. I was on the beach. It was night. The sand was warm and the palm trees were super crisp because the sky was clear and the moon was bright. It was half full, but the night was so clear, you could see the other part of the moon. I could even see craters. And the sand between my toes, the tiny grains of sand and the palm trees and the moon and even the air. I saw how everything was connected, from the sand between my toes to the air to the moon."

Julia didn't say anything, just kept looking at me. I was going to say, it felt like God, but I knew Julia didn't believe in God, so I stopped there.

At last Julia said, "I love how thoughtful you are."

There was no response to this, other than to look down.

"You've just described what it's like to take acid, and you've never even taken it."

If this is true, I want some of this acid, I thought.

The pine needles made a soft bed, and unlike in her car, we could stretch out. So soft. I could touch her whole body and she mine. I couldn't believe it. I was both in my body and outside looking down on us.

"Hey, dream boy," Reggie said, coming out of the walk-in with a pan full of the skate wings Chef had skinned and boned yesterday. "You got us covered?"

I looked at my watch. Four thirty. Shit. Lost track. Fortunately, the pots still had plenty of boiling water in them. I dumped the beans in. I ripped open bags of noodles and dumped those in.

I covered the pots. I looked at my watch again, trying to will the pasta to cook. It would be ready for family meal, but I still had to get it up the stairs and into hotel pans to serve it. I'd done three family meals so far, but Chef had really helped, as he had here. This was kind of my first semisolo venture in putting it all up myself. Now I was late from daydreaming.

Julia came out of the linen room and with a two-foot-tall stack of napkins strode to the stairs, not stopping but saying, "You good?"

I was now stirring the coq au vin and felt a lot of it stuck to the bottom where the flame had been. "Um, no? I think I burned this—and I don't have the hotel pans set up upstairs." By this time I'd scraped the bottom of the pan and the spoon came up with a wedge of black, burned sauce. Shit.

"Let me see," Julia said when she returned. "It feels like it's only burned in that one spot. Just don't scrape that stuff off the bottom."

"Does it taste burnt?"

Julia grabbed a spoon out of the bain and tasted. "Oh, man, it's *delicious*. But it's way too thick."

Luckily, super luckily, Amanda emerged from the walk-in hefting a humongous pan of strip steaks that had been soaking in olive oil, garlic, and pepper, and had overheard.

She paused, looking over Julia's shoulder. "Just add more water."

"Water?" I said.

"That's what cooked out of it. Use some pasta water. It's already hot."

I grabbed a ladle, knocking over the spoon canister, but I didn't care. Panic mode.

"Wait," Amanda said. "How hard did you season the water?"

"Chef tasted it, said it was fine."

Amanda set the pan of steaks on my worktable and stuck her finger into the boiling water, as if it weren't boiling, and sucked her finger. "Shit, Theo, Chef didn't okay that! It tastes like the ocean."

I clutched my head, realizing. In my haste, I'd dumped the beans into the pasta water and the pasta into the can't-be-too-salty bean water.

Julia said, "Okay, I'm going to set up family meal while you two figure this out. You've got four minutes." Even in my panic, a part of my brain registered how cute her butt was in those tight black pants, how beautiful her long blond ponytail was swishing across the back of her dark vest, the shape of her head with her hair pulled back so tightly. I looked back at my pots.

"Amanda, what do I do?"

She tasted the bean water on her finger. I honestly didn't know it didn't hurt to stick your hand in boiling water.

"Well, your problem is the pasta. It'll be way too salty to eat. Do we have any cooked starch?"

"Starch?"

"Noodles, rice, or potatoes," she said impatiently.

"No, we cleaned everything out for the long weekend."

"Shit." She picked up her pan of steaks and said, "I think Reggie is cooking the fettuccini upstairs. I'll check. In the meantime, fix the stew. With the bean water, not the water the pasta is in!"

She took the stairs two at a time. I stirred bean water into the coq au vin till it looked like the beef stew we had at home. I tasted it. It didn't taste burnt or too salty.

Amanda trotted downstairs. Casually! How could she be casual right now! I wanted to tell her there was an emergency going on here!

163

She gripped both my shoulders, hard, and said, "Theo." Long pause. Long valuable seconds. Long, long valuable seconds. "You've got. To settle. Down. You only make mistakes when you rush."

"But Chef is particular about timing."

She said, "No one's going to die, okay?"

"Yes, Chef."

"Here's what we're going to do. You're going to take that perforated round insert over there and drain the pasta in it. Then you're going to take that insert with the drained pasta and plunge it into Reggie's fettuccine water. The instant the water comes back to a boil, pull the insert, let it drain, taste a noodle, and if it's edible, dump it into the hotel pan Julia's setting up now. Hopefully a quick blanch in normal water will leach out some of the salt. Paul has a ninth pan full of soft butter. Throw that on the pasta and stir. Paul won't mind. He steals our meez all the time. I'll deal with your beans." She released my shoulders, paused again, then said, *"Go."*

I raced for the insert while Amanda found a big colander for the beans. "Were you doing anything else with the beans, almonds or anything?"

Almonds? What the fuck? "Was I supposed to?"

"No. Just asking."

I put the insert in the sink and drained the pasta, then raced the pasta upstairs to Reggie. He held out his hand to the giant pot he was cooking in.

"Just put it in, right on top of yours?"

"Just put it in."

I did, and raced downstairs to bring the coq au vin up. Julia was setting up the hotel pans on the central worktable, stacks of plates, silverware containers, serving spoons. Chef was on the phone, but I saw him look at his watch as I dumped "my" first coq au vin out of the rondeau into the hotel pan. The wall clock read 4:46. I could see the round spot of char, but it wasn't all burned. I brought it straight to the pot room, making sure Chef didn't see the scorch. Amanda arrived with a hotel pan of already buttered green beans. How had she done this?

She set it on the table. She tasted a bean and added more salt. Reggie's water returned to a boil. I pulled my pasta out of Reggie's pasta. As it drained, I tasted one—burning my fingers and mouth. The pasta was edible, definitely wouldn't need salt though. I dumped it into the hotel pan and raced to Paul's station where he carefully sliced slabs of terrine. I took his butter and ignored him when he said, "Hey!"

But in moments, with all the servers lined up waiting for food, I tossed the pasta with the butter, and it was done. I took a deep breath. The clock read 4:52. At least everyone would eat. Julia was at the end of the line. I went to her and put my forehead on her shoulder.

"Thank you so, so much."

"No problem, it only took a few and I'm in good shape with the side work. Look at you."

"What?"

"All red and disheveled. You're a mess!"

"I didn't want to be late. I didn't want to disappoint Chef." I saw Jackie head to the dining room with a plate. "It's too brown," I told Julia. I went to Paul's station and this time took his parsley. Before he could say "Hey," I said, "I'll chop more for you before service!"

I rained chopped parsley over the coq au vin even as people were scooping it out onto their plates. The green brightened it.

Chef appeared with half a lemon and squeezed it over the beans. He popped a bean into his mouth and, chewing, nodded. Phew. Cooked right and Amanda must have seasoned them right. He tasted the coq au vin sauce. He hesitated. Hmm.

Eating was the last thing I wanted to do now, but Julia, nearing the front of the line, said, "Want me to make you a plate? We can eat outside?"

"That would be great!" I said.

Chef was standing by with a plate tucked under his arm. "Next time, be early instead of late." I gave him my Yes, Chef nod. "And don't forget the salad."

"Shit, I forgot about salad!"

"That's all right for today. Oh, and I should have told you. The flour in the roux can stick to the bottom of the pan. You need to scrape the bottom after the roux goes in."

"Yes, Chef." *That* was his hesitation when he tasted it.

Amanda was at her station leaning against the range, eating. She gave me a thumbs-up. I pointed at her then pressed my palms together in thanks. Reggie was off dumping his own pasta, but I saw he'd already made a plate for himself.

Paul, standing and eating a chicken thigh with his hands, his mouth full. "Nailed it, Chef."

That was the first time I'd been called Chef. I bowed my head in thanks, but I'd totally fucked up. I'd scorched Chef's great sauce and he knew it. I'd been late. I'd forgotten the salad.

Julia waited for me at the door of the mudroom, two plates in hand.

"Oh, don't worry about it," she told me, taking a seat across from me at the picnic table. Two servers were already there, Brandon and Tony. The other table was filled up. "Oh God, this is delicious, Theo," Julia said.

"Yeah, way to go, Theo," Tony said. "This is great."

"I had a little help."

"But still," he said.

"Does it taste scorched?" I asked Julia.

"Not in the least."

"Somehow, Chef knew I'd scorched it. How did he know?"

"Because he's not real," she said.

"What's that mean?"

"He's not made of flesh and blood."

She leaned way over her plate to put her face close to mine. She whispered, *"He's your conscience."* She made her eyes go big, then let out a big open-mouthed laugh. She speared some egg noodles, looked at me, and said, "Now eat your delicious food."

I tasted. It was good. It was really good. But still.

As if she knew what I was thinking, she said, "Maybe it wasn't perfect to you, but everyone's loving it." She looked back at the other picnic table. Servers were already leaving with empty plates to get back to work. "I haven't seen people eat out here since Nando left."

"I guess you're right."

"We're gonna get hit early. I gotta bolt."

I watched her go. She was still finishing the meal as she walked.

I'd done okay. Chef would have made it clear if I hadn't. And people did seem to like it. But I couldn't linger. I had to replace Paul's parsley before service, which was in twenty minutes. And I had to prep tomorrow's family meal (an easy one, meat loaf). And check off about a hundred other items on my list. Mirepoix, thyme, shallots, potatoes, and on and on and on.

But I was already missing the nightly ritual of leaving with Julia and sitting in the car and talking about the night. And, well, her lips. Teeth clicking, hands roving. I refused to believe that what happened this summer was never going to happen again.

15

I couldn't stand to be at school. As September moved into October, classes grew from novel to confusing and difficult. Chemistry got super hard, superfast. More and more, I felt classes were just keeping me from the restaurant. And my classmates and former teammates increasingly annoyed me. They whined about the dress code. (I liked a dress code—you didn't have to think; but now my preferred dress code involved a chef's coat and pinstripe apron.) They passed around dirty magazines in the locker area. (I couldn't help but think about what Amanda or Chef would think—probably just shake their heads and get back to work.) Over in the corner of Monkey Island, a group of the richer kids gambled with dollar bills, folding them into paper airplanes and seeing who could float theirs closest to the brick wall without touching it. And in another corner of Monkey Island, my former teammates wrestled and shot rubber bands at each other.

Even Roger bugged me, constantly mooning over Sarah.

Restaurant Margaux was really the only place where I could be myself. I didn't like being at home, either—with Mom and Dad always riding me about homework and threatening to make me quit the restaurant if my grades fell off. I wasn't home a whole lot, which helped. Tuesdays through Fridays, from 7:30 when I left for school till 10:30 at night, I was either at school or at the restaurant, so home was just where I slept. Saturdays I took my books to the restaurant and did homework there at El 3, one of four tables on a small, elevated alcove at the back of the downstairs dining room that was also used for big parties. I could spread my books out and not be bothered by a mom or a dad. Sundays were all-study days at home; my only break, the Cleveland Browns game.

Weirdly, Dad started watching them with me. When I asked him about his newfound interest in our city's football team, he said he missed me. This made me confused at first—I'm not sure why. He'd always been kind of distant himself; when I became distant, he didn't like it. I should be glad for that. He was just so uncool. Cool was Chef. But I liked to watch the game with Dad. We didn't talk about schoolwork, just the game, so it was relaxing and fun. Also it was good to have someone to commiserate with when they lost and rejoice with when they won. And the Browns, despite losing their first two games, were looking to have one of their best seasons in a decade.

Also on Sundays, I cooked dinner and Mom loved that. Cooking for three was a breeze!

Also Julia was always at the restaurant, and I wanted to be where she was. I tended to work until she was finished so that I could walk her to her car. She usually parked across the street from the restaurant. I used to, too—I liked showing off my car. I thought it was too damn cool.

Until one day when I got to the restaurant and Jackie said, "Nice car."

I said, "Thanks."

Then she said, "Mommy and Daddy give it to you?"

"My father did."

"Figures," she said, and walked off.

I didn't care what Jackie thought anymore. But since then I started parking on the side street, behind Paul's car.

So after work, I would walk Julia to her car before walking around the corner to mine. She always began the talk with how much she made in tips, either grumbling a total or saying, "One guy gave me a fifty-dollar tip!" And there were usually tales from the front of the house. "I should write a book called *Stories from the Front*," Julia said. For instance, the time—oh happy day!— Jackie spilled red wine on a woman's white silk blouse. The night Clive, the maître d', kicked out a Cleveland city council member for being too drunk at the bar, calling him a taxi (the restaurant had a small, elegant bar with five stools). A major reseating headache when a man and a woman who were in the middle of a divorce were seated next to each other, by chance, with their new partners. The local news anchor who showed up in sweatpants and had to be denied.

The nights were cooling, and Julia wore a green army jacket she'd picked up cheap at the Army Navy store at the Golden Gate mall. She crushed out her cigarette and pulled its collar close to her neck.

Tonight, though, had been problematic. I was in the middle of hauling hotel pans of a beef and broccoli stir-fry up from the basement for family meal but a little worried because Julia was nowhere. I'd even asked Clive if she'd called in sick. So I was surprised to see her with a plate in hand waiting for family meal when everyone began to line up.

"Where have you been?" I whispered.

She pulled my arm close, alarm in her eyes (bloodshot!), and whispered, "I'm *stoned*."

"What? Why?"

"Stupid," she said. "Bennett got me high. My own fault."

"You don't even like getting high."

"I *know*."

"Are you going to be okay?"

She snorted and said, "We'll see!" She snorted again, stifling a laugh.

"Okay, just try to stay focused. Let me know if I can help you."

She made a mwah kiss in my direction, and I got in line with my plate, though I was almost never hungry after putting up family meal. I'd learned to eat, anyway, otherwise I'd be ravenous by eight.

I stayed upstairs in the mudroom for the first couple of hours during service, prepping stock mirepoix, to keep an eye on Julia. Normally I got tomorrow's family meal taken care of first. But I was doing spaghetti and meatballs, which was a no-brainer. Just had to shape one hundred or so meatballs and make the sauce—I could do that later.

She seemed normal, though she kept her eyes averted when she brought tickets to Chef and picked up plates. She appeared steady. Once Chef looked at her as she loaded three plates on her left arm and lifted a fourth with her right hand and said, "You got allergies, Julia?"

"Bad," she said, not wasting more time in his presence. He knew, but she was fine, so I finished up in the mudroom and took the mirepoix down to the walk-in and got to work shaping meatballs in the basement kitchen. It was well lit, and I kept it spotless. I liked cleaning as much as cooking. Chef loved this, and I loved that he loved it.

I was about fifty meatballs in when Julia rushed through the basement with an opened bottle of red wine. She lifted the door of the ice machine at the back of the room, against the walk-in.

"You okay?"

"I have a nightmare table." She'd jammed the bottle into the ice and was spinning it. "The first two bottles they ordered were eighty-sixed. And this one is too hot, they said."

"How's your head?"

"Still stoned but less so." She took a moment to let the bottle chill and studied her dupe pad. "Oh, fuck me!" she said. She ripped out a ticket. "Fuck!" she said again.

I wiped my hands on a side towel.

"This was supposed to go in like an hour ago. I thought it was in! I forgot. Fuck! Theo, what do I do? Chef knows I'm stoned, I'm sure of it. He'll fire me for this. I can't get fired."

"Lemme see the ticket." I took it from her. Halibut, lamb, and two lardon salads—Reggie's and Paul's stations. These were quick pickups.

"I'll take care of it. You take care of the bad table."

"This *is* for the bad table!"

"Ow," I said. "Tell Clive the kitchen is backed up, comp them some wine. I'll try to slip this in."

I bolted up the steps into the mudroom and waited for Chef to be distracted. I needed him to think I was hiding this, so I jumped on the line pretending to refill shallots, but I said, "Reggie." He owed me and I knew he'd help. "Julia gave me this ticket an hour ago and I spaced and forgot to give it to Chef. Halibut, lamb, two lardons. Table twelve."

"You got it, Chef," Reggie said. Then he said, "Paul, can you do two lardons on the fly?"

Paul shook his head—meaning he was buried—but he didn't say no.

"What's going on?" Chef said to me.

"Chef, I'm sorry, I was supposed to give you this ticket an hour ago. Julia was getting hassled by her table; she was getting wine and I told her I'd give you the ticket. And I forgot."

He held out his hand for the ticket. I walked off the line to his side of the Pass. He took the ticket from me, said, "Order-fire-pickup one lamb, one halibut, and two lardons." Then he stared at me. He pounded my forehead with the heel of his hand. "Think!"

I'd taken a million worse hits on the field, but Chef hitting me stung. He said, "I don't want to see you."

"Yes, Chef."

I spotted my dear pal Jackie bringing a load of plates into the dish room and caught her there. "Jackie, do me a favor?"

She looked at me like I'd just farted in her face.

"Please, just tell Julia I took care of it."

I presumed that she would, grudgingly, pass the info along. I disappeared down into the dungeon for the remainder of the evening. Fortunately, I didn't need to be in the kitchen, just finish the meatballs and sauce.

Service didn't slow down till 10:30. A busy fall Friday night. Julia appeared and fell back against the ice machine. "Worst night ever."

"How's your head?"

"No longer stoned, thank God. Theo, thank you so much. Chef didn't say a thing."

"I took the fall for you."

"You," she said. She gave me a long hug. "I got about an hour's more work. Will you still be here?"

"I will. Chef's pissed at me. I'll likely slink out. Let me know when you're leaving."

We leaned against the back of her car, both of us smoking, Julia outlining her long bad night.

She took a final drag and blew the smoke toward the sky. Ground the cigarette out.

"God you saved my ass tonight. Thank you."

"Just don't get high before work anymore!"

"That's for sure."

I'd finished my cigarette, and I couldn't think of a way to prolong the conversation. I didn't want it to end because I'd been aware all week that she'd called off tomorrow. Bennett was taking her to our Homecoming dance. So I only said, "Well, see you Tuesday?"

She squeezed her lips together and nodded. What did that mean?

"Bye," I said.

"Bye."

I turned and began to walk down the deserted street, around the corner to my car. I didn't know what her final expression had meant. And I figured I had nothing to lose. So I turned before she'd gotten in her car and called out, "Julia! You know I'm still crazy about you, right?"

I expected something cute, like, "You!" and a grin, at which point my heart would shimmer, and I'd take a deeper breath. But instead, her head fell forward as if all the muscles in her neck stopped working. I'd made her feel bad. I hadn't meant to.

I sat in my car, idling at the stop sign, watching Julia's car. It didn't move, just sat there with its red brake lights on. What was she doing? I waited. I wanted to wave when she passed, but she didn't move. Maybe she was waiting for me to leave first, so I did. I turned right onto Larchmere and headed home.

16

I got to work early the next day, Saturday, in time to join Reggie and Amanda for a smoke. They were both drinking coffee.

"Hey, Theo," Amanda said.

"Hey, brother," Reggie said.

"Hey," I said, lighting up and sitting down. It was a cool, cloudy, dry day. I could see Paul was already in the kitchen.

"Busy night last night," I said.

Amanda said, "And it's gonna be another busy one tonight. Plus another VIP dinner."

Reggie stared at me. With the hand that held his cigarette, he pointed at me and said, "That lost ticket last night."

"Yeah, what about it?" I said.

"Why didn't you just give it to Chef?"

"Duh. I didn't want to get caught."

"Just doesn't seem like you. You're always straight when you mess up."

"Yeah," Amanda said. "We thought maybe you were covering for someone? I wonder who?"

"Nope, just my own ass," I said.

Reggie pushed out his lower lip and nodded slowly, as if to say, *Okay.*

I was grateful to be really busy today. I tried not to think about Julia and Bennett. Not thinking, at *all*, about Julia and Bennett slow dancing to "Stairway to Heaven" and getting drunk at whatever after-parties seniors went to.

On top of the usual Saturday crush, that night we had, as Amanda had said, a VIP dinner, only this one was a super VIP dinner. Very Important Person dinners always involved extra effort, but this was one I hadn't seen before with new dishes I was unfamiliar with. Veal saltimbocca, fettuccine Alfredo, and something called steak Florentine.

I'd figured out by now I was at one of the best restaurants in the city. When I told my dad's friends where I worked, most of them raised their bushy eyebrows and nodded approvingly. (Only a few swished the air and said, "overpriced," or "pretentious.") It was common to have any number of Cleveland royalty in the restaurant. One Thursday night in September, we had Mayor Voinovich, the beautiful news anchor Wilma Smith, and the car guy Del Spitzer (his ads were everywhere), all on the same night.

But Chef never created dishes that weren't on the menu for VIPs, so this one must have been a V-VIP. It was fun because I got to learn a new dish (I pounded out pieces of veal and rolled them with what Chef called Italian ham), and Amanda showed me the two giant porterhouse steaks she'd be grilling, holding them both in her left hand and smacking the steak hard with her right hand.

"Beauts, no?"

"Who's it for?" I asked her.

"Big owner dinner, special request. All-Italian menu, eight-top, family style—everything's going out on platters."

I'd have to check this out.

In the meantime, I had a new family recipe to try, another braise, for Tuesday. Chef liked braises to sit refrigerated for a day or two, so I would almost always do some kind of braise on Saturday for Tuesday family meal.

Lamb navarin, which Chef said was a classic French stew usually done in spring, but I was going to do it with winter vegetables—celery root, carrot, potatoes, onions, and something I'd never heard of, Jerusalem artichokes, which didn't look anything like the artichokes Mom bought.

All the chopping gave me plenty of time alone in the basement kitchen . . . to think. And thoughts of Julia and Bennett having fun at a dance eventually just made me angry. Was I being a wimp? When I talked to Johnny about it, he said I was "pussy-whipped."

"Dude, she's totally using you," he said. "Stop pining for her, for Chrissake. It's embarrassing."

And he was right. I peeled and halved all my onions. Then I rough chopped them, cleaver-style, *bang bang bang bang bang*. Tony happened to be passing, three bottles of wine in his arms (servers were down here all night, usually for wine or for a fresh tablecloth when a guest knocked over a glass of wine). "Nice technique," he said.

"Chef taught it to me," I said, and gave the onions a couple dozen more whacks, chunks of onion flying. They disintegrated during the long cook time so beautiful cuts didn't matter. Johnny *was* right. I was being stupid. I should be trying to find a girlfriend. And maybe I would be if I wasn't working all the time. I decided to call Johnny to see if he could get together that night after work. I slid the stew into the oven at seven (it needed three hours). There was a phone in Maryann's office. I could see the door to Maryann's office was cracked open. Usually it was locked. I used the phone in there. Johnny was home and bored. He said he'd be "delighted" to run out for some Olde English 800.

As I left the office, Chef happened to be passing and said, "What were you doing in there?"

"I needed to call a friend."

"This is supposed to be locked. I've told you you can use the kitchen phone after the last entrée goes out." He took the keys he carried on a chain on his belt, concealed by his apron, and locked the door.

"Yes, Chef."

I had to get backup potato chips made for Amanda in case she got slammed. I had to get the veal bones roasting because Chef made the veal stock and demiglace Sundays and Mondays, our days off. Had to cut all the mirepoix for the stock as well. Tie up a sachet of herbs and smashed peppercorns, also for the veal stock. And just be available for the 8:00 p.m. hit, which we always, always got on a Saturday night. Which was also when the VIP dishes started to go out. Paul took over the Pass to call out orders as Chef plated this eight-top personally.

When Amanda put up the grilled porterhouse steaks, and Chef cut the meat off the bone, Amanda, facing the grill, called out, "How are they, Chef?"

"On the money."

She pumped her fist. And Chef cut the four chunks of meat into thick strips, then rebuilt the steaks on a platter with a salad of rocket, a peppery tasting green I'd never heard of, and lemon wedges. The whole kitchen paused to moon over the gorgeous dishes before Samantha, the de facto head server, whisked them away.

With the 8:00 p.m. push done, I headed back down to the basement to check on my stew. It still had a couple hours to go, so I figured I'd make sure the walk-in was organized and wipe down its shelves and mop the floor. This was a critical part of cooking as well, Chef taught me. Cleaning. Everything was connected, he said.

By the time I'd gotten the shelves wiped down and reorganized and the floor mopped, it was nearly ten and time to take the stew out. I left the walk-in with a bucket of dirty water and saw the office door open again and with the light on. As I passed on the way to a drain in the floor behind the stairs to dump the water, I heard voices trying to be quiet but not really succeeding. It was that guy, Jimmy Holliday, and Chef. Holliday had a fat cigar in his right hand and with the middle finger of that same hand, poked Chef's chest, hard. "Wrong answer," he said. Chef had one of those pouches in hand. When Holliday saw me looking, he kept on talking but reached over to close the door.

I hadn't seen Johnny in ages. He lived in a big house on South Woodland. His dad was an orthopedic surgeon at the Cleveland Clinic, and his mom was the quintessential suburban mom who was always available for rides in the middle of the afternoon and snacks after school. Johnny called them old hippies gone bad—they embraced the trappings of suburbia but didn't believe in private schools, which is why he went to Shaker.

Johnny was alone at the kitchen island reading when I tapped softly on the backdoor windowpane a little after eleven. He held his finger to his mouth.

Bundled up in his brown canvas jacket, Johnny closed the door softly behind him.

"Did you get the beer?" I asked.

He said nothing but gave my hand a firm shake. He was big on shaking hands. I followed him down the steps into the back-yard, which ended at a white picket fence, beyond which was one of the main fairways of the Shaker Country Club golf course. He'd stashed a brown paper bag with the beer behind some shrubbery on the other side of the fence.

"Man, I haven't seen you, like, all year," he said.

"I know," I said. Since school started, I'd checked in with him on the weekends by phone, when I'd moaned about Julia. But I really didn't have much time with school and work.

We followed a golf cart path to the sand trap he favored. You could sit on the edge and your feet would hang down to the slop-ing sand. The ground was dry and cold, and I could see my breath, but it was comfortably cold—a clear, dry October night and a crescent moon that gave off enough light to see by.

Johnny pulled a Swiss Army knife from his pocket and, using the leather punch, made a hole at the bottom of the first can and handed it to me, hole side up. "Gun," he said. Then he readied his own can.

He'd taught me this early last summer, shotgun.

"Oh, man," I said.

"Come on," he said, and we moved to the center of the sand trap.

When you held the hole in the can to your mouth and popped the top, beer shot out the hole and straight down your throat— whoever finished theirs first won.

His thumb on the hole, he lifted the can and, as ever, recited the liturgy: "Don't blame it on the music / don't blame it on the show / don't blame it on the date you're with / just blame the eight-oh-oh!" Then, "One, two, three!"

And we both put our mouths to the hole at the bottom of our cans and popped the top. I got about half of it down before I coughed the beer out my nose and got it all over myself. When I looked up, Johnny had already consumed his without a drop spilled.

"You gotta work on your technique."

Still coughing, I said, "I know." To save a little face, I chugged the rest and handed him my can. He put the empties in the bag and retrieved two more and we took our seats on the grassy edge of the sand trap.

"So let me guess," he said, cracking open his second beer. "You're here because it's US's homecoming dance, and your *girl-friend* is there with *her* boyfriend."

"She's not my girlfriend, but I suppose you're not wrong." I kicked at the sand. "It's just hard to forget about August. God, it seems so long ago."

"Theo, admit it. She played you. Her boyfriend was out of town, she found a fun play toy until Bennett got back."

"It wasn't like that. It was for real. And it wasn't like I wasn't loving every minute."

"But look at you now, six weeks later and you're still obsessed with her."

"I'm not obsessed. In fact, I'm done. Tonight did it. Enough."

"That's the spirit. But I'll believe it when I see it."

"Seriously, I'm done." I could feel Johnny staring at me. I drank my beer. "It's just . . ."

"Just what?"

"We just had such a good time together. It was so true."

"*Bwah-HA-HA-HA!*" he shouted.

Which I deserved, I suppose.

"Seriously, man," I said.

"Look at me," Johnny said. "Seriously. You broke your leg this summer and the whole course of your life changed, from known to unknown. For whatever reason, the gods sent you Julia who helped you find a new course. She did that. You were lucky to have her. Now her work is done. You need to let it go in *order* to keep moving forward. Understand what I'm saying?"

"I know, I know. Like I said, I'm done."

"And like I said, I'll believe it when I see it."

"Gimme another beer."

Reaching into the bag, Johnny said, "Not going to be easy—you see her every day at the restaurant."

"Yeah, I know."

"How's that going, anyway? What did you tell me you did? You cook dinner for the staff or something?"

"Yeah. They call it family meal. I cook for twenty people every day. I do other stuff but that's what's most important to me. It's really cool."

"Shit, that's impressive. I can't even make popcorn, let alone cook a meal, let alone cook a meal for twenty people."

"It's not hard if you're organized. There's a lot of pressure but it's such a rush that you feel great when you've done well. And when it doesn't, it's brutal."

"The agony of defeat," he said.

How many Saturday afternoons had Johnny and I sat in one of our TV rooms watching Jim McCay and the *Wide World of Sports* on ABC, whose intro featured those words as a skier, a distance jumper, wipes out just before launching off the ramp.

"But without that fear of defeat, you wouldn't be able to get it all done," I said. "And without that fear, the highs wouldn't be nearly so intense."

"I can honestly say that I have no idea."

"It's just like sports. I mean if we're going up against a team where all the kids are six-five and two hundred twenty-five pounds, it's scary. But you have to hit extra hard or else you'll get steam-rolled. And then when you beat them—there's honestly nothing like it. And there's nothing like *losing* by sixty points, either."

I got a little sting of missing football just then, which I pushed down.

"I think I might want to do this," I said. "For real."

"What?"

"To cook. Become a chef."

"That would be cool."

"My parents don't think it's cool, at all. When I told them, my mom said," and I imitated her, "'Oh, Theo, you're not going to become a cook, for goodness' sake. Only people who can't do anything else become cooks.'"

"Ouch."

"They don't understand. And it's not just the cooking and the food. It's the whole environment and the people and the stories."

I told Johnny about Chef, who was about the coolest human I'd ever met, and Paul who was always stoned but never missed a beat in the kitchen, and Reggie and how he was always really nice to me because I'd come through for him that first night I was there. And Amanda.

"I was afraid of her when I first met her. She has a tattoo. On her neck. Of a snake. I've never seen a woman with a tattoo. On her *neck*. She rides a Harley."

"No way."

"And I'm pretty sure she's a . . ." I paused and said softly, "A *lesbian*."

"And what makes you think that?"

"Because once, like a month ago, she told me she was married to a woman."

Johnny laughed hard. "Yeah, Theo, I'd say you can be pretty sure! Duh!"

"*I* don't know. I've never met a lesbian before." Both of us thought about this. I was definitely feeling buzzed by now, happy to be with my good buddy Johnny, whom I'd known almost literally forever.

He handed me another beer. I pulled off the pop-top and dropped it back into the can instead of throwing it on the fairway.

"It's like everybody's a misfit there," I said. "And that's kind of how I feel now. Maybe that's why I like to be at the restaurant." Just then, the image of Jimmy Holliday and his cigar flashed in my head. "Oh, I gotta tell you *this* story."

I told him about seeing the guy earlier and then about the time I'd seen him and that other guy at the restaurant with Chef.

When I got to the best part, about all those stacks of bills, Johnny stood up and walked to the center of the sand trap.

"What?" I asked him. He snapped around and walked toward me with his arms out.

"Theo, *Jee*-sus."

"What?"

"That's *mob* money."

"What?"

"Oh, come . . . *on*. You are so naive, Theo."

186

Johnny and I had both seen *The Godfather* (with our parents because it was rated R). Roger hadn't been allowed. That was about all I knew about the Mafia. And I couldn't believe that anything like that actually *happened*. Certainly not in leafy Cleveland.

"Didn't you say your chef called him the Hand?"

"Yeah . . ."

"Jimmy 'the Hand' Holliday? Come on, Theo."

It did sound like a mob name, the way Johnny said it.

"Theo, the guy's a fucking goombah."

"What's a goombah?"

"A mobster. Does he look like a goombah?"

"*I* don't know."

"Because you've never met one before, like the lesbian?"

I was totally confused now. I shook my head. "I just can't believe there's Mafia here. Or that Chef would be involved with the Mafia." *No way*, I thought when I heard myself say this. "There's no Mafia here."

Johnny made another I-can't-believe-you noise.

"Don't you read the *PD*?"

"Not really."

"Like three years ago. Remember that car bombing in Lyndhurst?"

"Vaguely."

"*That was a mob assassination.* Danny Greene."

"Just past Beachwood Place *mall*?" I asked.

"Walk down Mayfield in Little Italy someday. The storefront windows, the ones that are blacked out. Those are like mob social clubs. That's why the area is called Little Italy."

"If you're right, what does it mean? Should I do something?"

"No. Jesus. Keep your mouth shut."

"I just can't believe it. I mean, Restaurant Margaux is one of the best restaurants in the city."

"Maybe, maybe not, Theo. But I *do* know that stacks of small bills laid out on tables is not typically your legit business practice."

"Chef told me to steer clear of that guy."

"That seals it. The guy is one-hundred percent goom*bah*."

I stood in the sand trap to try to clear my head, but I got dizzy and fell forward.

"Ha, must be that bad leg of yours!"

I stood, brushed myself off. My leg was fine in terms of strength (just sudden out-of-nowhere knife-blade pain, but those were decreasing). Tonight I definitely had a serious buzz.

"I think I better get going," I said.

Johnny said, "Hey, what time are you picking us up tomorrow?"

"Tomorrow? Oh, that's right."

With all my angst over Julia and her being at the dance, I'd forgotten that my dad, in an effort to further bond, had gotten company tickets to the Browns-Packers game; four of them so that I could also invite Johnny and Roger. This was a huge treat as Dad's bank had season tickets on the fifty-yard line, and Dad was so high up, he could get them almost whenever he wanted to, I presumed. But this was the first time in forever that he requested them. This would help keep Julia out of my thoughts.

"Dad will want to be heading downtown at around eleven forty-five, I think?" I drank down the last of my beer, swayed a bit, and put the empty in the paper bag with the others. "I'll call you if anything changes. You gonna stay out here? It's getting really cold."

"One last eight-oh-oh and ponder the universe." He leaned all the way back on the grass with his hands behind his head. The sky was bright with stars.

"Don't fall asleep and die of hypothermia."

My head was definitely buzzing when I got into my car. I knew I shouldn't be driving, so I sat for a minute. I didn't usually wear a seatbelt, but I figured maybe it would be a good idea that night. I backed out of the driveway, and as I put the car in forward, I remembered what Julia had told me. When your hands are on the steering wheel, you need to be deadly serious. And follow the rules. Which is just what I did. And a good thing, too, as halfway home, a cop car was behind me, as if out of nowhere, and I hadn't even realized it. *It is super hard to drive the exact speed limit when you discover a cop car behind you.* But when I turned right, off South Woodland onto my street, the cop kept going straight. That was definitely not smart, but in a way, I felt Julia had gotten me home safely.

17

The following day, crisp and beautiful, the Shaker Heights foliage was ablaze, perfect fall football weather. Just a few days ago the weather had been in the seventies, but it got cold last night, and today was a fresh-smelling fifty degrees. Roger drove in from Solon, and the three of us left—Dad asked me to drive—to pick up Johnny and head downtown to the game. Dad had all the perks that went with his job, including parking right near the stadium. Game days in downtown Cleveland were exciting. The city felt more alive than it did at any other time. Rivers of people poured in from every direction. They streamed out of the Terminal Tower from the Rapid Transit. Packs of people strode down sidewalks in Browns jerseys, many with faces painted orange and brown, loud with excitement, everyone descending on Cleveland Municipal Stadium, a massive concrete cavern that held eighty thousand of maybe the most devoted football fans you've ever encountered, the kind that only perpetual also-ran teams develop.

Dad walked slightly ahead of us, examining the tickets and looking for Gate D. I walked behind him, and Roger and Johnny walked behind me to get through the crowd more easily. I heard Johnny use the word *goombah* and knew he was telling Roger what I'd told him last night.

I turned to Johnny, held my finger to my mouth, then whispered, "Don't let my dad hear."

Johnny quieted down to a whisper to a wide-eyed Roger. I didn't want to give Dad, and definitely not Mom, a reason to keep me from working at the restaurant. I could just hear myself arguing with Mom, telling her I wasn't "associating with gangsters." That's how she'd phrase it. And maybe she'd be right. If I was working in the kitchen, say, I don't know, cutting chicken, for instance, and a gangster was talking to me, I guess that would be associating with gangsters.

If Mr. Holliday was a bona-fide mobster, and *was* a silent partner of the restaurant, then I was basically on a mobster's payroll, wasn't I?

I'm associating with gangsters. That, frankly, was pretty cool-sounding. Could it be true? I was on a gangster's payroll? Ridiculous.

"Stick close," Dad said once he'd handed over our tickets and we passed through the gaping entry to the stadium. As always, the place teemed with Browns fans and a few brave souls wearing Packers jerseys. The place continued to fill and bustle, and the three of us stayed in a tight line behind my father, jostled left and right by the throng.

We walked up the ramp to section eight.

This was always my favorite moment, beholding the field. You walk up a dark, narrow concrete ramp and emerge into the light as if reaching the edge of a cliff looking out over rivers and mountains and sun and clouds, only what I saw was the glorious football field, my Browns warming up, the men in green on the other side, the band, the coaches, the cheerleaders, the photographers and reporters. It was the same field I saw weekly on television, but here in real space. It was the exact same size as the one I play on. Played on. The teams were out warming up. Life-size. I used to be able to pretend I might one day be down there, on the fields, running wind sprints, catching balls, loosening up. The lines were all freshly chalked and bright. I could see kicker Don Cockroft taking practice punts, far enough away that I didn't hear the sound of his foot against the ball until the ball was nearly at the height of its arc.

The majestic horns of the marching band played.

The air was a mixture of fall and turf and peanuts.

This was the first actual football game I'd been to since my leg broke, I realized. I still got that thrill, that rush, only now I couldn't even think about being out there myself one day, couldn't even dream.

We found our seats, right on the fifty-yard line, on the Browns' side. Fantastic seats. "Who wants a hot dog?" Dad asked. We all did. And peanuts and pop. The hot dogs were slathered with delicious mustard.

"Can we have two?" I asked.

"You all want two?" he asked, chuckling.

"And peanuts please."

"I don't know if I can carry all that."

"I'll help!" Roger said, on his feet. He was the kind of kid who loved to talk to adults. I suspected he didn't love football as much as the socializing that revolved around it from September till Super Bowl. He and my dad would talk about the stock market or something boring.

"Splendid, thank you, Roger," Dad said.

When they were gone, I shook Johnny's hand and said, "Theo Claverback, associate gangster." And we continued to crack up about this until Dad and Roger returned with all the food, just as the starting teams took the field and Cockroft set the ball on the tee. The crowd let out a cumulative rallying cry as he lifted his arm to signal ready, trotted to the ball, and launched it into the Packers' end zone.

To say the game was exciting was an understatement. But the Browns were always exciting this year—Brian Sipe pulling off so many multiple last-minute victories, people nicknamed our team the Kardiac Kids. Third down with twenty seconds left in the game—no hope of a field goal from the Packers' forty-six-yard line—Sipe, a brilliant scrambler, launched a moon shot to Dave Logan, who took it in for a touchdown: Browns twenty-six, Packers twenty-one.

"You boys still hungry?" my dad asked, negotiating the traffic on East 9th as we left the parking garage. "Want to go to Our Gang?"

I immediately said, "Yes." Excellent Swiss-cheese burgers and big fat beer-battered onion rings—I could eat those forever.

"Actually, Mr. Claverback, Johnny and I have an engagement."

I turned in the seat to look back at Roger.

"Double date. I'm fixing him up with Sabrina Finkle."

"Sabrina *Finkle*?" Sabrina went to HB, Sarah's school. "Doesn't she, like, wear a bandanna and stuff?" I said to Roger. And to Johnny, "Not exactly your type?"

"I'm not sure you necessarily know my type. I'm . . . open-minded."

What I wouldn't betray was my jealousy—how I would have loved such a diversion. Now, I knew that Dad would go to his Sunday fallback. Since I wasn't cooking he'd order takeout from Pearl of the Orient. Just the three of us, followed by homework.

Dreary Sunday night. If the Browns had lost, it would have been a truly miserable night.

After dinner I did homework. I would not call Julia.

I *will* not call her.

I won't.

I did.

She wasn't home. I didn't leave a message or say my name, though Mr. Bevilacqua surely knew the sound of my voice. Though maybe Julia got calls from all kinds of guys. What did I know? I didn't care. I was done.

I went downstairs the following morning at eight, not dressed for school.

"Theo, you haven't left yet?" Mom asked.

I was almost always gone before they were even downstairs. Mom had a pantsuit on, which meant she was in court today. Dad was pouring hot water into a cup with instant coffee crystals in it. He had two pieces of melba toast and one cigarette every workday morning. Without fail. He was a man of routine.

Mom would drop him off at the Attleboro Rapid stop to catch the 8:10 train and carry on to her office by car. Dad would walk from the Terminal Tower to the bank at the corner of Euclid and East 9th Street. How could he stand it? Day after day?

"I don't feel well," I told her.

They did their Mom and Dad thing: Mom reached up to feel my forehead, and Dad's eyes didn't leave the front page of the *PD*.

"You're not warm," she said.

"I think I'm just tired. Okay if I stay home and catch up on homework?"

Mom sighed with disappointment. "I honestly don't know if this restaurant job during the school year is a good idea. That's why you're so tired all the time." She kissed my cheek then loaded her briefcase with a stack of folders and said, "Bob, ready?"

He was already grinding his Lucky Strike out in the ashtray.

And they were gone.

It was strange being home alone on a Monday. It wasn't much different from the days I'd been stuck in my bedroom waiting for my femur to heal. I tried to sleep more, but I couldn't. I did over-due chemistry homework. I wrote the essay on *Invisible Man* that was due last week (Mr. Morgan gave me an extension). I watched *All My Children* (Erica up to her usual tricks). I made a seriously good grilled ham and cheese sandwich—in a last-minute deci-sion, I put sliced dill pickles on it and that turned out to be an excellent idea.

And I kept checking the clock—I didn't want to miss Julia Child's *The French Chef* and *The Galloping Gourmet*. I hadn't seen them since school started. *Galloping Gourmet.* Who came up with that name? I figured I could do my trig while I watched. Mom called at noon to check on me and ask me to take pork chops out of the freezer for dinner and asked if there was any Shake 'n Bake in the cupboard.

I told her no but that I could take care of them. Chef had taught me what he said was "Standard Breading Procedure": You dredge the meat in flour, dip it in egg, and dredge it in bread crumbs—"Dry sticks to wet, wet sticks to dry," Chef said.

Mom said, "You're a love. Get your work done *and* get some rest. I'll be home at the usual time."

Which was 6:40. Of course she would.

Dad would arrive at 6:25.

I don't know how they could stand it.

At 3:57, I loaded a bowl full of vanilla ice cream and spooned half a can of cut pineapple and some of its syrup on top. An excellent pairing, vanilla ice cream and pineapple. I took it to the den and turned on Channel 25 for Julia Child.

She opened the show by saying, "Beef Bourguignon, French beef stew in red wine. We're going to serve it with braised onions and mushrooms and a wine-dark sauce. A perfectly delicious dish." And, as if summoned by Julia Child's voice, a car in need of a muffler pulled into the driveway.

I wouldn't answer the door. I was just going to ignore it. But she always just walked in. I rushed to a mirror in the hall to see what I looked like. Jeans, T-shirt, and bedhead but no time to do anything about it, as Julia, *my* Julia, knocked on the back door. I would be totally aloof. I was not going to fall for whatever it was that brought her here. Which was *what*? I hoped nothing bad had happened.

"Hi," I said through the screen door. Dad had yet to put the storm windows in (which he unfailingly did on Daylight Savings Sunday, next week).

"Hi?" she said.

I waited. I had to be strong. She was so pretty, standing there. But I was done.

"Well," she said, "may I come in?"

"Sure," I said. "You used to just come right in." I opened the door for her. She didn't look at me. "So, what's going on?" I leaned against the kitchen island and folded my arms across my chest.

She put her purse on the island and leaned against the opposite counter. "Can we sit down somewhere?"

"Sure, we can sit in the den."

"Could I have some water, please? My mouth is really dry."

"Cotton mouth?" I asked.

"No," she said, annoyed by my jibe.

I got her some ice water, and she followed me into the den. I turned the television off.

We sat next to each other on the couch. She sipped her water and set the glass down on a coaster.

"Has something happened?" she asked. "Are you okay? You're acting weird."

I shrugged.

"What's that mean?"

"I've got stuff on my mind."

"Such as?"

(Such as keeping you off it.)

"School and stuff," I said.

"School?"

"I get home from work and I'm so tired, I can never seem to finish what I need to get done."

"I said I'd help you."

"Have you?"

"Have you asked?"

(Well, no.)

"How was the dance?" I asked.

"Not good."

(Hm, interesting.)

"Sorry," I said.

"Yeah, well."

And then we sat there. Julia staring at her lap. Me staring at the turned-off TV.

"I'm gonna go." She was already up and heading back through the kitchen.

"Wait," I said. I wasn't going to follow her but I leaped up, anyway. "What did you come here for?" I jogged through the dining room to the kitchen. *Julia.*

And the back door slammed. I opened it and said, "Julia, what the hell?"

She sat in her car but didn't turn it on. She got out and strode toward me.

"I forgot my purse."

She pushed past me into the kitchen and got her purse, then strode out digging for her keys. I followed her.

"Julia, you obviously came here for a reason."

"Yeah," she said, starting the car. She jammed the gearshift into reverse. "I wanted to talk about *us*, but obviously it's not the right time."

The car's front tire missed my bare toes by inches as she backed out of the driveway.

Wait. What?

My heart hammered against my ribs. "Us." The wind blew cold and I hugged myself. I went into the kitchen. I paced. What could I do? Obviously, nothing here at home. I took the stairs two at a time up to my room. Changed from a T-shirt into a fresh school shirt. Brushed my hair and teeth. And got in my car.

First, I drove by Bennett's house. If she was there, I didn't know what I was going to do. Knock? Maybe.

But there were no cars in his drive. So I drove to Julia's, not paying attention to the speed limit and only running one red light. This was not the defensive driving Dad always preached. "Talk about us." What did that mean?

199

I parked directly in front of her house. I saw her car in the drive and her sister's car in the open garage. I knocked on the front door. And knocked again. I called her name. Nothing. I tried to open it.

The back door. I walked up the driveway to the back of the house. A chain-link fence kept their black Lab, Ruby, in the backyard. She barked and barked but didn't do anything. The back door was open, and I squeezed in to keep Ruby out. "Julia? Julia!"

I'd only remember details of the house later—the dishes in the sink, the general clutter, the ratty living room furniture, a big water stain on old wallpaper—I was so focused on finding her. I moved through the kitchen into the living room foyer area and took the stairs up, saying, "Julia, I'm coming up."

The stairs had a small landing midway up and when I turned at the landing, I saw her waiting at the top of the stairs. She hugged me immediately, her face tight against my chest.

"You came," she said.

And my whole inner self uncoiled. I took several breaths. She *wanted* me here. She was glad I came.

"I'm just so confused," she said.

She looked up at me, into my eyes. I kissed her. I stroked her hair. I kissed her again, after which she held her head against my chest. We both took deep breaths.

She led me through her open bedroom door at the top of the stairs. It was a small room, just big enough for a twin bed, a dresser, and a desk. A cork board above the desk had neat rows of three-by-five note cards, concert ticket stubs, a beaded necklace. On the wall above her bed were two posters, Jerry Garcia and Janis Joplin. The room was tidy, the bed made. She led me to it, and we sat on its edge side by side.

I honestly didn't care what happened next. I was there. In Julia's *bedroom*. And she wanted me there. Right then, that was all that mattered.

Then she said, "I have a confession."

"This was why you came to my house?"

I'd never seen her like this. She was different. She was always so confident, self-assured, cocky even, and funny. This was a different Julia.

"Remember Friday night? After work? When you called out to me?"

"Yes, of course."

"I swear, Theo, it was like a lance went through my heart. I got in my car and cried. Just cried."

"You *did*?"

"I realized."

"Realized?"

Her eyes, enlarged through her round glasses, deep brown and flecked with gold. Her smell. Her pale lips. "And it's not *just* because of what you did Friday. You have always been so wonderful to me, and I'm such a fool for not seeing it."

"You changed my life."

"I've been trying to give me and Bennett a chance. I didn't think it was fair to him. We've been so incredibly close for so long. But then this summer. You. When I saw him for the very first time, the Saturday before school, I knew. I knew it wasn't going to work. It just wasn't there. And I tried to give it a go—I owed it to him and us. But now, all he wants to do is get high in his room."

"In his room at *home*?"

"He wedges one of his fancy skis against the door so his parents can't get in. It's just boring. Something happened on that

Asia trip. He did acid on a beach in Thailand and had some kind of 'awakening.'"

"Awakening?"

"He's a different person." She shook her head. "Maybe I'm a different person, too." She reached for my hand and looked at me. "Theo. I'm kind of in love with you I think."

"Well, you know I'm in love with *you*."

"But all fall at the restaurant, you were just buddy-buddy."

"You were in love with Bennett!"

"And today you were so cold, I thought it was all wrong."

"Oh my God," I said to the ceiling.

I pulled her chin toward me and kissed her. "Jules, I'm *crazy* about you."

She kissed me, and we hugged, there on the bed. No one could possibly know this mixture of joy and relief and happiness and love. One ounce more of it and I'd all but literally explode. It felt too much to contain. She hugged me hard. And I hugged her back.

Ruby bounded into the room, barked once, and spun in a circle as if chasing her tail. Julia stood abruptly, eyes large, skin paling. "Shit, Daddy's home." She left the room. I followed. Her sister Janice was already in the hall.

Julia said to Janice, with genuine panic: "What do I do?"

She said, "Well, at *least* get him down*stairs*."

I heard that.

I passed Darren Bevilacqua on the stairs. He was taking them fast. He said, "Theo." Cordially, it sounded. But he didn't slow, nor did I. I stood by the front door.

I heard this: "What is he doing in this house?"

I heard this: a flat hand against a face.

I heard this: "Get . . . him . . . out of this house!"

What was happening?

I heard a flat hand against a face and then a bump against a wall.

Then footsteps on the stairs as Julia bolted down toward me, passing me to unlock the front door. "Get out!" she said urgently. The left side of her face was bright crimson.

"I'm not leaving you!" I whispered.

"You'll only make it worse, *please*."

She meant it. But Darren was right there in my face. "You think you're bigger than me?" He moved in front of me as I tried to leave. "You think you can take me?" he shouted in my face. "Try it, punk!" I pushed past him to leave. He was right behind me, still screaming in my ear. "Try it, I'll kick the shit out of you! Punk!"

I hustled down the stone steps where Julia and I first had that conversation the day I broke my leg, got into my car, and drove away, shaking.

I rapped on the window of Johnny's back door. Mrs. Davis was in the kitchen.

"Hi, Theo," she said, welcoming me in. The warm kitchen smelled like cookies, which felt surreal. His little sister sat at the kitchen table coloring in a book.

"Is Johnny here?"

"He's in his room. Is everything all right?"

I took the stairs two at a time, through the hallway and up to the third floor. He had the whole floor—bedroom, a little living room area with a couch and a desk, a bathroom with a claw-foot tub. I'd spent hours up here, fourth, fifth grade especially, maybe years, listening to his 45s, like "Eleanor Rigby," and reading passages of *Go Ask Alice* aloud, astonished by the teenager-dom that was in our future. And here I was, finally in it, in those years, and I'm not sure I liked it any more than the narrator of *Alice*.

"Johnny?" I called. "Johnny?"

Damn, damn, damn. Gone.

"He isn't there," I said to Mrs. Davis, who paused while lifting chocolate chip cookies from a tray to a cooling rack.

"He must be out collecting," she said.

"Damn." His paper route.

"Honey, are you okay?"

"Yeah," I said, trying to think.

"Would you like some cookies and milk?"

I felt like I was in an alternate universe. "No, thank you, Mrs. Davis."

I heard her say, "Bye!" before the back door swung shut.

I knew what to do when I turned the key in the ignition. Chef. He'd be in the kitchen. I knew his routine now—he took Sundays off but worked alone on Mondays. I didn't even knock. Just raced in through the mudroom and into the kitchen. Sure enough he was there. I halted just for a moment. There was a pig's head all by itself on the corner of the table, staring at me. Half of the pig's body lay on the table where Paul normally worked. Chef stood over the other half at the worktable in front of the range. He had a saw in his hand, the kind the guy at the Christmas tree place used to cut the ends of the trunks off. I heard the rasp of the blade against the bone as he pushed the blade forward.

"Hey," he said, putting the saw down and picking up his boning knife to finish the cut.

"Chef, you gotta call Julia."

"What's going on?"

This whole time I could only picture Julia's dad beating her.

"I gotta make sure she's okay."

Chef set the knife down as I gave him the quickest version I could. He wiped his hands on a soft white side towel. "What do you want me to do?"

"Just call her, make sure she's not being hurt."

He put the towel down and strolled to the phone on the kitchen wall. I loved this guy—didn't ask a single question, just got things done. "What's her number?" I told him and he dialed.

He stared at his black clogs, waiting. I moved close enough to hear Mr. Bevilacqua answer.

"Hello, this is Chef Jackson. Is Julia there? I've got a scheduling issue."

It took forever for Julia to get to the phone.

"Hey, Julia, it's Jackson." Pause. "I have an agitated young man here who wants to make sure you're all right. Are you all right?" Short pause. Chef said, "I'm guessing you're not at liberty to speak freely. Just to be sure, if you need help or if you want someone to come to your house, say, 'Yes, I can cover Jackie's shift.' If you're really okay and *don't* need help, say, 'No, I can't cover Jackie's shift.'" Pause. "Okay, see you tomorrow?" And then, "Great, see you then."

"She clearly couldn't talk, but she sounds fine," Chef said, returning to the pig.

Okay, I could relax. A little. I was still kind of hyperventilating. And my heart hadn't stopped racing since Mr. Bevilacqua threatened to kick the shit out of me.

"Are you sure?" I asked.

"I'm sure she doesn't want either of us coming over there or to call child services."

Then I told him the whole story, from when Julia showed up at my house, to my going over there, to talking on her bed, to her dad's arrival. He didn't pick up his knife right away but leaned against the range behind him, arms folded and listening.

"We weren't even *doing* anything. Just talking. It wasn't like he caught us making out in her bedroom." I pulled my fingers through my hair. "He threatened to kick the shit out of me!"

Chef chuckled. He *chuckled*. "You coulda taken him."

"I didn't *want* to take him! I'm not getting into a fistfight with Julia's dad. Jesus." I'd never been in an actual fight in my life, let alone with a parent. I paced in front of him, on the other side of the pig. Chef got back to his pig. I said, "I mean, what he did was abuse."

"She sounded completely calm, so she's okay now. You can relax."

"But what if she's being seriously abused?"

Chef paused to think. "Nah, I don't think so."

"What would you know? Your dad used to regularly break your nose. That's not abuse?"

He grinned and said, "Not in my family, it wasn't. My dad was just a violent drunk."

"Mr. Bevilacqua wasn't drunk."

"No, he sounds like a prick with a temper."

"What if it's worse than that?"

"Has she ever talked about anything?"

"No. Hates him but still calls him 'Daddy.'"

"Because he's her parent. Even I needed a parent. Dad didn't break my nose *every* day. He bought me clothes when I needed them, put food on the table for me and my brothers, kept the house clean and warm. He even paid half the tuition for culinary school. He was just a mean drunk."

"But it's just . . . *wrong.*"

Chef shrugged, picked up his knife, pink with blood, flecked with bone, and gave it several swipes on the steel. He grunted a bit as he pulled the knife, held tightly in his fist like a dagger, through the front half of the pig, the tip of the knife blade rasping on the board as it cut through the tough skin. He put his left hand under the front shoulder of the pig, and he karate chopped the spine as he folded the pig over on itself, snapping the spine.

He unfolded the pig, dragged the knife through where he'd cracked the spine to separate the front third of the pig from the rest of the carcass.

Chef hefted the front half of the pig in both arms and moved it over to Paul's table with the other half of the pig.

He gave the back leg of the pig a loud swat. "Learn about the pig," he said. "It's infinitely giving.

"See this long muscle that runs along the top of the back, nestled on top of the ribs and along the spine? That's the loin. Not a heavily worked muscle so it's tender. It's where the chops are. I can leave it on the bone, turn it into a crown rack, cut them into individual chops, or take it off the bone. And this muscle, underneath the ribs?" He cut it out and held up the long tubular muscle. "This is the tenderloin. It's even less worked than the loin, which is why it's called the *tender*loin. I can sell these cuts here pretty much as is. These are the easy, expensive cuts. It's where we get the phrase 'living high on the hog.' The rest of the pig takes some work, but it's so much better. The belly, the ham, the muscles around the shoulder."

"How did you learn all this stuff?"

He shrugged. "Paying attention?" He steeled his knife. "These ribs here?" He caressed them. "We'll use these for family meal. Staff will be very happy. You can smoke them tomorrow out back. You have family meal squared away for tomorrow?"

"Yeah, that lamb stew."

"Navarin. Good. Serve it with couscous." I gave him a "huh" look. "I'll show you tomorrow, it's quick. Spareribs Wednesday."

I stopped pacing to find the pig's head staring at me. Just lying there flat on a half sheet tray, gazing impassively at me. Nonjudgmentally, but curious. It seemed at peace anyhow.

"What do you do with the head?" I asked. "Throw it out?"

"Every part of the pig can be cooked. Everything but the oink, they say. That's why the pig is such an amazing animal."

"Where do you *get* a whole pig? Like, can you go to Heinen's and order a whole pig?"

"Amish guy an hour south of here. Mr. Yoder. It's not exactly legal for me to serve it—supposed to be government-inspected slaughter—but it's the only way I can get some of these cuts. Remember that belly you tasted your first day?"

"I will *never* forget that." I asked, "So what *do* you do with a pig's head?"

"Headcheese."

"Cheese?"

"Not actual cheese." He cut and sawed as he spoke. "It's kind of like a pâté." He paused. "No, actually it's more like a braise that you set up in a pâté mold, slice and serve with some grainy mustard and bitter greens. I've got to brine it tonight. I'll show you how to make it tomorrow."

"Is this for the menu?" Chef had never let me prepare something that was to be served.

"Unfortunately, no one in Cleveland will order something called headcheese. Even if I call it *fromage de tête*, like they do in France. It'll be for family meal Wednesday or Thursday. I don't even tell the staff what it is. I just can't stand to waste any part of the pig. You're going to be plenty busy with the pig this week. It's an amazing animal. You're welcome to stick around and help."

I looked at the clock: 5:30.

"I need to go. I promised Mom I'd help with dinner. If that's all right."

"Of course—you're not on the clock. I'll see you tomorrow."

"I'm going to check on the stew, I mean the navarin, before I go." I trotted downstairs to the walk-in. I wanted to make sure it was set up and stored well. Sometimes people put something on top or the plastic wrap could blow off from the fan. Leaving the walk-in, I saw that the office door was open. On the desk were four of those pouches, each a different color. I paused, wanting to open them. But I didn't want Chef to catch me in the office. And I knew what was in them, anyway. Johnny was right. I guess Mr. Holliday paid regular visits on days the restaurant wasn't open, when only Chef was there. I just didn't know why.

"Bye, Chef."

"See you tomorrow, Theo."

"Hey, Chef."

He looked up from the pig whose parts had become smaller and more numerous.

"*Thank* you."

I turned to leave, but Chef called, "Theo." I stopped. "You're part of the family—you're welcome here anytime."

Walking to my car, I felt incredibly lucky. That I had somewhere to go. For help. Listening to Chef talk about the pig took my mind off Julia and calmed me. And then he said what he did. Part of the family.

It *was* like a family. A big family of misfits. But on the other hand, it wasn't like family—it was better. I would never, ever have told my parents what happened. That would be a disaster. Just the three of us in the kitchen. Me dipping pork chops in flour, in egg, in bread crumbs—which I did when I got home, after salting them, of course. And then frying them in a pan in oil.

Mom came home, kissed my cheek, took off her suit jacket, poured a glass of white wine, and looked at my golden brown chops in the skillet.

"Those are gorgeous, Theo. But I don't know if your father wants to eat just yet."

"I know." Dad needed a good hour, one martini, and one Lucky Strike in the den with the *Plain Dealer* before he was ready for dinner. Which would be in a half hour. "I'll undercook them a little and keep them warm in the oven so we can eat anytime."

She stood by the stove, arms folded, and shook her head. "How do you know how to *do* this?" Mom almost never looked baffled. But I didn't really know, either.

"I don't know," I said. "Paying attention, I guess?" I'd watched Reggie pan fry a thousand pork chops, and a thousand perch filets (Chef always put a fried fish entrée on Friday menus).

"I just hope you're *paying attention* to your schoolwork, young man."

"*Yes*, Mom."

19

The pig's head stared up at me from the stockpot, submerged in water and covered here and there by chopped leeks and diced carrot. It seemed to be asking me why.

"Because you're delicious?" I asked it back. I took a spoon from the bain-marie insert and tasted the broth. It was sweet from the vegetables and intensely porky. I'd never tasted anything so porky. It was the essence of pork.

Chef told me what to do with it: Take the head out and pick off all the meat, discard the fat that hadn't rendered, julienne the ears, strain the stock and skim the fat off, then call him for the next steps in making what sounded like maybe the grossest thing ever, headcheese.

Because I was cooking and the basement kitchen was quiet, just me and the pig's head, and because all I'd been thinking about was when I was going to be able to see Julia, I heard Julia's car arrive sputtering and backfiring. I threw off my apron and took the stairs three at a time.

Her last words to me had been "get out" and over the course of the next almost twenty-four hours I couldn't speak with her or find out what had happened or if she was all right. I was moving so fast I couldn't avoid Reggie, who was hefting a sheet tray loaded with dirty sauté pans. They went crashing to the floor.

I said, "Sorry, Reggie! I'll clean it all up in a second!"

Reggie said, "Settle down, man. She's going to be here all night."

Out the door and over the raised herb garden. Almost. My foot caught on a tomato stake, and I crashed onto the sidewalk, landing on my left butt cheek. It felt like someone stabbed my thigh with a glowing fireplace poker.

When I could see, when the sparkly blackness evaporated, there was Julia's face, her blond hair swooping down each cheek and onto my chest.

"Are you okay?" she asked.

"Julia," I said.

"Theo. Jesus." Julia pushed the bangs out of my face and said, "You gotta stop falling for me like this. Or you're really going to hurt yourself."

"I love you."

She was on her knees. She lifted my head off the sidewalk to bring my lips to hers and kissed me. A good long kiss. Just as she had months ago at the concert. And all the stress I'd been feeling all last night and all day today at school drained from my body.

I felt my left leg. No pain, all good. She stood and helped me get to my feet, at which point I heard hooting and clapping from the steps. Reggie, Amanda, and Paul were watching. I saw Jackie in the window of the mudroom but not, thank God, Chef.

I took a deep breath. Julia cupped my cheek, then drew me in and pressed her face against my chest.

"I'm so embarrassed. What happened yesterday. It's just part of my world. But I'm fine. Don't worry about me."

I kissed the top of her head, which smelled like flowers and cigarette smoke, the mixture that never failed to make me dizzy.

"I've been so worried."

"Kiss me."

I did. Reggie whistled and Paul whooped. Julia said, "Enough!" To me she said, "Can we go out after work?"

"Of course."

"We can go to the lakes. I gotta get changed."

I let her go first. Then I followed. Everyone pretended not to be laughing. Jackie passed me and said, "You are such a spaz." I didn't even care.

It was an easy night, slow and well-paced. The lamb navarin was such a hit, even Jackie told me it was a good one. Once I'd gotten the ribs smoked, I wrapped them in foil and put them in a low oven so they'd be ready for tomorrow. Then Paul let me take part of his garde-manger station, plating one dish, the pâté with a small bundle of frisée and a quenelle of whole-grain mustard and tiny pickles called cornichons. The only hard part was that I had to cut each one to order. Paul gave me this superlong knife that was rounded on the end. He showed me how to take the knife out of the bain of hot water, dry it, then push it once forward through the pâté, and then once back, making sure the knife was ninety degrees to the board so the piece wasn't slanted. He made me eat my first try because it was slanted, then showed me what I'd done wrong. Boy, it was delicious.

The last dessert went out at 9:15 and by ten, when Julia appeared in street clothes, I was wiping down my worktable downstairs, everything set up and ready to go for tomorrow. I loved wiping down the table—it meant work was done.

I followed Julia to the small gravel parking lot by the lake and parked beside her. She left her car running because the night was cold. We sat in her car because she had the tape deck. She'd just put in *Blues For Allah*, what I had been playing when I'd made us lunch, a day that now, in chilly fall with the leaves in full burning orange, seemed a lifetime away.

She pulled two bottles of beer and a bottle opener from her purse.

"Where did you get these?"

"These I actually swiped." She took a long swallow and set the bottle between her legs. "Theo. I'm so sorry you had to see that. Every so often, he just erupts."

"So, what, does he just have a temper?"

Julia took a deep breath. "There's more to it." She was quiet for a long time. She said, "My mom didn't die of cancer."

"She didn't?"

"I killed her."

"What?"

"Well, actually, some asshole asleep at the wheel killed her, but I'm the reason." She stared straight ahead through the windshield, her voice dull and trancelike. "I was in sixth grade; it was spring. I snuck out of the house to go spend the night at my friend Becky Marshall's. A spur of the moment thing we hatched talking on the phone. She lived a couple blocks away, across the tracks on Milverton. Mom and Dad slept in on Sundays and I could get back before they got up. It was a Saturday, just before midnight when I left. I had to wait till they were asleep. I got to Becky's fine but then we made too much noise and got caught. Mr. Marshall called my parents to let them know where I was, so they didn't worry if they found me missing. He told them I was welcome to stay. But Mom was furious and insisted on going to get me. I was really rebellious, even then, and I suppose she was trying to nip the worse behavior that might be coming in the bud. Dad told my mom, leave her, we'll get her in the morning. She went anyway. Some guy ran the light, slammed into her at the corner of Ashby and Van Aken. T-boned. Three a.m. She was thrown through the passenger-side window and broke her neck. Driver dead, too."

"How do you know the driver was asleep?"

"We don't know exactly, only that the tox report came back totally clean so . . . He coulda had a heart attack, I guess, or was just spacing at three a.m. We don't know. All we know for sure is, Mom wouldn't have been in a car at *all* that night if I hadn't gone to Becky's house." Pause. "If I weren't who I am."

I tried to absorb this and was quiet. I said, "Julia, you didn't *kill* her."

She looked at me. "Tell my father that."

"But it was an accident."

"Maybe. Either way you can't change the fact that if I hadn't snuck out of the house she'd still be here."

"Your mom didn't have to come get you. That was her choice."

"There's nothing you can say that will change the fact that if I hadn't done what I did, Mom would still be alive, and my dad wouldn't hate me."

"He doesn't hate you."

"He'd have kicked me out already if I wasn't a minor. And I'd have *left* already if I had enough money."

"Where would you go?"

"Cambridge, because that's where I'm going to college if I can get a scholarship. Even if I can't, I'll figure out a way. Harvard tuition is around eight thousand dollars. I can take out loans."

I was quiet, just drank my beer. That you could just up and leave home and move to a different state would never have occurred to me. But I suppose why would it, given all I had? I mean, I guess I *was* a rich kid. I'd never really thought about it.

"It's gotten worse as I've gotten older. I look a lot like my mom, sound like her, too, according to Jeanie. So I guess I'm kind of a walking reminder. My sisters don't blame me, but he does."

And my beautiful Julia put her forehead on the steering wheel and began weeping. I moved as close to her as I could in the cramped car, rubbed her back.

When the jag was over, she sat back and wiped her face. She pulled a wad of Kleenex from her purse and blew her nose. She inhaled deeply, let it out slowly. Then she pulled cigarettes from her purse and gave me one. We opened windows and smoked quietly.

"I need something stronger than this," she said. She dumped the remainder of her beer and put the bottle under the seat. She took the keys out of the ignition, unlocked the glove box, and pulled out a pint of something and the shot glass.

"Jack Daniel's?" I said.

"Yeah, all they had, my sister said. It's a little harsher going down, so, careful."

I spit half of the shot out it was so harsh. Julia laughed.

"You weren't kidding," I said, wiping my mouth.

"Here, you have to go like this." She poured herself a shot and said, "You gotta make that face after you shoot it."

"What face?"

"That face you see in the movies. Anytime an actor takes a straight shot of whiskey they make that grimace." And she did it, the corners of her mouth went wide and she bared her teeth. I laughed because I knew exactly what she was talking about. Then she threw back the glass, swallowed, and made the face.

"Okay, lemme try." I did, and I made the face, and it was still harsh but all of it went down this time.

"See?" she said.

"Let me try again." She filled the glass and I took it again. This one was even easier, and I felt the rush of the alcohol flush my face and relax me.

Julia took another shot herself, and returned the bottle to the glove box. "Just in case," she said. Once, during the summer, a police car skidded into the parking lot with its spotlight on us. We didn't get in trouble, just got kicked out. "Fucking cops," Julia had said.

"Can I do one more before you put it away?" She gave me another. I loved the dizzy feeling. And it made me want to talk more. And to kiss her. And as ever I felt like I couldn't get enough of her.

"Julia, have I told you I'm in love with you?"

"I think I'm kind of in love with you, Theo. Thee. Thee I adore." And she leaned in for another long, long kiss.

"Can I ask where things stand between you and Bennett? I mean, does he know?"

"It was kind of clear at the dance, but Sunday afternoon we talked, and I broke up with him. I wouldn't have come to you yesterday without telling him first."

"Did you tell him about me?"

"I wasn't going to but he asked, so, yes, I told him."

We kissed. I held her hand. She looked at her watch and said, "I should be going. One more for the road?"

We both did one more shot, then I kissed her and said, "I will see you tomorrow."

"Yes, you will," she said.

20

On the short drive home, I felt lighter than I had, maybe ever. I didn't have to hide my feelings about Julia. She wanted to be mine. I loved the restaurant and all the people. They were starting to feel like siblings I never had, with Chef like the father of us all. Chef had called me family. I even felt warm toward Jackie, since she liked my lamb stew today. And school wasn't all that bad. All I really had to do was not get kicked out, which just meant getting no Ds or Fs. I could manage, and Julia would help. My Julia.

I parked in the normal spot, beneath the basketball hoop; when the snow came I'd keep it in the garage next to my parents' Thunderbird. I stepped out of my car. The air smelled of dried leaves, which rustled in the October breeze. I looked up at the silhouettes of the trees, waving against a clear sky, with clouds beginning to roll in. I had the feeling of the inevitability of all things, the perfection of it all, how everything was connected. Like that time in Sanibel. A chill raced from the bottom of my spine through my neck. I felt so lucky.

Then I paused.

Why was the kitchen light on? Mom and Dad were always in bed by eleven. I entered the kitchen to find both of them up and drinking coffee. This meant they'd either had a fight and were making up, or they'd been having a serious discussion about something *me* related. Instant decaf coffee at night, I'd learned, was never good.

And I saw pretty quickly why. There was a crumpled soft pack of Marlboros on the kitchen table. *Damn.* I had the last cigarette on Saturday night after service, before heading to Johnny's, and stuck it in my pocket. Today was Tuesday, when Linda did the laundry.

Dad was noticeably not smoking.

"Hi, what are you guys doing up?" I tried to make it sound like the most natural thing in the world to find them drinking coffee at 11:30 on a Tuesday night. I had this covered.

"Where have you been?" Mom asked.

"At the restaurant."

"Until eleven thirty? I thought it closed at ten on weeknights."

"There's a lot of cleanup and getting stuff organized for tomorrow," I said. "And then Julia and I hung out for a while."

"Julia," Mom said, lips pursed.

Dad said, "Theo, Linda found that in your pants today."

Mom stood up in a way that I imagined she would in court. She walked around the island, picking up the evidence, and handed it to me. "What do you have to say?"

The only way to handle this was to come clean straightaway, this I'd learned. I took a deep breath and before I could say anything, Mom leaned up close in my face. "Have you been *drinking*?"

"No!" I immediately lied. I closed my eyes and scratched my head.

"Your breath smells of liquor."

"Oh, Paul gave me a shift drink. It was the first time. I didn't want to say no."

"So they get you drunk and let you drive home?"

"I'm not drunk," I said. "I'm not even buzzed." Also a lie.

"And the cigarette smoking?" she asked.

"It's just one pack—it's the only pack I've *ever* bought. Everybody at work smokes. I wanted to fit in."

Mom scowled at me. I wonder if she scowled at her defendants this way. "I think it was that girl who got you smoking. You smell of cigarettes!"

"One of the cooks gave it to me. Julia tried to stop me. And Dad smokes!"

"Dad's an *adult*." She looked at Dad. "You see what I'm saying, Bob. This restaurant, not to mention the girl, is not good for him."

"That's not true," I said, feeling desperation climb up my throat. "It's the opposite!"

Mom pointed her finger at me. "You skipped school yesterday because you can't keep up with your work, you're tired all the time, and now you come home smelling of *whiskey* and *cigarettes*? On a Tuesday night!"

It sounded so bad the way she said it, I immediately groveled. "I'll stop. I promise. Please. And school is fine. I *am* getting everything done."

"Okay, you two," Dad said. "Let's keep things calm."

"I am perfectly calm, Bob," Mom said, sounding quiet but not at all calm.

"Theo," Dad said, "we're going to ask you to leave the restaurant."

"No!"

"You can work there during school vacations, you can work summers—"

"I can't just walk in and out when I feel like it. I've got responsibilities." When neither spoke, I said, "And I love it there. I'm so happy."

That was a good tack. I could see a slight softening of Mom's expression.

Dad said, "We're primarily worried about school."

"And now smoking and *drinking*."

"Kate, that's behavioral. We can work on that."

"I'll stop! I promise!" I shouted.

"But schoolwork," Dad went on, "your intellectual development and growth, getting into a good college, these are things that you have to work at continually, and failure to do so will have permanent consequences for your . . . *life*."

"But I *am* keeping up. You'll see."

"That restaurant and that girl are bad influences," Mom said.

"We're not going to try to tell you who you can be friends with."

"Bob," Mom said, but he ignored her.

"But, we *can* dictate how you spend your time and where."

"When I broke my leg last summer, I thought I wanted to die. But now I don't and it's because of the restaurant." And to my Mom, heart hammering my ribs and whiskey-defiant, "And because of Julia." The softness in her hardened up again—shouldn't have said that. Tactical error.

"Kate, why don't you let me talk with Theo's teachers—"

"That's a great idea!" I said. "Talk to Mr. Morgan; he's my faculty advisor." Mr. Morgan, my English teacher, was cool. He was always going on about self-reliance and one man's destiny and stuff like that. I liked his class and was actually doing okay. He'd support me. And I couldn't risk Dad just randomly contacting any teacher—if he got my math teacher, Mr. Dalton, that could be trouble.

I told them I had to get up early to study and left the kitchen. Mom asked Dad, "What's a shift drink?" I didn't wait to hear if Dad knew.

I knew my plan. I'd find Mr. Morgan first thing, explain the situation. All he needed to do was assure my dad that my schoolwork wasn't suffering. If my first trimester grades were bad, then I couldn't argue. Like in a kitchen, excuses wouldn't matter.

This, of course, made it imperative that I actually didn't get any Ds or Fs. So I'd really have to stay on top of the books. And I would. That was part of why I got up early the next morning. This would be a new routine. Homework at night, after the restaurant, was too difficult. But after six hours of sleep, I could be much more productive.

I put the kettle on to make some instant coffee then sat at the kitchen island.

"Dear Mom and Dad," I wrote on a piece of white lined notebook paper. "I'm very sorry that I bought that pack of cigarettes. I won't do it again. And it's not right for me to be accepting an after-work drink along with the rest of the staff. I won't do it again."

These weren't lies. I *wouldn't* buy cigarettes. I would only smoke Julia's, or Amanda's. And I didn't get offered shift drinks, anyway, so that was an easy one.

Just as every day I had my prep list, I made a list of all the positive things I got from working at the restaurant.

- Developing a good work ethic, responsibility, and timeliness.
- Learning how to be super organized and how to plan ahead.
- It was my only form of exercise. Unable to do sports, I'd otherwise sit around eating and getting fat. Being a cook is very active.
- Learning to work with a team that wasn't on a football field, a real-life team.
- Learning about running a business.
- Half of Chef's recipes are French, so I'm learning French words.

I'd never heard of leeks before, a kind of onion, but now I know about leeks and that in French they're called *poireaux*. In French, *beef* and *egg* rhyme.

- Learning the metric system, as French recipes use grams and milliliters.
- I'm learning a skill I can use later in life; I might pay my way through law school by cooking.

I threw that one in specifically for Mom.

- I was learning how to cook, a lifelong value!
- Learning about other people's lives beyond school and family.
- Keeping my word to Chef.
- Earning a paycheck.

I almost didn't put that paycheck one in. I didn't really need a paycheck. I always got a generous allowance. I didn't even spend gift money; any money my grandparents or aunts and uncles gave me had been going straight into a savings account for years.

On the other hand, both Mom and especially Dad always stressed the importance of learning to manage one's money. So I revised it when I rewrote the list more legibly to include, "and learning how to manage my money."

I reread my note and my list. Then I made myself another cup of black instant coffee and opened my chemistry book to Chapter 4. "Bonding and Chemical Reactions."

Oh, God. How could I bear this stuff without the restaurant, without Julia? I had to keep this job.

Which was why I used the 10:30 break at school to work on trig. My mistake was doing it on Monkey Island, in the middle of a sea of boys. I leaned back on my little portion of Monkey Island with the book propped on my legs. I felt so separate from everyone that it gave me a sense of invisibility. Until my textbook was snatched away.

"Whoa!" I said.

It was Roger.

He snapped the textbook shut loudly in my face and said, "How could you not tell me?"

"How do you know?"

"Johnny called me."

I was so rattled on Monday after I fled Julia's that I called Johnny to explain why I'd shown up that afternoon. Told him the whole story.

"So let's hear it," he said. "I want it in your words."

We sat side by side on the blue carpeted platform. "It has been such a crazy couple of days." I shook my head and went through it all. How Sunday night after we'd dropped him and Johnny off after the Browns game, I was determined to end my obsession with Julia, how she showed up the next day. Roger's mouth fell open when I told him about Mr. Bevilacqua, and he put his hand on his forehead.

"Oh my God," Roger said.

"So, anyway, after work last night we went to the lakes to talk about it all, and she tells me she officially broke up with Bennett."

"Seriously?" Roger said, clearly happy for me.

"Okay, so I have these two huge days, right? And then I get home last night, and Mom's found a pack of cigarettes in my pocket."

"You smoke?"

"Sometimes. At work. Everybody does. So, anyway, they're waiting up to talk to me. And I come floating into the kitchen, never been happier in my life, then boom. My crumpled cigarette pack on the kitchen island. Then Mom smelled booze on my breath."

"Was there?"

"Julia and I were doing shots of Jack Daniel's in her car."

"What did your folks do?"

"They told me I had to quit the restaurant."

"They can't do that. You love that job."

"I think I can hold them off through Thanksgiving, until they get my first tri grades. I have to do well or I'll have to quit."

Roger leaned back and stretched both arms out behind him like he owned Monkey Island. "Doing shots of Jack with Julia fucking Bevilacqua."

"Yeah," I said, feeling my face flush.

"My good buddy Theo is officially going *out* with Julia Bevilacqua. I cannot believe it."

"Julia fucking Bevilacqua," I said.

"Julia fucking—" And Roger stopped. "Speak of the . . ."

Bennett Van Horn, hands in the pockets of his corduroys, loped easily toward us in his Doc Martens, casually flipping bangs off his face.

"Stick around, okay?" I whispered to Roger.

"Theo," Bennett said when he was standing over me. He removed his right hand from his pocket and held it out. I shook it, not sure at all what to expect. At least I'd have a witness in Roger.

"Well," Roger said, standing, "I'll let you two talk among yourselves," and was gone. Thanks, Roger.

Bennett took Roger's place beside me.

After a moment of silence, I said, "I hope there are no bad feelings."

He took a deep breath, then slapped my knee and kept his hand there. "Nah." He removed the hand. "It was probably time for us to split up."

I said nothing.

"Julia is a . . . *compelling* individual," he said.

"That she is."

"And she's so damn smart."

"I know. Not completely sure what she sees in me."

"That was my first thought. I even told her that I didn't think jocks were her type. So you must have something more than meets the eye."

"Well, I'm not a jock anymore."

He nodded. Awkward silence.

"Well," he said, "be good to her."

"Goes without saying. I love her."

"Yeah, I love her, too."

That made me feel worse. He was being so cool about this.

The bell signaling end of break rang, giving us three minutes to get to our next classes. We both stood and turned to face each other. He held out his hand again. We shook. He moved off first but after a couple steps he stopped.

He said, "Just be careful, for yourself. She may not always be who she seems to be." He waited for my response. I was not at all sure what *that* meant. Bennett flipped hair off his face and sauntered off with long, lazy strides, tucking hair behind each ear.

And that was the moment that everything seemed to lift. It was all done, at least for the time being. That was the last uncertain piece—would Bennett put up a fight? The rest of the fall was set. I knew Mr. Morgan would support me, and he assured me he could suggest to my parents that we wait until the first grades were out shortly after Thanksgiving. I had a plan of action for my schoolwork: Get up early each morning to do homework. Then use every free period for study. Use Saturday morning, all Sunday (but for the Browns, who were on their way to their first division title in forever), and Monday after school to get my work done. And I felt pretty certain I could convince Julia to come over on Mondays after school, when we had the house to ourselves, to help me study. And whatever else might happen.

But that cryptic comment from Bennett nagged at me until I realized he was, well, not being a dick, but he wanted to hurt me in some way. *May not always be who she seems to be.* Be careful for *myself*? He just wanted to throw a little granule of doubt into my brain.

Who else could she be? She was in class all day. She worked most nights. Her house told another part of her story. Dishes stacked in the sink in the middle of the day. Ratty furniture. A living room that smelled like wet dog. A water stain on the living room wallpaper the size of Texas. Julia's room, though really small, was neat and organized. I wouldn't have been surprised if she'd wallpapered it herself. She had made her bed, the desk was tidy. Even the stuff on the cork board seemed to be precisely placed. And after her revelation last night, well, if she wasn't what she seemed, it was only that she was a lot more complex than she let on.

It was a shitty thing of Bennett to say. Why didn't I ask more?

I arrived at work as usual and finished off the Indian curry for family meal. Which turned out to be a no-brainer. It was all about the spices, which I got at the Asian market. Sear the chicken thighs with onions and carrots, chuck in the spices, cook them, add some of Chef's amazing chicken stock, simmer for an hour and serve with some Chinese rice. Chef loved it. Raised his eyebrows and nodded while chewing. Like scoring a touchdown when I saw Chef make that face.

I guess the only problem, if you could call it that, was I finished all my work early and had to look for more stuff to do. I mean, once I saw Julia go into the wine room, I actually had time to just go in, touch her and kiss her.

"Theo! I am working!" she said.

I kept trying to kiss her and hold her.

"Stop," she said, laughing. "I'll meet you after work!"

At nine, I wiped my basement stations down. Tomorrow's pot roast and roasted root veg were done so all I'd have to do is cook the green veg and throw together a salad. By 9:10, I was actually leaning against my downstairs prep table twiddling my thumbs trying to think of something to do. Station clean; walk-in organized; family meal prepped. I toured the line nearing the end of service. "Reggie, Paul, Amanda," I called. "Free hands here if you need anything." They all checked their mise and said, "All good, Chef!"

It was so sweet they called me Chef—as if I were.

Chef took a ticket from Jackie as she circled back into the dining room. "Order fire halibut, lamb, steak mid-rare. Extra chips with the steak." They all called back, "Oui, Chef!"

"Those are the last entrées, folks," Chef said.

"Thank fucking God," Amanda said, still turning and burning at the grill.

"Anything you need, Chef?" I asked.

"I think we're good," he said to me. "Have a good night." He shook my hand.

I couldn't believe I was done so early. I trotted down the steps to the basement to the guys' changing room. Everyone had a hook and shelf space for their stuff. I changed into the clothes I'd arrived in. As I was leaving, Julia passed on her way up the stairs to the kitchen. Her ponytail swinging, that full body, muscular legs, slim waist, full chest so compactly contained by the vest, black slacks, long white apron. "Hey," she said, rushing past, two bottles of wine in her hands.

"Hey, you, I'm done. I'm going home."

She halted and spun. "What?"

"I actually think I can get my French homework done if I get home now."

"You're leaving me?"

"I'll see you here tomorrow!"

For a second, she looked pissed. And then quizzical. As though she'd sensed some change in me. And maybe there had been. I was leaving without her. I'd never done that. But really, I was exhausted from this insane week, and if I got French done tonight, I could get chemistry done tomorrow morning before I left for school. And see Jules here tomorrow.

But I could see it in her face. She saw it as my leaving her before I had to. There was an edge to her eyes, the way she looked at me slightly askance, pausing.

She pushed out her lower lip and nodded. "You go home and study," she said, and walked back toward the steps up to front of the house.

"Hey," I said.

She looked angry. Like "What, I'm busy," but she didn't say it.

"I want a kiss. Please."

She walked to me and raised those beautiful lips to mine.

"See you tomorrow," she said, and headed upstairs to finish her shift.

"Hey!" I called. "I'm crazy about you, you know."

She didn't stop her trot upstairs. But by then I knew her smile even when I couldn't see it.

I closed our kitchen door softly and turned the key in the lock. I was so used to getting home when my parents were asleep. But Dad was awake, in his study in the far end of the house.

"Theo?" he called out.

He was in his maroon leather chair reading, a Lucky Strike sending an unbroken string of smoke a foot in the air before it curled and split apart. He had his usual glass of whiskey beside the ashtray, pale from the melted ice, and he'd turned his book over in his lap. He still wore his suit pants and wingtip shoes, but he'd removed his tie.

"How was school today, young man?"

"Fine," I said.

"And work?"

"Great!" I said.

"Mr. Morgan called me this afternoon," he said, and I took a deep breath. "He said you were a pleasure to have in class. That your questions and comments were always great additions to the class conversation."

Dad took a drag from his cigarette. "*When* you've done the reading."

"I get behind in some things," quickly adding, "*but not because of work*. I'm just a really slow reader."

"I've talked with your mom and we've decided to let you continue to work at the restaurant."

Oh my God. "Dad, *thank* you."

"But it's dependent on your first trimester grades. A single D and that's it."

"Deal."

"And Mom insists you also have to get at least two Bs."

I quickly calculated. I was pretty sure I could get a B in Mr. Morgan's English class. And then I remembered art. I was good at art and might be able to get an A. I didn't ask if art counted. "I will, Dad, I promise."

I made to leave, but he said, "Not done yet."

He took a last long drag and crushed the cigarette out. He really smoked them down to the nub.

"I need to know what your final exam schedule is. I ask because I've got to buy our tickets to Florida."

"Tickets?" I asked.

"Grandma and Grandpa's? It's their year."

Shit. This was our year to spend Thanksgiving with my mom's parents in Sanibel.

"Thanksgiving is one of the restaurant's biggest days."

He closed his eyes, sighed. But different than usual. As if the world weighed heavily on him. I was just a kid and it weighed heavy on me. It had to be heavier on him.

"They *need* me."

"Can you stay with Johnny?"

"Why can't I stay *here*? I can certainly cook for myself. And take care of the house. Feed the cats. You should see my station at work. It's spotless."

"But you'll be alone on Thanksgiving. A holiday."

"No, I won't. I'll be working. That's what cooks do. They work on holidays. They work when everyone else is enjoying themselves. I'll be with my restaurant family."

"I'll have to talk with Mom about it."

I didn't dare get my hopes up that I would actually be able to stay home by myself on Thanksgiving. Though I wanted to. And really and truly, Chef would be seriously upset if I told him I had to go to some fancy island off Florida for Thanksgiving. I knew that would change things between us. He'd think, "Of course you do."

And I didn't want him to think that. I wanted him to know that I wanted to be on his team; I didn't want to be a rich boy who sucked at private school. I wanted to be a cook.

21

Julia spread out some books on the kitchen island.

"Let's study in my room," I said. "We can listen to music."

This was the second Monday Julia had come over to help me with my math homework. Last week, we studied at the kitchen island until Dad got home. I wanted him to see us at work. Being *diligent.* Julia would go over my lesson, help me with the first problem, and then while I worked on similar problems, she did her own work. It was a good system, and I loved that I got to look at her, smell her, while we did homework. It drove me crazy in the best possible way.

Dad was suitably impressed when he closed the back door, set his briefcase down, and said, "Well, look at this."

"We are going to get Theo through trigonometry, Mr. Claverback."

Dad smiled at her. I don't think he really knew what to make of Julia.

But that was last week. Today, in my room would be more fun, with music. We could study on the floor or on the bed. I poured us each a glass of orange Crush and filled a bowl with pretzels. She followed, carrying both our book bags.

I set the food and drink on my desk. She put the books on the end of my bed, which I'd made this morning. For just this reason.

233

I took both her hands in mine and kissed her, and then we were quickly really kissing. I pushed her backward onto the bed and we kept kissing, and my hands were kind of all over her. And when she kept kissing me I began to unfasten the buttons of her shirt. But I only got two undone before she held my hand and said, "Theo, you've got to *work*."

"Yeah, but—"

"What if your mom surprises us again?"

I rolled onto my back and sighed extra heavily.

She turned on her side to snuggle into me. She drew circles on my chest with her finger.

"The only time I get to be with you is in your *car*. It's really frustrating."

"For me, too."

"Like, when *can* we be together?"

"We'll know. Just be patient." She kissed my cheek.

I knew she was right. She was usually right. She just knew stuff. But I was very grumpy doing trigonometry, determined to ask her as few questions as possible, and to just figure it out on my own. When she said she was going outside for a smoke, I said I was good. I consoled myself with the fact that the Browns were on Monday Night Football tonight. After last week's victory over our enemy, the Pittsburgh Steelers (an Ozzie Newsome grab in the last minutes of the game, of course), if we beat Chicago tonight, we would be on a serious roll.

Julia couldn't care less about the Browns, but she pretended to be interested for my sake.

Julia *was* right again. Mom arrived at 5:45, early, and walked into my room (door open!) as if she was going to find something. Which she did. Julia lying on my bed, feet on the pillow end, writing her college essay, me at my desk, struggling through the math problems. And they were exactly that. Problems. That's why they were called *problems*.

"Hm," she said.

"Hi, Mrs. Claverback," Julia said.

"Actually, Julia, I should have told you this before, but I kept my name. Jones. My name is Kate Jones."

Julia rose to sit on the edge of the bed. "I so admire that."

"You do," Mom said, not a question, just skeptical.

"Why should *we* have to change our names? We're not changing who we are because we marry. Right?"

I saw an expression on my mom's face I had never seen before. I knew it was good. There was surprise in it. And then she smiled. Mom at that moment accepted Julia.

"Yes, Julia," Mom said. "Yes."

Mom folded her arms, thinking. She said, "Julia, will you stay for dinner? I don't know what Theo has planned but it's bound to be good."

"Thank you, Mrs. Jones, but—"

"Kate. Please call me Kate."

"Thank you, ma'am," Julia said. "But my dad will be expecting me. Theo is a *fabulous* cook. He feeds us all at the restaurant."

"He does?"

"Hasn't he told you? He does family meal every day. For all of us."

"All of you?"

"The cooks and the dishwasher and servers."

"How many would that be?"

I said, "Twenty people." But I didn't look up from my math book.

"Oh, it's great," Julia said. "He's a natural."

"Well, you're welcome to stay for dinner if you change your mind. What's it going to be, Theo?"

"A surprise!" I said.

After Mom left, Julia closed her notebook (she was writing about her mom, I knew, for her college essay) and said, "I gotta go."

This always broke my heart, so before she could get off the bed, I rolled on top of her and began kissing her neck.

"Theooooo!"

"I can't help it."

She rolled out from under me, stood, smoothed her hair.

"I love your mom, by the way," she said.

"I do, too," I said.

I walked her to her car. Dad, briefcase in hand, walked up the drive from the Rapid stop.

Life was *good*.

According to Julia, Thanksgiving, less than three weeks away, was the start of the busy season. It seemed pretty busy to me already and I was glad to be finishing up the week. I arrived before ten that Saturday to do homework at my usual table, El 3. Chef always had good coffee made. Reggie and Paul arrived around eleven on Saturdays, and now that the weather had gotten cold, Reggie, Paul, and Amanda usually sat at the bar drinking coffee and gabbing for an hour before putting their aprons on and getting to work.

After three hours of book work, I was ready for the pleasure of cooking, little reading necessary, no writing, and no math harder than quadrupling recipes out of Chef's books.

At 12:30, Reggie came back to the dining room. "Theo, *you* don't know where Amanda is, do you?"

"No," I said.

He looked troubled and said, "Usually here by now."

A little before one, as I was stuffing my textbooks into my bag, Chef called out from the kitchen. I zipped up my bag and brought it with me to the kitchen. Chef leaned against the main prep table in front of the ranges, Paul on one side, Reggie on the other, and all of them staring at me as I walked in. This couldn't be good.

"I know you're in the downstairs kitchen most of the day, but you watch a lot of service, yeah?"

"I try to."

"What dishes come off Paul's station?"

Chef looked at Paul when I didn't say anything.

I closed my eyes and I could see all three of their stations. I said, "The pâté with greens, mustard, cornichons. Leeks vinaigrette. Salmon rillettes. The mesclun salad, soup of the day, lardon salad, then cheeses and desserts."

A smile gradually took over Chef's expression.

"What am I forgetting?" I asked.

"A couple hot dishes, but I'm going to cover those. You're officially on garde-manger tonight."

I didn't speak.

"Think you can handle it?" he asked.

I don't know! Last time I was on the line you kicked me off. Can I? But I said, "Yes, Chef!" And then my senses returned, and I asked, "What's going on?"

"Amanda hit a slick patch on the way to work and took a spill," Chef said. He held up his hand seeing my alarm and said, "She's fine, mostly. Broken arm, not serious, but she needs a cast and can't work tonight. Paul's going to take her station. I'm going to pick up his fish dishes and expedite. You're going to prep and plate all those dishes you just named. Paul will go over his prep list with you."

"Don't worry, man," Paul said, leaving his spot at the prep table. "Nothing difficult. You just got to be organized."

He took me to his station. "You have something to write on?"

I tore out a piece of notebook paper and folded it in quarters. I did this every day, wrote my own prep list this way. Now I'd have almost double the work. I wish they'd have told me sooner.

We leaned on the prep table across from one another.

"How's family?" he asked.

"Beef stir-fry and sesame cabbage slaw," I said. "Everything's ready to fire, half hour."

"Excellent," Paul said. His eyes were their customary pink with pale blue irises, his smile easy and comforting. "Okay, write these down. I'll explain how to do it all. Nothing difficult, like I said."

And then he went through his list:

- Make soup
- Make salmon rillettes
- Cook leeks
- Make red wine vinaigrette
- Make balsamic vinaigrette for the mesclun
- Poach eggs
- Hard-cook eggs

These had to be pressed through a sieve, whites and yolks separately; garnish for the leeks vinaigrette.

- Cook lardons

I looked over the list. "What do you mean *make* soup?"

"Soup of the day. Whatever kind you want, it's your call."

"I've never made soup before."

"You had a ton of black beans left over from a few days ago. They still good?"

"I think so?"

"Do a black bean soup." Seeing my expression he said, "Sweat diced onion, add cumin and coriander, a handful or so of each, throw in the beans. There should be plenty of veg stock in the walk-in from yesterday. Bring it to a simmer and burr mix it, check for seasoning. Don't even need to strain it. We'll serve it with some crème frâiche and chives. Put chives on your list."

- Cut chives

"Okay, what else?" he asked. "What's on your normal list?" This I knew:

- Mince shallots
- Chop parsley
- Peel potatoes
- Pick Chef's thyme
- Peel and dice carrots
- Dice onion
- Cut celery
- Start family meal at 4

"Okay, looks good," Paul said. "Do your standard stuff last if you have time. Start with the soup—get that out of the way. Then let me know and I'll go over the next item. Do the leeks, then the rillettes, those need to chill for at least an hour, then you can do the vinaigrettes. Once garde-manger station is set, do your other prep."

"Got it."

Chef passed by just then and said, "Let me see your list." I thought he wanted to make sure it was complete, but he said, "Why are all the items squinched over on the right?"

"I'm a leftie? That's just where they wind up."

"You ever been checked for dyslexia?"

"What's dyslexia?"

"Some brains are just wired different—dyslexia makes it harder to read and write."

"How do you know that?"

"Because I'm dyslexic."

I didn't know what this meant, but I'd have to think about it later. With service four and a half hours away, I'd have to get moving. "Thank you, Chef," I said, then pounded downstairs, and as I changed, I went through my moves. I'd chop all the onions I needed for stock mirepoix, but also for the soup. Then get the beans cooking. Then go to Paul for the leeks method. And then the salmon rillettes, whatever those were—I knew they were salmon and we served them in small jars, cold with toasted baguettes, but I had no idea how you made them. I'd have been excited had I not been so nervous.

Julia appeared as I was sautéing the onion for the soup. She always came by when I was cooking onions. I'd have to remember this. Maybe she liked onions, or maybe onions were just kind of magical and drew her to them.

"Oh my God, I just heard! You're on the line tonight!"

"I'm going to piss my pants." I kept stirring the onions.

"You'll get it done."

"How do you know?"

"Because you don't have a choice!" she said. And she bounded up the stairs. But she stopped at the top and called back down. "Like Chef says, people are usually surprised by what they can accomplish when they don't have a choice!"

She said it happily, but I wasn't happy. I was scared. But that was also something Chef said. "You can't run a kitchen based on fear. I worked in French kitchens where they scared the shit out of you on purpose. And it's true. Fear motivates. But it's not sustainable." And I thought, okay, fear for now until service, then I'll be organized. Super organized.

Paul brought down a hotel pan with a side of salmon that he'd poached in fish stock, still steaming. "You got butter at room temp?"

"Yes, Chef," I said.

"Take the skin off. Robot-Coupe half the salmon with the butter, salt, and white pepper."

"The whole pound of butter?"

"Flake the rest of the salmon, stir till it's all mixed together. Put it in the jars, be neat about it. Then pour a thin film of clarified butter on top to seal them and put them in the walk-in to chill. Then get family meal up."

"How much salt and pepper?"

He headed back up to the kitchen, saying, "Till it *tastes* good!" He did not say it nicely.

"Yes, Chef!"

And he was gone. I thought, *Jars? Butter?*

But then I saw, Paul had put a sheet tray on my prep table, lined with small jars, the kind that had a rubber lip around the lid and that clicked shut with a metal clasp. Superfast, I pulled the salmon out of the stock. Burned my hands but I didn't have time to get spatulas to do it carefully. It was all going to be shredded and pureed, anyway. I tossed the skin in the garbage and put half the salmon in a big metal bowl. I seasoned it with salt, raining the salt from high up like Chef did with the potato chips. All the spices were lined up alphabetically on a shelf above my workstation. I found the white pepper and, because I didn't like white pepper, just added a little. I couldn't really believe Paul, or Chef, was letting me do this, actually make the food they were going to charge people for.

I put the rest of the fish in the Robot-Coupe, which was like Mom's new Cuisinart Dad gave her for Christmas, only bigger and heavier, and used regularly, unlike ours at home. I seasoned this with the salt and white pepper. I threw in the whole block of butter, and pulsed it till it was smooth, spatulaed it into the bowl with the half salmon, and stirred. The half salmon broke apart easily, so the mixture was both smooth and chunky. I tasted it. I don't think I'd ever had salmon. At home, I'd only eaten Mrs. Paul's fish sticks with tartar sauce, so I didn't really know what it was supposed to taste like. It wasn't as bad as I thought it was going to be. I thought it was going to be like our cat food, but it was actually okay.

I was officially going to be *on the line*. I couldn't believe it.

I ran it up to Paul and handed him a tasting spoon. He tasted. Thought. "A little more white pepper, then you're good."

I ran it back downstairs, added a small four-finger pinch of white pepper. Worked this in. I tasted. So this was what it was supposed to taste like.

I quickly filled the twenty jars with the salmon, smoothing the top. The bain of clarified butter was warm, not hot. I poured just enough of each to coat the top, got them in the walk-in. While there I pulled everything for the stir-fry: rice, slaw, beef, and veg, all of which I'd cut yesterday. I remembered some peanuts in dry storage; I'd throw those in there as well. I put the Robot-Coupe and blade in the hotel pan that had held the salmon and ran it up to George in the pot room, grabbed the peanuts, ran down the stairs.

The pot of black beans with veg stock was at a heavy simmer.

I got the burr mixer out of the pot room. This was a stick blender, huge. You could dunk it in the water behind a boat and drive the boat. I put the rondeau with the beans on the floor, plugged in the burr mixer and buzzed the soup hard until it was all smooth. I ran a spoon of it up to Paul, who was cutting potato waffle chips. He tasted, closed his eyes. "Good." Then he said, "You put cayenne in there?"

"Yes, Chef, just a little."

I ran to the stairs and almost knocked Chef down as he was coming with a case of frisée.

"Theo."

"Yes, Chef." I didn't need this, I had stuff to do.

"Don't work faster, work smarter."

"Yes, Chef." He stepped past me. I'd file that away and try and figure out what he meant later.

I got the leeks cooking in veg stock as Paul had told me. I went down my list:

- Make soup
- Make salmon rillettes
- Cook leeks

On to the vinaigrettes, then I'd start family meal. After family meal I'd poach eggs. Paul kept these in ice water after they were poached and reheated them in butter for the lardon salad. I got a tall pot of water going, put a sheet tray on top to make it boil faster. I could do the hard-cooked eggs at the same time. I put those into the cold water figuring by the time all that water came up to a boil, they'd be done.

That's what Chef meant I guess.

I had to get the leeks cooling. Once you could slip a paring knife right through them, they were done, Paul said, and into cold veg stock. When cooled, I poured the red wine vinaigrette over them in a hotel pan and put them in the walk-in.

The water with the hard-cooked eggs was at a boil by the time I had the lardons cut. I took one egg and cut it in half to see if it was cooked. Almost. I threw the lardons in the clean rondeau George had mercifully brought back to me. I poured a bunch of water on top of the lardons, as Chef had taught me. This worked great because while they boiled away, shedding fat, I didn't have to think about them till I heard the water crackling off and fat sizzling in the pan. In the meantime, I poached thirty eggs and pulled them out with a big slotted spoon, two at a time, and put them directly into ice water.

At four, I got the beef stir-fry cooking while the already-cooked rice reheated in the oven. I poured rice vinegar and some sesame oil over the shredded cabbage. I ran all this food up to the main kitchen and set it out. Everyone was surprised it was up early. I was soaked with sweat, even though it was a gray, windy, chilly afternoon, classic Cleveland fall.

Julia and Tony got plates and bins of silverware and the plastic cups and paper napkins we used for family meal.

I couldn't spare the time to eat, let alone wait in line.

Julia came down the stairs with a plate of food for me. "I knew you didn't have time. You need to eat."

"Thanks, but I think I'll throw up."

"Well, try anyway." And she was gone to finish up her work.

Whenever I didn't know something, I asked Paul. He just kept whipping something thick in a pot, sweating, his face as pink as his eyes, and said, "Cup and a half of oil, half cup vinegar, shallot, salt, pepper, blend."

To which I said, "Yes, Chef!"

- Make red wine vinaigrette
- Make balsamic vinaigrette for the mesclun
- Hard cook eggs
- Poach eggs
- Cook lardons

By 5:10 I was running all my food up the stairs to Paul's station—*my* station—the soup, the leeks, the eggs and lardons. I checked the lowboy and saw that Chef had prepped the frisée for me. I found a serrated knife and began cutting a baguette for the salad and the pâté, got them toasting.

I saw that Tony and Julia were covering the Pass with a white cloth. That meant service was coming up.

The rillettes were still in the walk-in downstairs. I needed to get them up here so they could temper, otherwise they'd be too hard to serve.

I set them out at Paul's station, lining them up neatly in the corner of my prep table.

Chef called, "Fifteen minutes."

I joined the rest, shouting back, "Fifteen minutes!" It sounded like a team.

Chef appeared at my side, put his hand on my shoulder. He said, "You got this."

"Yes, Chef."

"You're just going to be responsible for four dishes, okay? You're going to ladle soup, using the eight-ounce ladle, into a bowl, put a dollop of crème fraîche on it and garnish with chives. You got the chives?"

"Yes, Chef." I held up the ramekin covered in wet paper towel, filled with minced chives.

"When I call 'leeks,' you're going to put two leek halves on this plate." He reached down and pulled out an oval plate. "You know the plate. You'll spoon a little more vinaigrette over them, sprinkle egg white across them this way, then top them with the yolk."

"Yes, Chef."

"I'll show you how to make each plate the first time the order comes in. The only tricky one for you is going to be the lardon salad. Lardons are hot in their fat above the stove?" I pointed to the pan that sat on a shelf above the stove, where they stayed hot but didn't cook. "Heat some butter in this one small Teflon pan." He held it in front of my face. "It's the only thing we use it for. The poached egg. Drop an egg in it, gently or the yolk will break. While the egg heats in the butter, put frisée in a bowl, spoon some bacon fat over it, give it a shot of red wine vinegar from this little bottle here, plate it. Top it with the egg. Keep a sizzle pan right here." He slapped the edge of the stove. "With plenty of C-folds." C-folds were what we called the brown paper towels, stacked on top of each other. "Use this spoon." He hunted in the water-filled bain for Paul's small slotted spoon. "Let the egg drain, then place it on the frisée and send it to me at the Pass."

"But, Chef," I said. "It's got red powder and coarse salt on it when it goes out."

This halted him. But I knew I was right. I could see it in my mind exactly.

He smiled at me. "I finish it at the Pass."

"Yes, Chef."

"Cut and plate ten pâtés so they're ready to go, right now, okay?"

"Yes, Chef."

Samantha walked into the kitchen and said, "Order in, Chef."

I couldn't believe it was here already.

Chef took the Pass and said, "Ordering!"

The rest of the night happened like a dream. The first orders were pâtés and soups, the easiest of the pickups.

Chef said, "Theo, I'm firing a lardon in two minutes."

I made sure all the mise was ready for him. He left the Pass to demo it. He made it look so easy that when he fired the next one and my turn was up, I moved too fast and carelessly. The yolk broke in the pan, and I had to waste valuable seconds wiping the pan out and reheating butter in it. I'd be careful from there on in.

When I set that first salad at the Pass, a new kind of movement took over. I wouldn't recognize this until later. Time seemed to change. Or I changed and everything around me slowed down. I hit some kind of groove and I just re-created those plates I'd been watching Paul make all those weeks. Like I wasn't even thinking, just moving.

There's a certain groove you hit in a football game when everyone, every single player is executing their position perfectly, play by play, and you just steadily march down the field. It's as if everyone is connected, and the end zone is inevitable. It felt like that, like an incredibly choreographed march down the field for the touchdown.

Clive seated the last table at 8:30, and twenty minutes later, it was Julia who arrived and said, "Order in—this is the last seating, Chef."

Julia normally just headed straight back out to the dining room, but instead, she stood at attention behind Chef, hands behind her back.

Chef, reading as he stepped in my direction, called out, "Order fire! One rillette, one leek, one soup, one lardon."

"Rillette, leek, soup, lardon!" I called back.

She pumped her fist at me.

One of each, I thought, perfect, this is it—plate the cold ones first, finish the hot ones last. I'd done it.

When I put the last plate up, Chef dragged a white towel around the rims, his long gold-brown curls hanging down, obscuring his face as he checked each dish. He was so cool to look at. I wanted to be him.

"Pickup, table eight!" he called, then, without looking at me, he said, "Thank you, Theo."

I cleaned my station, got all the trays to George, stored the soup, took three unsold rillettes to the walk-in, then wiped down Paul's station. I could help him get set for cheese courses. Chef and I had gotten a few early desserts out already, but there was still a lot of night to go.

But I was done. Now all I had to do was lend a hand, and was happy to do so. After Paul had finished his entrées on Amanda's station, he took over desserts. I went to the downstairs kitchen to knock out the mirepoix so it would be ready to go when Chef started the veal stock tomorrow. Then I wiped down the prep table and cutting boards and cleaned my knives.

"Hey."

It was Jackie, snarling at me as only she could. She was quiet a long time and I almost said, *What?*

She said, "Nice job tonight. No one thought you were gonna be able to do it, and we were going to suffer. It was a good night."

Once I got over my shock, I said, "Thanks."

"Hey, you made that soup didn't you?"

"Yeah," I said.

"People really liked it."

I said my official good night to Chef, Reggie, Paul, Amanda, and George. Paul and Reggie high-fived me. I changed back into jeans and my dry shirt. I felt exhausted and elated. I looked into the dining room but didn't see Julia, which meant she was changing. I went downstairs, filled two-pint delis with ice for the two of us and waited outside the girls' changing room.

I was ready to *celebrate*.

Julia opened the door, looking beautiful and transformed, as ever. "Shift drink?" I said, grinning, holding up two ice-filled delis.

She lowered her head and stared at her feet, her long hair cascading forward so that I couldn't see her face.

22

"Jules," I said, deli cups in hand, "what's the matter?"

"I can't tonight, Theo."

"It's only eleven o'clock."

"I told Bennett I'd meet him after work."

I'd had the wind knocked out of me three or four times, hit so hard in such a way that I literally could not breathe. It's scary the first time, when your lungs simply won't expand with air, not knowing when or if it's going to end. It's a horrible feeling.

"Why?" I said, when I could breathe.

"He's been calling. And calling. He says he's got something important he wants to say."

"So what's wrong with the phone?"

"He said it had to be in person."

"Why did you say yes?"

"I owe it to him."

"Julia. Do you still have feelings for him?"

No is what she said. Then she said it again.

She said, "I'll call you first thing tomorrow." She hurried toward the stairway leading to the front of the house.

"Hey," I said, desperate to stop her, to make her stay. "Can I steal a cigarette?"

She fumbled in her purse and handed me a flattened pack of cigarettes. There were two. She was halfway up the stairs already.

"But these are your last ones," I said.

"I've got a spare pack in the car." And she was gone.

It was that split second before she said *no*. I went over and over it in my mind to make sure I wasn't making it up. But it had been there. The slightest of pauses. "Do you still have feelings for him?" Pause. "No." And she threw in an extra *no*, I reasoned, because when you're lying, you overexplain. One *no* would have been fine. But she knew that she'd paused so she added an extra to try to cover the lie.

The descent from euphoria to crushed was brutal. I didn't know what to do or where to go.

I drove around for an hour, listening to music. The same music we'd listened to all last summer. Grateful Dead. Neil Young. Pink Floyd's "Wish You Were Here." Torturing myself. I gave it an hour.

Then I headed down Shaker and turned right onto West Park and toward the lakes. I drove past the parking lot where we always went and saw what I'd expected. Julia's Bug. And beside it, Bennett's car. A blue Mercedes. I knew it from the parking lot at school.

The night was cold enough that I could see exhaust coming from Bennett's car. Running to stay warm.

I still couldn't go home. I parked across the street from Johnny's house. I zipped up my jacket, headed down his driveway, and out the back gate to the golf course. I found our sand trap. I sat on the edge of it, my ass getting wet. I lit a cigarette and looked at my watch. I planned to give it one more hour. I took out the second cigarette and threw the pack into the sand trap.

I looked at my watch again. It's amazing how slowly time could pass. When you're cooking, three hours go by and you don't even notice it. On a golf course in the middle of the night, with your ass getting wet, five minutes feels like three hours.

Pretty soon I got too cold to keep sitting and went back to my car.

I don't know how I did it—the music, I suppose, every song connected me to Julia—but I lasted an hour from the last time I drove past the parking lot. It was 1:30. I turned right off of Shaker Boulevard onto West Park. At the stop sign, I could see Julia's car but not Bennett's.

My heart lifted. Thank God. I'd at least speak with her. Good or bad, an end to this anxiety, this crushing feeling that I was losing her. I sped into the parking lot, gravel crunching. I slammed the door and ran to Julia's car.

It was empty. I cupped my hands around my face to be sure I wasn't missing something. Vacant. I stood and turned a full circle.

"Julia?" I said. "Julia?!" I jogged toward the woods. "Julia!" I called again. I walked down the cement embankment to the lake. *"Julia?"*

"Julia!" I called one last time. Dead silence. Not even an echo in response. A black lake, a black sky.

23

Julia sat on my bed.

Julia?

Where am I? I looked around. Okay, bedroom, but what's Julia doing here?

"I've been trying to call all morning."

And slowly I remembered last night. "What are you *doing* here?"

"I left a message with your mom hours ago. Then I called again and nothing. I called every hour and then thought, Fuck it. I'll just go there."

I heard Julia's loud car outside even through the closed windows. "Is that your car?"

"Battery's dead. If I turn it off it might not start. Bennett had to drive me home."

"I thought you were *with* him. I drove by the lakes and saw your car. I thought you were . . ."

"Silly *you*."

"I thought you were still in love with him."

"Theo. I love *you*."

I threw my arms around her and hugged her. I just hugged her. I hugged her and hugged her, rocking gently back and forth. "I love you so much."

I didn't want to release her, but I finally did. "Can you tell me what Bennett wanted?"

"He wanted to get back together."

"And that was that?"

"And that was that."

I just sat there until Julia said, "Well, I'm gonna run out of gas if I don't get moving and find a battery."

"Wait, I'll go with you." And I jumped out of bed to use the bathroom and brush my hair and teeth. I was just in a T-shirt and boxers when I got out of bed, but I didn't give it a thought, walking before her basically undressed.

"Cute boxers," she said.

When I left the bathroom and hunted for a clean pair of jeans, Julia said, "I had a really good night last night, and paying for this will completely erase it. All that work."

"No it won't," I said. I reached into my top drawer and pulled out my envelope which had $160 in it. "Don't even try to stop me."

The mechanic, skinny, unshaven, with a big mustache and wearing a gray jumpsuit with "John" sewn on it, greeted us with a rag over his shoulder and an adjustable wrench in his hand. "What can I do you for?" he said.

I explained that we needed a new battery and the muffler had been shot for months.

John said, "You can probably get a muffler for ten bucks cheaper at Midas."

I had the cash and told him if he could do it today, we wanted both.

Julia hugged my arm as we crossed Warrensville. "I can't believe you, Theo. Let me buy you the best greasy burger and griddled onions. And a fantastic vanilla malt. To thank you."

"Where might that be?"

"You don't know Mawby's? Right here at Van Aken, between the cleaners and the art store," she said, surprised. "I am about to change your life."

It was there, on cracked leather stools, at the counter in front of a big flattop heaped with browned onions and sizzling burgers, that I told her my news: My parents, after much back-and-forthing, and much hand-wringing from Mom, had agreed to allow me to stay home alone so that I could work Thanksgiving at the restaurant while they went to Gram and Gramps in Florida.

"I'm guessing you probably need to be home for Thanksgiving," I said.

"Yeah, they'll be holding dinner till I finish at the restaurant."

"But," I said, "we have Friday off."

"I think I know where this is going," she said.

"May I make dinner for us on Friday?"

"Well, I'm not going to say no to that!"

I took her hand in mine. "Will you stay the night?"

She looked into my eyes for the longest time. I mean, the *longest* time. And I held her gaze.

Finally, she said, "I'll figure a way."

It was the best burger and vanilla malt I ever had.

24

Unbelievably, Amanda returned the following Tuesday, just two days after her accident, having missed only one day of work. She'd broken the smaller bone in her arm, the ulna. I said, "Welcome to the club." She gave me a gentle fist bump with her casted hand. It was her right arm, her dominant hand, so she asked the doctor if he could put on her cast so she'd be able to hold a knife, a sauté pan, and the throttle on her bike. She was badass.

When she was prepping her station that day, I said, "Doesn't that hurt?"

"Even with all the pills they gave me, it hurts like a motherfucker," she said, not looking up from the rack of beef she was breaking down into one-and-one-quarter-inch strips. "Riding my bike is no pleasure, either." She held up her cast. "This is my throttle hand, and I can't use my wrist."

"Why are you working, then? I can keep covering Paul's station."

She said, "Money, duh. I don't work, I don't get paid. I don't get paid, I don't make rent." And she kept on cutting. I walked away, embarrassed.

But still, it was a golden time. I stayed on top of my studies. I fed the staff every day. The Browns were winning. And I had Julia. My love. With the day after Thanksgiving glowing like a beacon before me.

Golden.

Until the money went missing.

25

Thanksgiving prep began on the Saturday before Thanksgiving, with thirty turkeys arriving from an Amish farmer who'd driven them in from Middlefield, about an hour east of Cleveland. The following day, Sunday, was unlike any other Sunday of the year that the cooks worked. Over the course of two days, the four of us would prepare an entire Thanksgiving feast for 150 reservations.

First trimester exams were Monday, Tuesday, and Wednesday morning. So I got up early Sunday to study. Chef said we'd be finished by six and I could finish studying for my hardest day, Monday: chem in the morning, trig in the afternoon. Tuesday was American history and French. And Wednesday morning was my last final, and the one I was most confident about, English.

I felt prepared, and even Julia, who'd stopped by Sunday mid-morning to quiz me on the French verbs, said, "You've so got this, Theo."

The stakes were high. I used the discipline and hard work Chef had drilled into me to get my schoolwork done. I think Mr. Morgan would have liked this "irony." We'd been talking a lot about irony in class. Working at the restaurant, learning to cook, had not *hurt* my studies, it had made me a *better* student. That's almost ironic, I think. Learning to cook family meal taught me how to study. As Chef said, people are usually surprised by what they can accomplish when they don't have a choice.

Sunday at noon, Chef, Paul, Reggie, and Amanda got to work breaking down the turkeys.

I couldn't really wrap my head around what Chef was up to with the birds. But he kind of treated them like the chickens, only we used all the dark meat rather than saving it for family meal. Paul pushed his steel worktable up against the long worktable in front of the ranges, which doubled as the Pass when it got covered with white cloth. Amanda, Chef, and Reggie stood along that table with Paul facing them at the end. Each had a big heavy cutting board. I was in charge of keeping everything organized, bringing them turkeys as they needed, and storing what they cut.

First, all the skin had to be removed. The skin was to be salted and spread out on sheet trays with parchment paper, stacked one on top of the other to be roasted till all the skin was flat, golden, and crisp.

They removed the wings. These all went into a big gray tub. Along with all the bones, a ton of bones, they would get roasted and used for the stock we'd turn into gravy. There was not a single bone that wasn't used for stock. They boned out the leg and the thigh, a real pain because of all the bonelike tendons in the drumstick. Chef had a big communal cleaver they could all use to whack the knobby ends of the drumsticks off. All the leg bones went in with the wings. All the dark meat went on one tray. They took off both sides of the breast and kept those whole on separate sheet trays.

I got the wings roasting, and when there were enough thigh bones and carcasses, I got those roasting, too. I had to use all the ovens. George was there to wash as we needed.

Reggie brought a big radio in so we could listen to the Browns-Bengals game. By the end of the first half, the kitchen smelled so much like Thanksgiving from the roasting bones, I could almost taste the turkey in my mind. Chef ordered sandwiches from the deli across the street, so while I was eating Thanksgiving dinner in my head, we were actually eating egg salad sandwiches with potato chips and drinking Pepsi Light.

By the time the Browns had thoroughly trounced the Bengals, all the birds were broken down. All the turkeys were separated by part. The bones were all being roasted and would go into the stock-pot overnight (along with roasted veal bones, which Chef said made the gravy magical). He carefully salted all the skin and the meat, telling me this seasoned them, but also helped to keep them fresh till he cooked them.

Chef tied all sixty breasts into tight roulades. He could do these so fast I could barely follow how he did it. His plan, he told me, while tying, was to sear them, then poach them gently in turkey stock and refrigerate them in the stock so they'd stay moist and juicy when they were reheated and sliced and held for service in warm broth.

He first roasted the dark meat till it was golden brown and delicious-looking but still tough, then he braised them in turkey stock till they were tender. When they were cool enough to handle, Reggie, Amanda, and I picked the meat off the bones, pulled it apart, and put it in big steel bowls. Chef folded in a massive amount of sautéed shallots and seasoned it and then, using cheesecloth, he made a dozen logs of braised dark meat, which he would also refrigerate submerged in stock.

I offered to work Monday afternoon to watch how he did all this. I was all studied out, and I'd be finished with the toughest of my five finals. I changed from school clothes into the black pants and white chef coat and was unfolding a fresh apron as Chef went on: "Just so you know, these are the fun days, these are the cooking days."

"Yeah?" I said, putting the apron over my neck and tying it around my waist.

"I just don't want you to think that actual Thanksgiving is fun. This is the fun part."

I stuck two side towels in my apron strings. "I don't understand."

"Thanksgiving is just an assembly line. It's pure heat and serve, everyone gets the exact same plate. It's like a factory. Cooking the entire meal days before is the only way we can serve all those people. The only thing I'll actually cook on Thursday will be the mashed potatoes, roasting the skin, straining the stock to turn it into gravy."

Then he sent me to help finish off the green bean casserole. Chef hated it, but too many people wanted it. He did make a great béchamel with mushrooms and fried his own shallots to top the three massive roasting pans of casserole. We'd cut up all the baguettes on Sunday so that Chef could make the stuffing today as well, a traditional celery, onion, and sage stuffing.

On Thanksgiving, every plate would get three slices of breast meat; a slice of the dark meat roulade; and a thick disc of stuffing, each piece cut with a ring cutter (leftovers would go home with staff). Green bean casserole, a scoop of mashed potatoes, and a corn pudding. The turkey got a ladle of gravy, and the plate got finished with a big shard of roasted turkey skin, thin and crisp as a potato chip. Like Chef said, everyone got the exact same plate. Like a factory. Every table got its own gooseneck of gravy on the side (at home I called it a gravy boat, but I got laughed at when I called it that here—*gooseneck*).

"I love roasting the skin shortly before service," Chef said, "because it's delicious but also because it makes the whole place smell like a Thanksgiving home when people arrive. Oh, and I whip the bourbon cream to dollop onto the pumpkin pie for dessert."

"When do we do the pies?" I asked.

"Are you kidding? They're all ordered from Hough."

Hough Bakery was famous in Cleveland.

So, by Tuesday, when we opened for normal service, practically an entire Thanksgiving dinner for 150 customers and two seventy-five-seat turns, one at noon, one at three, had already been prepared, and Amanda could tend her steaks and salmon; Reggie, his halibut and lamb.

"Not that Thanksgiving is not fun. People tend to drink a lot so it's a pretty lively crowd. And it's Thanksgiving!" Chef said, almost giddy.

I don't think I'd seen Chef so happy, preparing for this holiday meal.

26

It was fun being alone in the house. Feeling all grown-up. I drank a few Olde English 800s Johnny bought for me that afternoon. I picked him up on the way home from the airport after I'd dropped off Mom and Dad so that he could buy a bottle of red wine at Shaker Beverage for my dinner with Julia. And a bottle of Southern Comfort, of course.

Instead of a bag, he came out of the store with a box. He put it in the back seat.

"What's all that?"

"What you asked for. Plus two sixes of Olde English, one for you and one for me. You'll want it for the game on Sunday. And I got you two bottles of wine, not one."

So you can see why I loved Johnny.

On Thanksgiving at the restaurant, late morning, the entire long steel worktable got filled with plates, completely filled. Food got put on them, each one identical. Everyone had their job. The only thing that had to be worked over were the mashed potatoes, which Chef made at ten that morning—they had to be "refreshed." You could make them ahead as long as you didn't let them get cold. Then you had to reheat them in fifteen portion batches with more butter and half-and-half. These got dumped into a big pastry bag with a star tip so that plating them was both fast and pretty.

There wasn't even any ordering done. Julia and Jackie and Tony and the rest didn't order anything. They just picked up and set down. Clive and Samantha handled special wine orders, but the servers' main duties were trotting up and down the stairs to replenish wine. Chef had a house white and something called a Beaujolais, which was the red and a big deal.

The only variation came when the restaurant's owners arrived with their families. The Treadwells and the Welches were booked for the noon seating, the Hollidays for the 3:00 p.m. seating. Clive had Samantha and Julia covering the noon tables. Samantha would handle the Hollidays.

Chef told them, "The owners get an extra course, so get their salads out first. The Treadwells and the Welches have asked for artichokes vinaigrette. That's done and ready to go. Sam, let me know when Jimmy arrives. They're starting with pasta pomodoro, served family style. I'll plate all that over at Paul's station, just keep me posted."

"Yes, Chef," they said in unison.

I knew the Hollidays had finished their desserts because I could smell Jimmy's cigar smoke all the way in the kitchen. They were really loud when they arrived, and only got louder the more wine they drank.

The Hollidays were among the last to leave, very much "in their cups," as Dad sometimes put it. Julia, finishing up her tables, stopped by the central worktable where I was putting the last of the pie on eight plates. "Mr. Holliday is making Chef do shots of grappa!"

"What's grappa?"

"Some kind of alcohol he shipped over from Italy."

Julia picked up four plates of pie after Paul had piped bourbon-spiked whipped cream.

"I've never seen Chef drink before," she whispered to me.

"Where are the stars?!" a voice boomed. Jimmy Holliday barreled into the kitchen, fat cigar in hand, a bottle in the other, and Chef right behind him. "Yous guys!" Holliday said. "You are the *real* stars. Isn't that what you said, Chef?"

Chef set six shot glasses on the stainless-steel worktable.

"And I wanted to show my appreciation and wish you a happy Thanksgiving!" Holliday said, and he poured a clear liquid into each glass. "This is grappa, from my homeland, Italia! Water of life!"

He filled the glasses to the brim.

"I remember you, youngster," he said, handing me a shot.

"Theo. How do you do, Mr. Holliday?"

He let out a big *bwah-ha-ha*, and said, "The kid's got manners! You'll go far, kid." He handed a glass to Paul, then Reggie, then Amanda, saying, "That's some serious artwork you got there, girlie!" *Bwah-ha-ha!*

He handed Chef a glass, then held his own glass up. "To the chefs. I thank you for another fine and profitable year, and I look forward to many more! Happy Thanksgiving!"

Then he threw his glass back. I smelled mine, grapey and strong. I braced myself and swallowed it down. Oh my God, it was like drinking *gasoline*. I made that face Julia taught me. Reggie was coughing and wiping his eyes. Chef just sipped his. "You like?" Mr. Holliday said to me.

"Yes, sir," I said out of habit.

"Splendid, have another!" And he refilled my glass. "Anyone else?" He held the bottle aloft. Paul and Reggie waved him off, but Amanda held her glass forward. "Atta girl," Mr. Holliday said, filling her glass and his. He set the bottle down, shot a plume of cigar smoke into the air, and drank. I muscled through mine in one go again.

Mr. Holliday reached into his pocket and pulled out a fat wad of cash. "They in there"—he pointed his cigar at the dining room—"they get tipped, am I right? But you guys, nobody ever tips you, do they?" He peeled off four twenty-dollar bills and smacked them down on the table. "A token of my appreciation for your excellent work."

"Jimmy," Chef said quietly, "George, the dishwasher. He's probably the most important person in the kitchen."

"The dishwasher?"

"If he doesn't work, we've got no pans to cook in or plates to serve on or glasses to fill."

Holliday frowned, trying to process this, then smiled and said, "What the hell! It's Thanksgiving!" and he dropped another twenty on the table. He gripped Chef's head (his cigar never left his left hand) and gave him a wallop of a kiss on both cheeks and stumbled out.

We each took a bill. Amanda said, "Sweet." And it was. Twenty bucks was a lot. I mean, I made thirty-two dollars a day, so it was more than half a day's pay for me.

Then Chef hurried downstairs. Reggie and Paul high-fived. Amanda picked up the remaining twenty and said, "Hey, George, got something for ya."

Chef burst through the basement door having flown back up the steps. His eyes were wild. He looked at each of us. "Paul!" He pointed to the back door. "No one leaves through that door. Lock it and bring me the key."

Paul did as he was told. I watched Chef go to the dining room. I followed him out and saw a final deuce just paying. I heard Tony at the cash register running a credit card through the machine, the knuckle-buster they called it, with a clunk forward, and a clunk back. The servers could see that something was up. They watched Chef talk in animated whispers at the front with Clive. Clive went to stand by the door.

Julia put a handful of silverware on a table, caught my attention from across the room, held her hands out, and mouthed, "What's going on?"

I shrugged.

Ten minutes later, at 8:15, after Clive had personally seen the last two guests to the door with a fake smile and a "Happy Thanksgiving," we were all seated in the main dining, everyone except Paul.

Chef said, "At approximately five p.m. tonight, I put five pouches on Maryann's desk. As of about twenty minutes ago, there were only four. Which means someone in this room took one of those pouches. Those pouches contain money, obviously. So this is a serious crime. I'll say right now, no questions asked, and no consequences for anyone who has any information here: Say if you took it, return it right now, and there is no shame and there will be no consequences. I won't even fire you, I give you my word. I will chalk it up to a bad impulse followed by a courageous admission. Right now."

Chef waited for what felt like forever but was probably a full minute.

Everyone kept looking around at everyone else, people murmuring to each other.

Paul came in from the kitchen and shook his head at Chef.

"I'm sorry I had to do this," Chef said. "But Paul has been through every purse and bag, every winter coat pocket in both changing rooms."

A number of servers shouted out, "You can't do that."

"Evidently," Chef said, "he found nothing." He rubbed the back of his neck. "Listen. The owners of this establishment, one in particular, has, let's call them, very strict and definitive business principles and methods of dealing with problems. This will be a major problem. If you were the person who took the money"—he looked each person in the eye for one second, me included—"you may be in danger. If you are not in danger, then I am in danger and the restaurant is in danger."

It made sense that Paul was not a suspect. First and most importantly, he hadn't been downstairs all night, certainly not after 5:00 p.m.; only Reggie, and Amanda, and I had. And besides, he was like Chef's little brother; they'd been friends since high school, worked in the same restaurants. He was like the only family Chef had.

Paul walked around the room with a fist full of pens and a dupe pad, setting a blank ticket and a pen beside each of us, Clive included. Eighteen of us, Paul and Chef excluded.

"Here is an opportunity to anonymously give me information," Chef said, "whether to say it was you, and that you would like to return the money, or that you have information. Again, you can do so anonymously. Everybody must write something down, and I want each one signed. Again, I will not reveal anything, but I have to know. Seriously. I beg you. These people are *not* to be fucked with. *Please*."

While we wrote, Paul retrieved a pot from the kitchen and collected the pieces of paper in it. I wrote, "Chef, I didn't take the money, I promise you. Theo." I folded the ticket in half and dropped it in the pan.

Chef first counted them, then read each one. When he finished, he folded the whole stack in half, stood, and said, "Clive, Julia, and Jackie. Come with me to the kitchen please. Everyone else wait here, please."

After an eternal five minutes, they came back. I tried to make eye contact with Julia, but she just looked straight ahead.

"It appears that we will not recover the money tonight. Please consider this. On Wednesday, when Maryann is in to do the books, the discrepancy *will* be discovered. I pray to God that whoever took that money finds a way to return it, no questions asked. After Wednesday . . ." And he just trailed off, shaking his head.

"All right," he said, resigned. "You're all free to go." Everyone stood, with varying degrees of relief. I saw Chef say in his normal, if distressed speaking voice, to Paul, "I don't know what else to do!" And then, "God*dammit*."

Paul whispered something and Chef called out to us: "I'm sorry to have to do this but everyone's going to get patted down and bags checked as you leave."

I went down the front basement stairway with Julia.

"Someone wrote they'd seen me leaving the office," she told me, panicked.

"Did you?"

"Clive sent me there, but it was before the second seating even started."

"What did he want with the others?"

"I gotta get home," she said, still rattled from all of it. "I'm late already. My sisters are holding dinner for me." When we got to the bottom of the steps, she said, "Shit, forgot my wine key," and she went back upstairs. I changed with Paul, Reggie, and the other guy servers.

I waited by the front door. Julia and Jackie were the last up the stairs.

"What took you so long?" I asked her. "I thought you were in a hurry."

She just went to Chef, holding her purse open. He checked it. She held her arms out, and he dragged his hands down her coat, front, sides, down to her thighs. "Good night, Julia," Chef said. I hadn't brought a bag, but I wore a puffy down jacket. I suppose I could have stuffed the pouch in there if I'd stolen it. After he'd searched me, front, sides, and back, I said, "I'm so sorry, Chef."

"Let's just hope it shows up."

From the porch of the restaurant, I watched Julia do a U-turn from her parking spot across from the restaurant and speed off down Larchmere. She didn't even wait to say goodbye.

At 10:10, the phone rang. I raced to the kitchen and got to the receiver on the second ring. "Finally!"

"I've only got a minute."

270

"Do you have any idea who would have taken the money?" I asked.

"Jackie thinks it was Clive, because he has kind of unfettered access to the office."

"Maybe it was Jackie."

"She may be a bitch," Julia said, "but I don't think she'd do it. What about Amanda or Reggie—cooks are famous thieves."

"That would make me really sad," I said.

"We all knew something crooked was going on at the restaurant. Believe me, I don't think money is a problem for them, not in that small amount. Can't imagine it would be, like, $100,000— they wouldn't be so casual about that. So it's small. They'll get over it."

"What about putting the thief in danger?"

"I think he was just trying to scare the money out of whoever took it."

"Yeah, well."

"It's not *your* problem," she said. "Unless . . . did you take the money?"

"No!"

"Hey, I never said something to you."

"What?"

"Happy Thanksgiving. I'm thankful for you."

"Happy Thanksgiving, Jules. I too you. Wait, that sounded stupid. I'm so grateful for you."

27

The next morning was the first morning in ages I could sleep in.
With the incredibly busy week preceding it, without a day off at
the restaurant and with exams and Thanksgiving, my brain and
body were exhausted. I slept till eleven. I took my time waking
up. Called Mom and Dad to say hi. Then I went to Heinen's to
do the shopping for my dinner with Julia, the day here at last. I
found Joe, the store's manager, and when I told him what I was
there for, he brought me back to the meat department and told
Tom what I needed. An inch-and-a-half-thick T-bone steak. "It's
for his sweetheart, so make it perfect."

I'd been planning the meal in my head for a week. I was going
to do the steak Florentine I'd seen Amanda and Chef make for
Mr. Holliday. I'd grill it and roast a Vidalia onion in the coals.
Chef had let me take a bag of rocket, that spicy green he used, on
the last night of service before Thanksgiving, because it wouldn't
keep till the following Saturday, anyway. And I'd roast some
potatoes.

I got everything prepped. Salted the steak as soon as I got
back from Heinen's and left it out, the way Chef did. Washed the
greens. Minced the shallots. Cut the potatoes and put them in
water to keep them from turning brown. Peeled the Vidalia, cut

an X halfway through the top so the center would cook, slathered it with butter, salted it, and wrapped it in foil.

I set the dining room table for two. Put out wineglasses in the kitchen.

And I took a shower. For good luck, I put on the same clothes I was wearing when Julia and I met, and then the first time I cooked for her.

First, I got the potatoes roasting since they took the longest and they would hold.

I started a fire in the living room, which Julia thought deserved velvet roping. It wasn't that perfect. Soon, the mantel would be festooned with ribbons and pine roping and candles, and the table in front of the bay window looking out onto the street would be moved to make room for the Christmas tree. We'd probably do this on Sunday when Mom and Dad got back. It was cold outside, and a fire would be nice in here.

I began pacing when Julia didn't arrive right at five. I could feel it, something was going to mess this up.

Five fifteen by my watch.

I was all the way in the living room when I heard a knock on the back door. And then her wonderful, lilting, heart-lifting "Hellooo?"

Thank God, I thought.

"I forgot, I keep thinking I'll hear it when you arrive!" I said. Her car was now too quiet.

I lifted an opened bottle of red and said, "Can I pour you a glass?"

"Impressive."

"Oh, wait," I said, suddenly nervous. "We should probably put your car in the garage. I don't want the neighbors to see it here in the morning." That sounded wrong, so I added, "I mean, if you think it will still be here in the morning."

She stood on her toes to kiss me. "Remember when I said it was important to wait for the right time? Now's the right time."

I exhaled.

She said, "Pour me that wine. I'll pull into the garage."

I quickly poured two glasses, then went to the door off the kitchen leading to the garage and hit the door opener. She pulled into the space where I'd be parking once the snow and ice really started. I clicked the button again and the door closed behind her.

"Wow, a heated garage. Must be nice!"

I'd never known anything else, so I hadn't thought about it before.

She hung her coat on the hook by the door. She wore patched jeans and a blousy white shirt, a summer shirt, which tied at the neck, the one, I realized, she'd been wearing when I first saw her. She regarded my mise en place. "Steak!" she said. She strolled into the dining room, sort of inspecting the place and the table settings, the silver candlesticks moved close to the placemats. "Nice." She strolled into the den then moved into the front hallway toward the crackle of the fire.

She turned a full circle to take it all in.

"Let's sit by the fire," I said.

And we did. She'd brought cigarettes and we sat cross-legged in front of the fire, smoking and sipping our wine.

The first thing we talked about was the previous night's theft, of course. I stuck with Jackie, she stuck with Clive, but only after I'd convinced her neither Reggie nor Amanda would have done it.

"You'd be surprised what people will do because of money," she said. "Oh my God. I bet the money is still *there*."

"What do you mean?"

"Paul checked our changing rooms, bags, and pockets, and they frisked us on the way out. That means, whoever took it knew this might happen and hid the money somewhere in the house!"

"I bet you're right," I said. I wondered if Chef had thought of that, too.

But Julia drained her glass and announced, "This topic is over till tomorrow at work, when everyone will be talking about it."

Dinner was perfect. The steak bloody rare, with spicy lemony greens, crispy browned potatoes, and that sweet buttery roasted onion. After she got over the praising—"Oh, my God, Theo!" she said, with the first bite of steak filling her mouth—and I opened the second bottle and we settled into the meal, Julia talked and talked. First about the colleges she'd applied to early decision.

"I may not get into Harvard or Yale, but I should at least get into Wesleyan in Connecticut."

I knocked on the polished dining room table.

She put her hand on mine. "I've made a decision." I put my silverware down and sat back. "As soon as I graduate, I'm out of here."

Next school year seemed so far away, I hadn't really thought about the fact that she would be leaving town eventually.

"It's just a few months earlier than when I'd have left for college, anyway. And you can visit!"

"But . . . but . . . where will you go?"

"I'm working on that with Jeanie."

When we were done with dinner, Julia asked, "Anything sweet?"

"I do have some Southern Comfort."

"You couldn't be more perfect."

We sat quietly in front of the fire, having a cigarette and our shift drink and not talking much.

"So," Julia said, "where are we going to sleep?"

"I was thinking the guest room?"

"I've got a better idea. Let's make a bed right here and sleep in front of the fire!"

And so we did. I got all the bedding and pillows from the guest room, plus two more down comforters to make sure we had a soft bed. Julia lit candles on the mantel, and the lighting was perfect, soft but not dark, not with the fire blazing. Romantic.

"Just to be sure," she said as we spread a sheet over the comforters, "there is zero chance of your parents surprising us, yes?"

"They're in Florida. I called them this afternoon."

We set four pillows at the head of the bedding. Julia looked at our work, at the fire. "This is just so perfect." She stepped to me, put her hands on my waist, and we kissed. She stopped to say, "Do you have protection?" I nodded. She said, "Can I have it?"

I reached into my pocket and gave it to her. She set it on a pillow.

Standing beside the bedding, she slowly began to unbutton my shirt. I untied hers and lifted it over her head. Julia, being Julia, led me the entire way, making me feel completely comfortable. It was, well, beautiful. It was over far too soon. I told her I didn't mean for it to be over so fast. She shushed me and told me I was wonderful. She took my hand and continued to lead the way.

28

I awoke to see the living room lit by a gray November morning. I checked my watch beside our bedding. A little before eight. Julia curled on her side, facing me, her hair in a tangle across the pillow. I lay on my back, reliving last night. It had happened, and in the most beautiful way possible. Did I feel different? No. Nothing had changed in me. Julia and I had changed. We were now as close as we could possibly be. I let out a long, heavy sigh, staring at her, feeling so incredibly lucky.

Her eyes slowly blinked open. "You're awake," she whispered. She smiled and inhaled, and her cheeks turned rosy.

"Your cheeks just flushed," I said.

She closed her eyes, made a long, sleepy *mmmmm* purring sound and said, "I can feel it. That would be you."

"Keep sleeping, my Jule," I said.

I rekindled the fire. The embers were still warm, so with only a short hit of gas, the fresh logs caught quickly. Never in my life had I felt such—what?—*peacefulness*. Except maybe that time on the beach long ago when I was given a sense of the oneness of the world.

I stumbled to the kitchen to make coffee, then returned to get warm by the fire. I spotted Julia's cigarette pack and reached for it. One left. This and a cup of coffee, how perfect. But then I thought, *Julia is going to want this.* The coffee finished perking. I remembered she always kept a spare in her glove box. I reached for her purse and found her keys.

I was on a second cigarette, drinking coffee, when Julia stirred again. She made sweet cooing noises as she woke. She'd put her glasses on and covered her chest with the comforter.

"Already dressed?"

"Mm," I said.

She wrapped the comforter around her shoulders and sat next to me. "I'll have one of each," she said looking at my coffee, then the just-opened package of cigarettes. She picked it up, puzzled. "Wait, where did these come from?"

"Your glove compartment," I said.

Long pause.

"Obviously, you saw," she said.

"Yep, I saw."

We sat at the kitchen island on stools, Julia slouched over her coffee, propped on her hand.

"Why did you lie to me?" I asked.

"I never actually lied," she said.

"*Maybe the money is still in the house!*" I said, with sarcastic enthusiasm.

"It was important you not find out; that you have no idea. It makes you a kind of accomplice, and I didn't want to do that to you."

"I can't believe *you* stole that *money*."

"That money is my way *out* of here," she said, severely, as if angered. "Do you know what I can do with five thousand dollars?"

I looked away.

"Theo," she said, shaking my arm till I looked at her. "You're not going to tell on me, are you?"

"Of course not," I said. "I love you." I looked out the window at a fine snow beginning to fall in the gray light. "It's just . . . Julia, it's a felony."

"That money isn't legal, anyway, so I'm just stealing from another felon."

"But you could get into real trouble. I mean serious trouble." She said nothing. "Can you tell me what happened?"

"The office door was open, I saw the stack of pouches and I took the top one. I hid it in the ash trap in that gap between your worktable and the walk-in. Then when everyone was changing—when I told you I forgot my wine key, and you went to change, that's when I retrieved it. I stuck it in my boot. Chef didn't frisk that far down."

I just kept shaking my head in disbelief.

"This is my ticket to freedom, Theo. I could leave tomorrow if I wanted to!"

"But if you left tomorrow, it would be obvious who took the money."

"That's why, like I said, I'm leaving immediately after graduation."

I loved her, but I didn't know what to do.

29

I got to work the next day at two. When I entered the kitchen everyone was working quietly. Chef portioned a side of salmon. Paul cooked lardons. Reggie strained his lamb sauce. And Amanda, as ever, was cutting her waffle chips.

"Morning, everyone," I said. They all acknowledged without looking up. When I was dressed and back in the kitchen I whispered to Paul, "How's Chef?"

He shrugged.

"Theo," Chef said.

"Yes, Chef."

"I stored all the leftovers, stuffing, potatoes, corn, turkey, and so on. You can use all that up for family meal. Just reheat. There's still plenty of turkey stock. Make some more gravy if you think we'll need it."

"Yes, Chef." This was a bit of luck as I had no plan what I was going to make for family meal. Now all I had to do was reheat it, and maybe thicken some stock.

Julia was wrong that everyone would be talking about it. *No one* talked about it. No one said a thing. It was weirdly quiet all day. Everyone was avoiding the subject, like a stinkbug in the corner.

We were done by ten. I waited in the mudroom for Julia. We usually left together. When we hit the street, I asked, "Anyone say anything? Anyone suspicious?"

"No, thank God," she said. She got in her car and started the engine, cranked down the window.

I leaned in and said softly, "You're not going to spend any of that money right away are you?"

"Not till I'm out of Ohio. I'm not stupid."

"Okay, good," I said. I kissed her goodbye and watched till her taillights disappeared down Larchmere.

I knew Johnny would likely be home. He wasn't a big partier, and since he didn't have a girlfriend at the moment, if he weren't doing something with Roger, he'd likely spend Saturday night reading. And that's where I found him, in his attic room, stretched out on the couch, a copy of *In Cold Blood* on his chest.

"Theo, you have to read this book," was the first thing he said when he saw me. He didn't even say hello.

"Yeah?" I pulled out his desk chair and sat heavily. I looked around the room, at the place where I'd spent so much of my childhood.

"What's up?" he asked, putting the book face down on the couch and sitting up. "You okay?"

I told him everything, exactly as it had happened, starting with Thanksgiving at the restaurant. Blow by blow. Johnny sat stone-faced throughout. Didn't even respond when I got to the losing-my-virginity part. Just listened. And when I got to the end, which was, "Nobody said anything at work tonight," he just said,

"Hoo boy. If that *is* mob money, boy oh boy. I mean those are the kind of people who blow people up in cars."

"I know, Danny Green, you told me."

"I think your chef was right. You do not fuck with these people."

"I don't know what to do."

"The thing is, if Julia doesn't return the money, they might, I don't know, mess with your chef, break his kneecaps or something."

"God, I don't know what to do," I said again.

"If I had five grand lying around, I'd give it to you."

Wait.

I had five grand lying around. Almost. I had more than $4,700 in my savings account. It was supposed to be for college. But I was working now. I could make that up by the time I got to college in two years.

The mudroom and kitchen were dark, but the door wasn't locked. I called out hello, but got nothing in response. I walked through the main dining room to the side room where the bar was, the only lights on in the house.

"Chef?" I said.

He jerked alert. Turned and saw me. *"Theo,"* he said. His voice was thick. "You got any news for me?"

"I'm afraid not."

"That's too bad." There were two glasses on the bar. One was empty but still had some ice in it. "Want a drink?" he asked, filling the empty glass with bourbon. I sat on the stool next to him.

"I don't think that's a good idea right now, Chef."

"Probably right," Chef said. He finished what was in his glass then took the one he'd just filled for me, what I assumed had been Paul's glass. I didn't know how long they'd been sitting there, but it wasn't like Chef *not* to be in complete control. He wasn't sliding off the stool or anything, it was just something in his voice. Also that he'd offer me a whiskey at all wasn't like him.

"I came to ask you a question."

"Shoot," he said.

"How much was in that pouch that was stolen? I mean, it wasn't like a hundred thousand dollars or anything, was it?" I already knew this, but I couldn't let him know I knew it.

"Not even ten thousand," he said, staring at the bottles behind the bar.

"I've got this savings account for college, and I could maybe get close to what was in the pouch."

"You've got five grand?"

"Almost."

"And you'd just give it to me?"

I nodded. "Because I'm worried about you, and I care about the restaurant."

He sighed heavily, smiled sadly at me. "Regrettably, it's not the dollar amount that matters. *I* could come up with five thousand dollars."

"Then what . . . ?"

"You know the kind of man Jimmy Holliday is, don't you?"

"Yeah," I said, remembering Johnny's term. "He's a goombah."

"That's right. And the important part of what's in those pouches is the serial numbers. What I need are the exact bills in the sequence they're stacked in."

"Why?" I asked, deflated. Did this mean I couldn't help?

"Those pouches I get weekly, sometimes more, are filled with what's called dirty money. Mob money, money from ill-gotten gains. How ill, I don't know. Prostitution, gambling, drugs—I don't know, and I never ask. But that's what this place was built for. Those guys can't just deposit tens of thousands of dollars into a bank. It comes in here dirty, and it gets spread around to staff, to customers, my farmers. My heating and cooling guy. That's why I always pay in cash. Once it leaves that way, it's clean. Untraceable.

"The danger to them is if that money gets deposited somewhere or is spent in a big lump, it could lead the Feds back to their operations."

"Chef, how did you get mixed up with these guys?"

"I didn't know when I accepted the deal. It was just a good gig in my hometown. They built this place out beautifully. They got some French guy in here to design the kitchen, both kitchens, up and down. All of it brand-new. It's frigging gorgeous. The upstairs suite was mine to live in for free. It's got two bedrooms, a living room, and a bath. And when I asked them what they expected in the way of food cost—"

Chef took a swallow of whiskey.

"This is something you haven't learned because we don't have to worry about it. It's the amount of money you spend on food, as opposed to electricity or dry cleaning or payroll. Food cost should be under thirty percent, rule of thumb. It's one of the few things you can actually control, costwise. So if they were going to say they wanted it under twenty, I wouldn't have taken the job, I wouldn't have been able to do the kind of food I wanted to do.

"But the two owners I was dealing with shrugged and asked me, 'Forty?' Which told me two things. They didn't know shit about the restaurant business, and that if I wanted to have a forty percent food cost I could do really incredible food. What I learned at Chez Panisse was that a chef is only as good as his or her ingredients. And I know how to find really good ingredients."

He went behind the bar, filled his glass with ice, then more whiskey.

"So I pack up all my shit and drive across the country. I move in here, I've got a month to staff the restaurant and create a menu. The menu was easy, staff was hard. But we got 'em. It was only when we were opening, when I thought about how much cash I was handing out rather than checks, that I knew something was up. I hadn't met Jimmy yet. But I figured, none of my business.

"I thought if I can get enough attention from the press, maybe even some national press, I'd have enough cred to lure investors to open my own place. I figured three years and I'm out of here."

"Will they *let* you leave?"

"I think so. They know I'm not going to say anything. This all may change come Wednesday."

"Could you get hurt?"

"This has never happened before. But when I said these are people *not* to be fucked with, I meant it."

"Are you scared?"

He paused, lifted his glass, and said, "You ever see me drink?"

30

I arrived Tuesday at work at three, as usual, dressed and quickly got a Bolognese sauce going, since I hadn't prepped anything on Saturday, and this was quick. I always started a Bolognese with bacon, per Chef's suggestion. Once the bacon was going, I went up the front steps into the dining room. Clive was in his customary brown suit, going over the reservation sheet.

"How many covers do we have tonight?" I asked.

"Eighty right now, slow night." He dragged his finger down the list. "But we're kind of jammed in the beginning."

Once the bacon was cooked, I added onions till it was soft, then the ground beef. I stirred till that was browned and rendered its fat. There was a lot of beef and bacon fat. When Chef first taught me this dish, I asked if he wanted me to drain off the fat. He looked at me like I was crazy.

"Never, Theo," he had said, "never discard fat. Fat is flavor."

"But isn't fat unhealthy?" I'd asked.

"It probably is, but you know what? I'm not running a health-food restaurant! I'm running a tastes-good restaurant!"

That one exchange totally changed my relationship with food.

I opened two enormous cans of chopped tomatoes and dumped them in. Then I went to dry storage for a bottle of Open Pit barbecue sauce. This was Chef's little secret. His brothers had told him that their mom made meat sauce this way, and so he always spiked it with this tangy barbecue sauce. Weird, but it was good.

I had everything up early: pasta, sauce, garlic bread, salad. A few servers, Tony and Julia usually, ate family meal standing with me.

"This is so good, Theo," Julia said, tapping my shoulder with the side of her head. Then she whispered, "But not as good as Friday night's."

As if nothing had happened, as if she hadn't stolen the money, as if I didn't know she did.

"Thanks," Tony said. "Really good."

I went back downstairs. Peeled potatoes and cut them into waffle chips on the mandolin for Amanda in case she needed more toward the end of service. I minced a whole quart deli of shallots, because by nine, they often ran low. I carried the bain of waffle chips to Amanda, set them off to the side for her.

"Thanks, Theo, but I'm good," she said.

"Just in case," I said. They were good in cold water for a couple days. I set the shallots on Paul's station and said, "If anyone runs low later."

"Thanks, brother," he said, which he often said, but this time the knot in my stomach tightened.

I returned to the basement and got to work on mirepoix for Chef's veal stock.

I'd learned after all these weeks down here to gauge how busy the kitchen was by the foot tread on the boards above. Chef had put in a dropped ceiling and lights, but I could still hear footsteps. Once they hit a near continuous rhythm, pounding into the kitchen meant the first push was there. All the servers would be super busy.

That's when I went into the girls' changing room. We didn't have actual lockers, just hooks and shelves. Julia always kept any cash she might be carrying in her pocket during service, so she could leave her purse on a hook. Which was where I found it. I took her keys. I heard footsteps coming down the front steps. I waited. I heard clinking bottles, and then footsteps trotting back up.

I left the changing room and returned to the potatoes.

At 6:30, I took off my apron. I went upstairs to the kitchen. It was at full bore. I entered the mudroom and exited the restaurant. It had been weirdly warm today, fifty degrees, but the temperature had suddenly dropped. It was freezing.

I went to Julia's car. I unlocked the passenger-side door. I sat in the passenger seat.

I unlocked the glove compartment.

I removed the pouch. I unzipped it to make sure she hadn't moved the cash. I zipped it shut. I stood with my back to the restaurant and slid the pouch into my trousers. I pulled my chef coat over it. I locked the car.

I returned to the restaurant. I went downstairs. I wrapped the pouch in a side towel and hid it behind some bowls. I returned the keys. I put my apron on. I got back to work. Waiting.

After the first push, I went up to the kitchen. I saw Chef finish a six-top and send the plates out. Things were slowing, so I said, "Chef, I need to make an emergency private call. May I use the office phone?"

Studying the tickets he said, "Yes, you may."

"It's locked, Chef," I said.

"Right," he said. "Paul, I'm stepping away for a sec." Paul gave him a thumbs-up.

I followed him down the stairs.

He unlocked the door and said, "I'll leave the keys, just lock it when you're done and bring the keys to me."

"Actually, Chef. I need to talk with you."

I stepped into the office. He followed and closed the door behind him.

I pulled out the pouch and the look of relief on his face was so strong, so deep, I thought he was going to fall down.

I held it out.

"You told me you didn't take it."

I shrugged.

"You're aware that if you don't tell me who did, I've got to fire you."

I just looked at him.

"I'm glad you understand. If I didn't, it would be like telling everybody that it's okay to steal. I just can't. You leave me no choice."

Chef closed his eyes. When he opened them, he said, "You won't tell me who took it?"

"I took it, Chef."

"Theo, I've got no choice, then."

"I understand, Chef." I untied my apron, lifted the strap off my neck, and held it out to Chef.

"The apron's yours. Hope you'll keep using it." He shook his head at me.

I stored and labeled the stock mirepoix and put it in the walk-in. I cleaned my station till it was spotless. I dressed. I left the kitchen without saying goodbye to anyone, apron in hand. I'm sure they noticed, but I didn't look back.

31

Mom and Dad were in the den watching the end of the CBS news with Walter Cronkite.

"Hiya," I said, popping my head in.

"Why are you home so early?" Mom said.

"We were really slow, so Chef sent me home."

"I just put two TV dinners in the oven. Do you want me to put one in for you?"

"You eat TV dinners when I'm not here?"

"When I don't feel like cooking. They're easy."

"Theo?" Dad said. At first I thought it was grave, but when he put his hands behind his head, I knew he had good news. "Mr. Morgan called. You got an A- in English. He was so excited and knew we were concerned, he had to let us know."

"I thought I did okay, but not that okay."

"I thought you'd be thrilled."

"It's trig and chem that I'm worried about."

Mom stood with her mom instinct.

"What's the matter?"

"Nothing, I'm just exhausted."

She felt my forehead and said, "You're not hot."

"I'm *fine*." I retrieved my book bag from the kitchen and headed up the back steps to my room.

I tried to do homework, but it was too hard to focus. I figured Tuesday night with a slow finish, Julia would be out by ten, which is when I expected the phone to ring.

Instead, I heard a pounding on the window of the back door. Urgently. Then the backdoor buzzer. I stayed at my desk. A minute later my father came to the bottom of the stairs and called my name.

"It's Julia," he said. "Everything all right?"

"I don't know," I said, passing him. Julia stood by the back door, coat still on. Her glare burned holes in me instantly.

"*We* are *talking*," she said. "Outside." And she left the kitchen. I put on my coat, went outside. She was in her running car. I got in the passenger seat.

"How *dare* you?" she said.

"How did you find out?"

"I came looking for you. Chef said you'd left but didn't say why, only that he'd have an announcement after service. I knew that instant. I thought, 'He would never do that to me.' When I got a break, I checked my car." She closed her eyes and shook her head. "I *cannot* believe it."

"I didn't rat you out. I took the blame."

"Jesus."

"I was worried about you. And about Chef."

"That money was *my business*. Not yours."

"That money wasn't yours."

"Now I'm stuck here!"

"What do you mean, you were going to be here till graduation? So really it just means you're here for the summer."

"I was planning all this Sunday and Monday with my sister Jeanie and her husband. She has a friend, an assistant professor in Syracuse. She's arranging for me to stay there until I can finish high school. I'm leaving the day after Christmas." She snorted. "*Was* leaving."

"Julia, you'd have left?"

"Like I told you," she said with a hardness I'd never felt before.

"What about us?"

"Are you fucking kidding me?"

"I'll make it up to you."

"Yeah, *how*?"

I didn't want to tell her my plan—the money in my savings account—in case it didn't work. "I'll figure it out."

"A lot of good that does me. Fuck!" She slammed her hands on the steering wheel.

"What did Chef do?"

"Called a post-service meeting. Said the money had been returned and that you would no longer be working at the restaurant. He did *not* say you confessed. I think he knows you didn't take it. Which means he knows I did. Because who else would you be covering for? But he couldn't fire *me*, not without a confession from one of us. God, this fucking sucks!"

I felt sick to my stomach. I didn't know what to say.

"Okay," she said. "We're done."

I sat, unmoving.

With what sounded like enormous fatigue, she said, "Get out."

I still didn't move.

"Theo, if you don't get the fuck out of my car, I will go in there and tell your father to get you out."

She paused only a moment before she opened her door and began to get out.

"All right!" I said. "All right, I'm going."

I watched her back down the drive and vanish, tires screeching.

32

Instead of going to the restaurant after school, where I no longer had a job, I returned home to retrieve my savings account passbook, deposit slips, withdrawal slips, and some kind of bank card, which Dad kept in a plastic baggie. I drove to the AmeriTrust branch where Dad and I had opened my savings account and where I went every other week to deposit $320.

I recognized the teller. She was younger than my parents, but I wasn't good at guessing adults' ages. She had prettily tangled hair and wore a pin on her blouse that read "Elizabeth."

"Hi, um, I want to withdraw my savings account."

"You want to close your account?"

"No, not close it."

"You need a minimum of $250 to keep it open."

I examined my passbook: $4,778.16. I did a quick calculation. I said, "Okay, I'd like to withdraw four thousand five hundred dollars."

"Here, let me see that. And a driver's license?"

I gave her the passbook and my license.

She examined my license, looked up at my face, back to the license, back to me, and said, "You're only sixteen."

"That's right."

"This is a custodial account. It's yours but technically, it's managed by your parents."

"What does that mean?"

"It means you need their permission to make that kind of withdrawal."

I was so immediately crushed that I put my head on the counter.

"Are you in trouble, honey?"

"No, a friend is."

She pushed my license and passbook toward me. I slipped them into the plastic bag with the withdrawal and deposit slips.

"I see your parents gave you an ATM card."

"What's that?"

"It's for the automatic teller machine."

"Yeah?"

"You can make a small withdrawal with it. You won't need your parents' permission for that. You will need the PIN number they gave you. They should have set you up with one."

I closed my eyes. They had—that's what the card was for. I hadn't understood. Dad suggested using the last four digits of our phone number so I'd remember it.

"Yes, they did."

"Well, it sounded like you needed all the money today, but I think you can take out up to $200."

My heart leaped.

"Where is this machine?"

"Right out front."

"Thanks!" I said, but I turned back and said, "Two hundred per . . . ?"

"Per day," she said as the next customer took my place.

First thing I did was see if this thing really worked. I'd never used one before. When it asked for my PIN I pressed 5, 8, 6, 1. And then I hit *Withdrawal*. And it worked! Out came four $50 bills.

I'd really been hoping to give Julia the money today so that maybe she wouldn't hate me anymore. But that wasn't going to happen. When I returned home, I found a pen and pad and divided 4,500 by 200: twenty-two days. It would take me twenty-two days to get Julia the money I wanted to give her. I looked at our calendar and counted off twenty-two days starting today, December 3. Christmas Eve. I'd have $4400 by Christmas Eve.

Three weeks. Julia would hate me for three more weeks, but I could last, knowing that I'd be redeemed in the end.

33

By the end of the week, I had withdrawn $600, learned that my lowest grade was a C- in Mr. Dalton's trig class, and I told my parents that the restaurant had let me go because they were overstaffed.

Mom said, "Oh, Theo, that's a shame."

"I thought you didn't like me working there."

"Well, we saw how happy it made you, and how much you wanted it. That letter you wrote to us?"

"I know." I felt sick to my stomach but tried my best not to let it show.

On Friday, when I told them my grades, they were incredulous, basically three Cs, a B, and that A-. When they saw I did not share their enthusiasm, Dad knew why. He put his hand on my shoulder and said, "I know you put in all that effort so you could keep your job at the restaurant."

"Yeah, well," I said, thinking, that's only half of it.

"The irony of fate," he said.

"You sound like Mr. Morgan."

He chuckled, grateful I'd made light of the moment.

"Well," Mom said, "you'll be able to put all your efforts into your studies. Now that we know you're capable of it, we have higher expectations."

What she didn't understand was that I could only *get* those grades *because* of the restaurant.

On Saturday, after I'd returned from the ATM with another installment, I lay on my bed, not even listening to music. Mom came in and sat on my bed. "Honey, is everything all right?"

"Yeah," I said, and I had a huge desire to let myself cry. But I managed to exhale it out of me.

She asked, "How's Julia? I haven't heard you on the phone with her at all."

"We sort of broke up."

"Oh, I'm sorry, baby." She stroked my cheek. "Did something happen when she came over Tuesday night?"

"Yeah."

"Want to tell me what?"

Shook my head.

I wanted to say, *Mom, help me. I lost my love, my Julia, my jewel. I can't set foot in the only place I feel like myself. What do I do now?* But I had to rely on my plan. I shook my head again without looking at her.

And so began my new life. Without work after school, I had way too much time on my hands. Of course this went into increasingly elaborate meals for Mom and Dad. I got a copy of Chef's favorite book from the library, *Great Chefs of France*. I made my own veal stock, which I learned how to turn into a demiglace so that I could make a classic Sauce Robert to serve with grilled medallions of pork, sautéed spinach, and potato croquettes. I even floured and fried shallot rings as an extra garnish.

It's hard to explain, but only when I was actually cooking did life seem to make sense. When I was cooking, Julia was so far in the background as to not hurt me. When I was cooking, Julia hadn't stolen money. It was only after dinner, alone trying to study, that things vibrated in my head.

I just kept marking off the days on my calendar. By Christmas she would be back in my arms. Or so I thought—if there was one thing I knew now, it was that you never knew what was going to happen from hour to hour. As I said, sometimes you jump and when you land, the world has changed.

I had a fantasy that she'd get it, work the Christmas Eve service, then call me that night. Or maybe, more dramatically, show up Christmas Day and throw her arms around me. And once she was in my arms, my whole being could unclench, and I could breathe again.

What was harder to keep out of my thoughts, when I wasn't actually cooking, was the fact that this girl I loved was capable of stealing $5,000. Did I know this part? Did I even know her? What did I know? What I knew was that she was smart and strong and had changed my life, and I was in love with her. But what didn't I know? Was this what Bennett had been trying to lead me toward? I told myself that I'd deal with this once she was back in my arms.

Another week went by. The weather grew increasingly cold. Slowly, wrapped packages accumulated beneath our tree, which Mom had decorated this year with silver and red ribbons (weird). Snow fell. On Sunday, I drove out to Beachwood Place mall to look for Christmas gifts for Mom and Dad. When I began withdrawing money to give to Julia, I still had $160 in cash from the Friday before Thanksgiving. This meant I had $60 for gifts, and still had $4,500 by Christmas Eve.

I got Mom three pairs of tennis socks, two pink wristbands, and a pink visor at a shop called the Tennis Lady, which she liked.

I got Dad a history of the building of the Brooklyn Bridge at B. Dalton Bookseller, because he loved history (and it was in paperback). I felt so opposite from how festive everything looked that the festiveness felt phony, the fake snow on the big tree glaring, the big, gaudy, wrapped packages with nothing in them. The fake Santa and the line of kids and parents. I sat by a fountain and stared at the rising shoots of water. I kept seeing, in these bubbling shoots, figures praying, as if they were leaping toward the sky, praying.

I took another pass through the mall, both floors, slowly. It was possible Julia, too, was shopping for Christmas gifts. This was where everyone went. But nothing.

I was hungry and had enough money for a Chick-fil-A sandwich. I could eat it in the car on the way home. I didn't want to be here anymore.

A week before Christmas, Mom and Dad had their annual Christmas party. It was, as Mom called it, "a cocktails and passed hors d'oeuvres affair." I was required to wear a coat and tie and the candy-red corduroys Mom bought me specifically for this. I was in charge of helping the caterer, but there wasn't much to do. They brought everything already cooked and just reheated their little mushroom tarts and bacon-wrapped water chestnuts in the oven.

I took drink orders and delivered them to the bartender, who had set up in the den. I was also in charge of keeping the music going, but mostly I sat in a chair in the living room and watched the adults get tipsy and loud.

In a way, it was gorgeous. All these people, dressed in bright Christmas clothes, the red poinsettias Mom had filled the room with. The tree. The presents under the tree. A soft snow fell outside. The fire crackled. It was happy and festive and beautiful.

I couldn't help but wonder what Julia's house looked like now. Did they decorate it? How do you decorate a place with a sagging torn couch and water-stained wallpaper? Then I tried to imagine Reggie and Amanda and Paul, cooking away at the restaurant. What would they think if they were there? They probably wouldn't be comfortable. And I didn't *like* that they wouldn't feel comfortable—there was something wrong about this.

And then I realized that *I* was uncomfortable here. Maybe I was just depressed about Julia, but I didn't want to be here. I wanted to be at the restaurant.

The day after the party was the last day of school before the Christmas break. So now I had too much time to fill up. But I was getting closer and closer. The next day I took out another $200. That made $3,600, plus the $100 I already had. Four more days.

On Tuesday, the day before Christmas Eve, Gram and Gramps arrived from Florida, and I was grateful for the distraction. Anything that would help pass the time.

A heavy wet snow began on Christmas Eve day. We hadn't had much accumulation, but now it was really coming down. The weather report said the temperature was going to drop drastically, maybe to single digits. I arrived at the ATM for my final withdrawal. I felt weirdly nervous. Like officials were going to burst out of the doors and catch me. Or the machine would be broken or out of cash. But it remained reliable. I had it all. Eighty-eight fifty-dollar bills, and my five twenties. It all fit into a legal-size envelope but didn't close neatly. I found a manila envelope and put the white cash-filled envelope in that, taped it all up so that it was the dimensions of a fat letter. I wrote on the front in large letters:

To: Julia
From: Theo

I had thought about writing something like *I love you*, or even *Merry Christmas*, but decided to keep just that "to" and "from."

"Where are you going?" Mom asked. She was making sandwiches and tea for Gram and Gramps, who were reading newspapers in the living room.

"Some last-minute shopping!" I said as I put on my winter coat and shoved the envelope in the pocket, then zipped the pocket.

"Drive carefully! The roads are getting worse."

I arrived at the restaurant at 1:30. That's when Chef butchered salmon. Every day. You could set your watch to it.

I kicked my shoes against the steps before entering the mudroom. Chef stood at the center of the central table, back arched and dragging his long slicing knife along his steel. Before he made the first cut, I said, "Chef?"

He looked up. Paul and Reggie turned to look at me. Amanda came up from the basement with a crate of spinach, saw me, and brought the crate to her station. No one said anything. Not part of the family anymore. Who could blame them? Chef paused. I didn't want to cross the kitchen threshold. He set his knife down and came to me.

"Hi, Theo."

I unzipped the pocket of my down jacket and pulled out the envelope. "Will you give this to Julia when she gets here tonight?"

I handed him the envelope. He bobbed it in his hand as if he were weighing it to determine the contents.

"I can do that," Chef said.

"Can you, like, keep it on you until she gets here? I don't want any chance that it will get lost."

He smiled slightly and said, "I promise. I will put this into her hands myself." He pulled back his apron, and stuffed the envelope into his front pocket. It stuck out some, but it looked secure. The apron fell over it. Chef patted the envelope through the apron. "Any message?"

I shrugged. "Merry Christmas?"

"Done."

"Thank you, Chef."

I turned to leave.

"Theo."

"Yes, Chef?"

"You have a merry Christmas yourself."

"Thank you, Chef. Same to you. And to the others."

And it was done. I could do nothing more.

The phone didn't ring till 2:00 p.m. the next day, Christmas Day. By then we'd already had our coffee and coffee cake and brown-sugar-sweetened bacon and eggnog in front of the fire as everyone opened their gifts. We'd stuffed all the wrapping paper into a large trash bag and organized the gifts into their piles. Mom had the standing rib roast in the oven. I'd finished setting the dining room table and was heading up the stairs to shower, when the phone rang.

"I got it!" I shouted a little too loudly, bolting up the stairs and to my bedroom.

34

"Hello?!" I said into the receiver.

"Theo?"

I was so surprised that it wasn't Julia I didn't know what to say.

"Theo, it's Jackson."

"Hi, Chef."

I couldn't *believe* it wasn't Julia. I felt like crumbling to the carpet.

"I'm calling because I'd like to give you your job back. I hope you'll say yes."

"I don't understand, Chef."

"Julia gave her notice . . . well, not notice. She quit last night. She told me you didn't take the money."

"Did she confess?" I asked.

"She did not, not explicitly, confess. She told me how much you loved it here and hoped I could see my way to asking you back.

"We're open tomorrow and Saturday as usual," he went on. "And we stay open through New Year's Eve, then it's our break. I'm hoping you'll be with us?"

"Yes, Chef."

I put the phone down. Then I lifted the receiver and dialed Julia's number.

Mr. Bevilacqua answered.

"Is Julia there?" I blurted.

"No," he said.

"Do you know where she is or when she'll be back?"

"Do you?" he asked.

"No," I said.

He hung up.

35

I'd been gone three weeks but when I arrived the next day, it felt like I hadn't missed a single hour. Nobody knew what had happened, only that *something* had happened. I had to assume Chef figured out exactly what, but he didn't say anything. Everyone told me they were glad I was back at family meal, most of all George. The night was slow and went smoothly. It was just weird without Julia zipping through the kitchen with orders, heading out with plates on her arms, the lovely surprises downstairs when she could take a thirty-second break to say hi.

I guess it showed, because as I was cleaning my station at the end of the night, delaying going home for as long as possible, Amanda left the changing room and stopped to speak to me. She was back in her leather jacket with a huge scarf that covered her tattoo, her knife kit and helmet in hand.

"I'm sure everyone has said this—I hope they have, anyway—but it's really good to have you back."

"Thanks, Amanda."

She headed upstairs.

"Hey, Amanda?" I called to her. "You don't know where Julia is by any chance?"

"We were never close," she said. She was quiet for a moment. She returned to me saying, "Aw, Theo." And she gave me a great bear hug and as soon as I felt her arms securely around me, I started crying. I couldn't believe she was gone. I felt lost and confused. Amanda held me till I stopped.

"Thanks," I said.

"She's tough, she'll be okay," Amanda said. "And so will you."

I didn't feel so sure.

36

New Year's Eve. Time to end this horrible, miraculous year and start a new one, I thought as I arrived at work that day. I'd only been back four days by then, having worked the Friday and Saturday after Christmas, and then yesterday, Tuesday, and tonight, December 31. I was still trying to get back up to speed on family meal, but Chef helped me out today. He liked to welcome every table with Hoppin' John, a dish of black-eyed peas and hog jowl that he cured himself, along with collard greens in their pot liquor and corn bread—good luck for the coming year, he said.

This was also going to be family meal, and together we figured the quantities I'd need to have enough for all the guests and staff meal. I always loved learning a new dish. As I cut onions and the jowl for the beans, servers would pass behind me. I turned every time. Something in my brain kept insisting I'd see Julia, smiling, her ponytail swishing as she trotted up the stairs.

I got family meal up but went straight back down to the prep kitchen. Wasn't hungry. Too much positive energy up there. This was the last service before the restaurant closed for two weeks. Servers would make good tips tonight. Reggie, Paul, and Amanda were ready, knowing that diners had high expectations on this special night.

Chef called me up to the kitchen to plate the Hoppin' John and collards, which I served in small dishes for deuces and soup tureens for tables of four or more. The corn bread was as delicious as birthday cake. This was a no-brainer, service-wise, as everything was already cooked, and everyone got the same thing.

I stayed upstairs to watch service. This being the last night, there wasn't a family meal to prep. The only thing would be to clean and clear the walk-ins and reach-ins for our two-week break. Amanda was her wonderful, bizarre self. She said wearing a cast for six weeks had made her a better cook. Reggie was getting a divorce, Paul told me. And Paul said he'd sworn off weed, which I found hard to believe. Everything changes, I suppose. Always and forever. But how do you brace yourself? I guess by showing up early for work and making sure your counter is clean at the end of the night.

"Ordering, two steaks mid-rare, one salmon, one lamb, two lardons!" Chef called.

"Order fire two pâtés!" he called.

"Picking up two halibuts, salmon, and steak rare!"

Jackie pushed through the swinging door, calling out, "Order in!" handing the ticket to Chef.

Chef had asked me to help Paul on desserts. There were just two, a chocolate tart with a raspberry sauce, which he called a coulis. And the usual crème brûlée. But it was my job to tap powdered sugar out of a fine mesh strainer over a stencil that read "1981!" over all the desserts. When I finished with the last dessert, I told Paul, "I'm going out for a smoke."

He gave me a thumbs-up.

"But, hey," he called. "Come midnight, cooks do a champagne toast with Chef. They're humping in the dining room and refilling glasses for the countdown, but our work is done. So back in fifteen, okay?"

I still had my apron on, which was bloody from all the strip steaks I'd been butchering earlier after getting the Hoppin' John course out. I sat on the steps. It was freezing, and the snow was coming down, but because I was so hot from the kitchen, it felt refreshing, heat coming off my body almost like steam. I shook out a cigarette and lit it. It was a new year. I couldn't not think back on it. Just six months since it happened. A lifetime. In a way it was. Another life.

Was this the "more of something else" my dad had talked about? It didn't feel like it. Julia was gone. I'd held out hope that I'd hear something, that I'd get a call saying she'd arrived in Syracuse, or anything to let me know she was safe and sound *somewhere*. But nothing, and I knew at that moment, there on the back steps, with a shock of bedrock certainty I hadn't allowed myself till then, that I would not hear anything. Maybe ever. She was gone, gone, gone.

Maybe Johnny was right, what he'd said on the golf course two months ago. The gods sent me Julia, who helped me find a new course. Now I needed to let her go; she forced me to let her go so that I could move forward.

But I loved her.

I took a deep drag of the cigarette and exhaled. And with it, I felt the pain leave my body. I thought I might cry, but I didn't. I felt a kind of sadness I'd never known before. This sadness had no tears attached to it. There wasn't really a name for it—not that I knew. And it was bigger than just Julia. She was the core, but the bigger sadness radiated out from this core, big as the universe and connected to everything.

"Dude, it's champagne time." It was Paul, standing in the mud-room behind me. His apron was off, so I knew service was done.

"Be right in," I said.

I took a last drag on my cigarette and flicked it as far as I could, watching the ember arc into fresh snow.

Here's what happened next: I brush my backside off and reenter the mudroom. I stop and look at the big butcher-block cutting table and remember slicing those shiitake mushrooms for Reggie my first day here last summer. I *see* the sizzle platter with its silver spoon filled with peas and carrots Chef had left for me. I remember that sense of simply loving where I was on my first day in this kitchen. This strange family. Coming in from the cold, seeing the mudroom, the dry goods on the shelf next to me, the bowls below the worktable that Julia helped me to find that first day. I could see her clearly, too, as she was that day, and as *I* was that day. Everything appears uncommonly crisp, as if the air has been filtered to crystal clarity.

"Theo, get in here," Chef calls out. "Our work is done until next year!"

I step over the threshold into the kitchen. The minute hand on the clock has yet to reach twelve. We have one minute left till next year. I see Paul looking at me and Reggie and Amanda. And Chef, who is holding a full champagne flute out to me, the bubbles bright as stars. Chef is smiling, too.

"Happy New Year," Chef says.

We all touch glasses. I am flooded with relief, as if a fever has broken. I am on a new course. I hold my glass to theirs, touch each one, knowing, feeling in my spine, this is where I belong.

Thanks to Julia. A roar comes in from the dining room, like a wave crashing. Midnight. All those people, here for the food, here to be served, here to be happy. And we are here to make it happen, me and Amanda and Reggie and Paul and Chef, my misfit family.

ACKNOWLEDGMENTS

Before I thank a few people who were fundamental to this book, I feel obliged to note that there is a lot of drinking and smoking and driving after drinking in the story, which we know is not a good idea. We did not always have this understanding. This story is a faithful rendering of the time when, and the place where, I grew up: Cleveland in the late 1970s and early 1980s.

I'm grateful to Francesco Sedita, head of Penguin Workshop, for giving me the opportunity to write this story, and for his pairing me with the perfect editor, Nick Magliato, a young father who has done his own time in restaurants and food service. Nick's assistant, Celina Sun, was a welcome and productive addition to the team (books are a group project, and I had a great group). Even the copy editor, Shona McCarthy, was superlative—rigorous, thoughtful, and diplomatic. And thank you Mary Claire Cruz, Penguin Workshop's art director, who led the design front for the cover.

The crux upon which this story turns comes from an actual story told to me by Matthew Accarrino, executive chef of SPQR in San Francisco. He was helpful in providing physical and practical details of his specific circumstances. The events in this story are entirely fictional. Orthopedic surgeons Greg Fisher and

Christopher Furey—who was in my class at University School—helped me with details related to my character's medical condition and treatment.

Chef Thomas Keller, who has taught me so much, helped to inform the character of Chef Jackson, and I thank him for all he's given me. I must thank the actual Paul, Reggie, and Amanda for letting me cook beside them at Sans Souci in Cleveland in the late 1990s—it was a comfort to attach your names to characters who are not you but let me be with you in spirit. I hope you're still cooking.

Laurence Edelman, chef and co-owner of Left Bank and Poulet Sans Tête in New York City, read this manuscript to ensure the accuracy of the kitchen details. My friend Chris Hudson also read and commented on the manuscript, offering changes that were invaluable.

My wife, Ann, an extraordinary novelist, was with me for the whole journey of this story and improved this book immeasurably. It was at her encouragement that I began it. She also cut roughly twenty thousand beloved but unnecessary words, and there are not enough thanks for that task.

Thank you all.